FRIENDS IN HIGH PLACES

The Liberty Lane Series from Caro Peacock

DEATH AT DAWN
(USA: A FOREIGN AFFAIR)

DEATH OF A DANCER
(USA: A DANGEROUS AFFAIR)

A CORPSE IN SHINING ARMOUR
(USA: A FAMILY AFFAIR)

WHEN THE DEVIL DRIVES *

KEEPING BAD COMPANY *

THE PATH OF THE WICKED *

FRIENDS IN HIGH PLACES *

* *available from Severn House*

FRIENDS IN HIGH PLACES

A Liberty Lane Mystery

Caro Peacock

Severn House Large Print
London & New York

This first large print edition published 2015
in Great Britain and the USA by
SEVERN HOUSE PUBLISHERS LTD of
19 Cedar Road, Sutton, Surrey, England, SM2 5DA.
First world regular print edition published 2015 by
Severn House Publishers Ltd., London and New York.

British Library Cataloguing in Publication Data

Peacock, Caro author.
   Friends in high places. – (A Liberty Lane mystery)
   1. Lane, Liberty (Fictitious character)–Fiction. 2. Women
   private investigators–Fiction. 3. Murder–
   Investigation–England–London–Fiction. 4. London
   (England)–Social conditions–19th century–Fiction.
   5. Blessington, Marguerite, Countess of, 1789-1849–
   Fiction. 6. Detective and mystery stories. 7. Large type
   books.
   I. Title II. Series
   823.9'2-dc23

ISBN-13: 9780727870827

Typeset by Palimpsest Book Production Ltd.,
Falkirk, Stirlingshire, Scotland.

Printed digitally in the USA.

ONE

It was the first day of September, a Tuesday. I'd been away on a case in the country and, after the clean Cotswold air, the smell of the Thames seemed even worse than usual, the streets thinly coated with horse dung, trees starting to shed leaves more from sheer weariness than the nearness of autumn. Since the summer season was over and parliament was not sitting there was nobody in town, apart from the two million or so of us who had to scrape a living there and did not own a grouse moor. In spite of that, I'd returned to find a dozen or so missed invitations to musical evenings, tea parties and 'at homes', carefully laid out on my work table by my housekeeper, Mrs Martley, along with three bills, various advertisements from tradesmen seeking my valuable custom, two letters from people wanting to consult me about their problems and the latest unsatisfactory note from my landlord about the cesspit. Every sort of letter except the one I wanted, with my name in that familiar eager handwriting, sent from Switzerland, Italy or goodness knows where by now. I tried not to think about it and to turn my attention to business – necessary in view

1

of the bills – but my mind felt as jaded as the yellowing grass in Hyde Park across the road. Perhaps the case in the country had taken more from me than I'd realized. I was asking myself a question: did I want this life forever? I was twenty-five years old, living from hand to mouth doing work that most people would hardly recognize as respectable. True, there were people I'd helped as a private investigator. Equally true, there were men in high government positions who raised their hats to me when we met, knowing I'd done the state some service, though I was rarely invited to their dinner tables. It was all very well now – sometimes much better than very well – but what would I be in, say, ten years' time? An ageing woman living in a few rooms above a yard at the back of Park Lane, with a crotchety housekeeper and an elderly cat for company, a keeper of old scandals and gossip nobody cared about any more. Intolerable. I'd half resolved to go travelling. I'd been able to put a little money aside from my more profitable cases and acquired a few jewels and trinkets I could sell. It might amount to enough to go out and see my brother in India. If not, I might go to France or Italy. With the prospect of a London winter I yearned for sun, blue sea, lemon trees. For the present, only one thing from the collection on my table gave any prospect of entertainment – a note on fine ivory paper wafting Lady Blessington's favourite scent of carnations.

2

Gore House,
Kensington.
28 August.

My dear Miss Lane,
Where have you been? We've missed you.
I do very much need to speak to you. I
take it you've heard about the misfortunes
of our poor friend LNB. I shall be at home
from two o'clock every day for the coming
week and should be very pleased to see
you.
Marguerite Blessington

Then a postscript: *Mr D will not be present.*

So she'd heard that I'd quarrelled with Mr Benjamin Disraeli, MP. Not surprising as he was a close friend of hers and would probably have told her about it himself, at goodness knows what disadvantage to me. Still, it was kind of her to reassure me. As for the unfortunate friend, that was no mystery since even in rural Gloucestershire the newspapers had covered his latest piece of buccaneering. LNB was Prince Louis Napoleon Bonaparte, favourite nephew and political heir of his uncle, the late Emperor Napoleon. Recent resident of No. 1 Carlton Gardens, London, thirty-two years old, reasonably good looking, especially when seen on horseback which made up for his short legs, possessed of a moderate though over-strained fortune, a fine stable of horses, the best cook in London and an unshake-able belief that France was waiting for him to become its next emperor. It was this last quality

3

that accounted for his current place of residence being a prison in Boulogne. I didn't know the details, but if the newspaper reports could be believed he'd attempted a coup against the French king by landing at Boulogne on – of all things – a Thames steamer with fifty men of assorted nationalities equipped with Birmingham rifles and a tame eagle as mascot, marched on the garrison and tried to rouse the soldiers to join his cause. Unsuccessfully. He was a good friend of Lady Blessington and her son-in-law, Count D'Orsay, so it wasn't surprising she was worried. I could claim him as no more than an acquaintance, though I quite liked him. It was Lady Blessington who had introduced us, at a ball given by a grateful client of mine.

'Miss Lane, I don't think you've met the prince.'

She'd handled the introduction with her usual tact because it presented difficulties. If he'd been a British prince, it would have been, 'Your Highness, may I present Miss Lane.' But Prince Louis was a different thing altogether. Here he was in England, living in exile, because in the peace treaty after the Battle of Waterloo, one thing all the European powers agreed on was that none of Napoleon's large family should ever be allowed to set foot in France. As far as most political commentators were concerned, he had as much chance of becoming Emperor Napoleon III as a cab horse has of winning the gold cup. But racing and politics both throw up surprises, so British diplomacy and society mostly danced careful circles round him, not including him entirely but

4

not cutting him out. He was aware of this. When we were introduced he gave me a polite bow, as any gentleman would, then waited for a split second to see whether I'd curtsey. A deep court curtsey would imply devotion to the house of Bonaparte, a polite bob a discreet compromise. As it was, I only dipped my head briefly, as any lady would. My father, a committed republican, had practically worshipped Napoleon as a revolutionary leader then changed his mind entirely when he'd declared himself emperor. My father's daughter didn't care for curtseying but I can't deny that my heart was beating faster for being close to a man who'd called the terror of Europe 'uncle'. The band was playing. He asked me if I'd care to dance. He smiled, but mostly had a pale and serious look as if the sense of destiny never left him and he waltzed like a man determined to leave nobody standing on the dance floor. He spun in circles like a skater, almost whisking me off my feet, avoiding collisions with the other dancers by no more than a slither of satin or swirl of silk. He asked me for another dance, a mazurka. I've had cross-country gallops on my mare Rancie that didn't leave me so nearly breathless.

Rather than deal with the dispiriting correspondence I decided to ride over to Kensington that very afternoon. I changed into riding costume and told Mrs Martley I might be late back. Down in the yard, I lingered for a moment in case there was any sign of my apprentice Tabby but there was nobody except Mr Grindley at his forge by the gate, repairing the brakes on a carriage. Tabby, no lover of the country, had fidgeted in the Cotswolds and would probably be absent now for days, catching up with the news of her street urchin friends. She was in funds too. I'd given her half a guinea from the fee from our country case and when she had money she spent it, mostly on treating her friends. In the past, I'd tried to convince her of the advantages of saving but I might as well have saved my breath. 'If I had money, I'd only worry about people taking it so I might as well spend it,' she said. Secretly, I more than half agreed with her. What to do about Tabby was one of my problems if I decided to go travelling. Taking her away from London, where she knew every kerb stone and back alley, would be like prising a crab from its shell – but I couldn't abandon her. I thought about it as I walked across the park to the livery stables on the other side of the Bayswater Road where my friend Amos Legge worked as head groom. He was out with some ladies, so a stable boy helped me groom and tack up Rancie. I had no hesitation about riding on my own to Kensington. Rancie is the best-tempered mare in the world, as long as you're light-handed. We walked for a while alongside the Serpentine, enjoying the sparkle of the sun on the water and the sight of people skimming across it in rowing boats, then turned towards the Kensington Road. By fashionable standards Kensington Gore was far enough from Parliament and St James to count as out in the country, although a few large houses had been built there in the previous century. The sinister-sounding name had nothing to do with blood but came from the triangular shape of the plot of land beside Kensington Road. Lady Blessington had moved out there for the sake of economy although you wouldn't have guessed that from her style of living. I knew from experience that her 'at homes' were usually more than tête-à-têtes over the teacups. It would probably be a salon, with a dozen people there at least. Lady Blessington's occasions were invariably entertaining, often surprising, sometimes blessed with a breath of scandal, just like the lady herself. Because of that, half the fashionable world was prepared to make the pilgrimage out to Gore House to enjoy her company – the male half, that is. Owing to some events in her past and gossip about things that might or might not be happening in her present, ladies who considered themselves respectable rarely visited. But respectable gentlemen, along with artists, writers, wits and cabinet ministers, were regulars at her salon, where behaviour was every bit as polite and conversation a lot livelier than in the circles that bowed and curtseyed at court. She'd been a friend of Lord Byron, which was enough to make me like her from the start. We'd become acquainted when I did some small service for a relation by marriage of hers and she was kind enough to count me as a friend, perhaps because my strange way of earning a living and the fact that sometimes people gossiped about me too made for fellow feeling.

Gore House was a neat three-storey Georgian mansion surrounded by three or so acres of gardens and orchard, with a porch in the classical style that looked as if it were waiting for somebody in a toga to come and make a speech between the pillars on the balcony. A porter opened the gates as soon as we set hoof on the gravel and a boy appeared to take Rancie to the stables. A footman in powdered wig and green and gold livery opened the front door before I knocked and a maid showed me into a side room where I might tidy up – very necessary after the dust of the journey. Then the same footman led me not into the drawing room as I expected but the library, where he said her ladyship was working. It was a spacious room the full width of the house, with looking glasses in between the book cases that reflected carved marble fireplaces, Italian statuettes and towering arrangements of fresh flowers from the garden on a dozen small tables, white-and-gold chairs, curtains and couches in apple green damask. I caught reflections of myself from several different angles and wished I'd taken longer to tidy my hair.

Lady Blessington was as immaculate as ever, in an ivory silk afternoon dress. She got up from her chair at the long library table and came towards me, stretching out her hands to clasp both of mine. Her favourite dog, a white poodle the size of a Shetland pony, paced beside her and looked up at me with eyes the colour of amber.

'Miss Lane, how very kind of you to come.'

Her voice still had the soft accents of southern Ireland, although it was a long time since she'd lived in her native country. Twenty years before she'd been a famous beauty. Now a widow of fifty or so she was still pleasant to look at, with clear, pale skin, grey eyes and a lissom way of moving. But plumpness had become a settled fact rather than a tendency and the silk scarf she wore round her head and throat, like the wimple of a worldly nun, probably concealed a double chin. She told the footman to bring tea and sat me down beside her at the table, alongside piles of manuscript and page proofs.

'Please excuse the mess. Deadlines, as usual. It's like doors in a nightmare. You run with every breath in your body to get to one before it slams in your face, then there's always another door and another, *ad infinitum*.'

Her hands were pale and soft, but the insides of the first two fingers of her right hand were black with ground-in ink that no pumice stone would remove. That was one of the other things that made me like her. Her late husband had left her with a title and a taste for rich living, but no money to support them. So she worked hard for her luxury, turning out novels, magazine articles and a fashionable annual called *The Book of Beauty* – the sort of thing that people who don't like books give people who don't read books for Christmas. Everything from the footman's gold braid to the poodle's meat came from her pen. The tea arrived. As we drank she asked if I'd enjoyed my trip to the country. It was easier to say yes than talk about the complicated case that had taken me there. Mostly she did the talking, about things I'd missed in my absence – a quarrel at the opera, engagements made and broken, a

9

political scandal just avoided – carefully not mentioning anything to do with Disraeli. It was only when a maid had taken away the tea things and we were alone apart from the poodle that we came to her reason for wanting to see me.

'No company today then?' I said.

'I'm simply too busy. And we're too worried about poor Prince Louis.'

I decided not to point out that poor Prince Louis had been the author of his own misfortunes. 'What will happen to him?' I said. 'America again?' As it happened, Prince Louis had made a similar attempt at Strasbourg a few years earlier and suffered temporary exile to the United States.

'Worse than America. They may shoot him. Poor Alfred is almost frantic, as you may imagine.' Another misplaced 'poor', in my opinion. Alfred was Count D'Orsay, her son-in-law, who had contrived to lead a spoiled and petted life simply by being beautiful – admittedly a privilege more common with women than men. In his youth people compared him to the god Apollo. The cut of his coat was imitated by every fashionable young man in London, and parfumiers, boot makers and glove makers competed to load gifts on him for the cachet of his custom. I'd met him several times at Lady Blessington's and liked him well enough. He was affable, well read, a good conversationalist. But he'd done nothing with his life except paint an amateur picture or two. He was also as completely dependent on Lady Blessington for his living as the white poodle lying by our feet under the table. That was one of the reasons why people still gossiped about

10

her. Count D'Orsay's marriage to Lady Blessington's daughter had broken down some years ago and he now lived as a close friend in his mother-in-law's house. Some people said much more than mother-in-law. As far as my opinion is of worth, I think not. People gossip about me too and get it wrong more often than not.

'Some people are even saying that Alfred and I helped him plan the attempt on Boulogne,' Lady Blessington said. 'Total nonsense, of course.' Her limpid grey eyes gazed into mine. Quite possible, I thought, but didn't say. I was still waiting to find out why she'd wanted to see me so urgently. I hoped I was not expected to smuggle the prince out of prison. I said, experimentally, that I supposed we'd have to wait and see what happened at his trial.

'Yes. But meanwhile, there are other . . . complications.' Hesitation was unusual with her. She laid a hand lightly on my arm. 'Miss Lane, you and I haven't known each other for very long and you are young enough to be my daughter, but I feel I can trust you as I would one of my oldest friends. I shan't insult you by asking for your word that what I say will go no further, but I know I can depend on your kindness and good sense.'

'It will go no further.' She was clever. What else could I say?

She nodded. 'There are some things about the unhappy affair which did not get into the news-papers. They give the impression that all Prince Louis's men landed at Boulogne and were

11

captured. There was one who remained on the ship. He's a French gentleman of good family, much attached to the prince. Nobody doubts his courage but nature never intended him for a soldier and he's not a young man. His position on the prince's expedition was that of treasurer. The prince knew that he'd need money to pay his men during the march on Paris, but it would be foolish to land it until the barracks and castle at Boulogne were secured. So the money and some important papers remained on board the steamer, the *Edinburgh Castle*, with the gentleman waiting for a pre-arranged signal. Of course, that signal never came. After the prince's arrest, the French authorities seized the steamer. The gentleman and his valet, who sounds like a resourceful young man, managed to get away in the confusion while the boat was being searched and took passage on a fishing boat to somewhere on the south coast, then a coach to London. The gentleman knows very few people in London, but he did recall being welcomed at one of my salons a few months ago as a friend of the prince. In his desperate need he presented himself at my door.' She looked at me, head on one side. 'So, have you guessed yet?'

'Guessed what?'

'And you an investigator!'

'The gentleman is now lost and you want me to find him?'

'Oh, no. We know exactly where he is.'

'Well then?'

'He needs to get back to France with some

papers that may help the prince at his trial. In fact, they may even ensure that he never even comes to trial. But there are people who might be embarrassed by what's in those papers and he might be in some danger. We've discussed it and decided it might be safest to go by boat from Gravesend to The Hague.'

'A very sensible arrangement,' I said, still waiting.

'He believes, rightly or wrongly, that the French government has somehow found out about the papers and sent agents to kidnap him before he can leave England.'

'Has he thought of notifying the police?'

She gave me a look that said not to ask stupid questions. 'Our own government isn't exactly sympathetic towards Prince Louis. The last thing Pam wants is another Napoleon.' 'Pam' was our mighty foreign secretary, Lord Palmerston, also an occasional guest at her salon.

'Is there any evidence about these kidnappers?'

'Possibly yes. Two nights ago I looked out of my window and there was a man behind a statue on the terrace. I sent a couple of my people out to get him, but he escaped. It must have been over the wall or out of the back gate. It's not locked at night.'

'An ordinary burglar perhaps?'

'Also possible. Another thing – my house-keeper tells me that a young man presented himself last week wanting employment as a footman. She told him there were no vacancies and sent him on his way, but she thought he seemed too curious about the habits of my household. Also, he was a foreigner. He said he'd formerly worked for a Swiss gentleman.'

'That hardly proves he was a French government agent.'

'Indeed not. But it seems strange he should have come out all this way to look for work. It's possible that I'm being infected too much by our friend's suspicions, but we can't take the risk of letting him walk or drive out of here if people are looking for him.'

That confirmed what I'd already guessed. 'He's under your roof, then?'

For some reason she seemed to find that funny. 'Very much so. The question is how he's to be spirited away safely and on to a ship.'

'Lots of ways, I'd have thought. In a laundry basket. Or disguised as one of your maids.'

'There's his dignity to consider. He's already ashamed at having deserted the prince, as he sees it. If the story spread that he'd been cowering in a laundry basket or dressed as a woman it would humiliate him entirely.'

I was rapidly losing sympathy with the man. 'So he wants a guarantee of safety and dignity. Anything else?'

'A sister.' She waited until the expression on my face must have told her I'd got the drift. 'A much younger sister you'd have to be. They'd be looking for a man on his own. Travelling with a woman, he'd be less conspicuous. You could make the travel arrangements, even let it be known that your brother's an invalid, going abroad for his health. I'm sure he'd have no objection to that. And you're so observant and

14

resourceful. You'd notice anything amiss long before anybody else.'

Nobody flattered better than Lady Blessington. That soft voice, the wide grey eyes fixed on my face as if I had the power to grant or blight her dearest wish, would have swayed hearts harder than mine. Then she laughed and I found I was laughing with her.

'I already have a brother.'

'Then take another. I promise you, you'll find him entirely the gentleman, though perhaps not very conversational. But you can speak French to him. That will help.'

So it seemed I'd agreed. I wasn't unhappy about that. In fact, the service she was asking might be a useful distraction from other things. It seemed straightforward too. Amos Legge would drive us to Gravesend and discourage any lurking agents, French or British.

'Do I have to go as far as The Hague with him?' I said.

'It should be enough to see him on to the ship, but we'd leave that to your discretion. He's kept enough money to pay expenses.'

No mention of a fee, though, so I was probably doing this for friendship. 'When does he want to go?'

'As soon as arrangements can be made. This week, if possible.'

'I'll see what I can do. Now, am I to be allowed to meet my brother?'

She rang for the footman, who appeared so quickly he must have been waiting outside the door.

'Will you please present my compliments to Monsieur Lesparre and bring him here. Say there is a lady I'm anxious for him to meet.'

While we waited she talked about plays and concerts I'd missed. It seemed a long time before the library door opened and the gentleman walked in. He was in his late forties, slim in build and a little below average height, sharp featured and so clean-shaven that the razor must have scraped over his high cheekbones like a boat keel grounding on sand. His hair was cut short, with more grey than brown in it. He moved quietly and with some dignity, like a man who was used to good carpets under his shoe soles. When Lady Blessington introduced him to me as Monsieur Lesparre, he bowed gravely and looked at me with sad brown eyes. I could see why, in a military expedition, he'd be the one left on the boat. If I'd had a choice of elder brothers I'd have opted for something more lively. He was neatly dressed in black and white with a plain silk waistcoat, clothes a little too tight fitting. I guessed that they might be D'Orsay's cast-offs. Lady Blessington guided us over to an alcove where three armchairs in green and gold stood between a bust of Homer on a pillar and a small table with a vase of yellow and white chrysanthemums. Monsieur Lesparre waited politely for her nod before sitting.

'Miss Lane and I have a plan,' she told him.

I decided not to protest that it was her plan, not mine, and said nothing while she described it to him in French, studying his face. I couldn't see any enthusiasm in it and wondered why she

16

hadn't discussed it with him earlier. When she'd finished he said he was grateful to both of us for taking such trouble.

'I can see you have reservations,' she said.

'There are risks.'

'There are always risks. The alternative would be staying here indefinitely and not getting those papers to the prince's lawyers. The French government will want to put him on trial and get the matter over as soon as possible.'

She spoke a little sharply. I guessed that she was anxious to get him out of her house and was using me to speed up the process. I couldn't blame her. If she and D'Orsay had been as deeply in the plot as I suspected, she wouldn't want to draw attention to them.

'Risks for Miss Lane, I meant,' Lesparre said. 'It seems hardly right to involve a lady in my concerns.'

'Miss Lane is used to risks a lot worse than this,' Lady Blessington said. 'Besides, our plan avoids them as much as possible. What could be more innocent than a sister helping her invalid brother?'

'When were you hoping to arrange this?'

'As soon as possible. In the next few days if there's a boat sailing.'

Again, I had the impression that he was less than enthusiastic, but he nodded and then added, 'There is the question of Bruno.'

'Mr Lesparre's valet,' Lady Blessington explained to me.

A smile flickered over Mr Lesparre's grave face and his tone became warmer. 'Indeed, I can hardly

17

do anything without Bruno. He is a most loyal and capable young man. Without him, I shouldn't have managed to get away from Boulogne.'

'Is he with you?' I assumed he'd have been found a place in the servants' hall, but Mr Lesparre shook his head.

'Bruno thought it best that we should separate in case the servants gossiped. They can be very curious about new arrivals. He has friends among the Italian community in London.'

Annoyance flickered in Lady Blessington's usually serene expression at the idea that her servants might gossip. 'But you know where he is?'

'Not exactly, no. He thought he might move from place to place. But he told me how I might get a message to him.'

She looked at me, appealing for help. Like her, I wanted to get the business over as soon as possible. 'If you like, I could take a message,' I said. She fell on the suggestion as if I'd said something brilliant and within a minute Mr Lesparre was established at her work table with pen, paper and an ink stand in front of him. She drew me to the far end of the library, claiming she wanted to show me some book or other, and pulled a volume out of the shelf at random.

'Well, what do you think of him?'

I thought that if the life of Prince Louis depended on him it was a long bet, but didn't want to add to her worries. 'He seems in no great hurry to go.'

'Yes. I think the valet may be the better man. But you can understand if he's nervous – all the planning and then everything going so badly wrong. You don't mind taking the message?'

'In his place, I'd jump at the chance of moving on. After all, Gore House is hardly a hermitage.'

She laughed. 'It certainly isn't. Would you believe, last week we had Pam and the French ambassador in the salon and poor Mr Lesparre just three floors over their heads.'

'Over their heads?'

'When we have company that might be inconvenient we send him up to the loft. We've made it as comfortable for him as we can, but it's not easy with his poor stiff knees. Still, *dans la guerre . . .*'

We walked back to the table, where Mr Lesparre had folded his note and was heating a stick of red wax over a spirit burner to seal it. He blobbed on the wax and slid a heavy gold signet off the little finger of his left hand. He pressed it down, waited for the wax to harden, glanced at Lady Blessington, then handed it to me. The seal was a phoenix surrounded by a laurel wreath. I turned the note over and saw it was addressed to Bruno Franchetti, care of an address I vaguely remembered as somewhere near Hatton Garden.

'Will there be a reply?' I said.

'No. I've asked him to come back here by Thursday night. Is that soon enough?'

Lady Blessington glanced at me and I nodded. It would take two days or so to organize the passage. I told them that I'd let them know as soon as I'd booked a sailing for The Hague. Lady Blessington said she'd walk with me through the garden to the stables so we left Mr Lesparre in

19

the library. The poodle followed us through a garden full of late summer flowers, with espaliered apples and pears ripening along the paths of the kitchen plots, fountains splashing and birds singing in aviaries. Lady Blessington stopped outside one large cage that contained nothing but an enormous black raptor on a perch.

'The imperial eagle,' she said. 'The one Prince Louis took with him to Boulogne.'

I decided not to ask how it had got from Boulogne to the garden of Gore House. The bird twisted its head round and glared at us with black pale-rimmed eyes. I looked at the wry neck and the bald blue skin of its head, most un-eagle like.

'I think it's a vulture,' I said.

'I thought it might be,' said Lady Blessington.

If I were superstitious I might have taken that as a bad omen.

TWO

Amos and I discussed it when we rode in the park early on Wednesday morning – I on Rancie, he on an ex-cavalry horse he thought had the makings of a useful hunter. Neither of us could see any great problem. The livery stables where he worked could supply a closed two-horse carriage and Gravesend was an easy day's drive from London. All that remained to do was find a ship sailing for The Hague in the next few days. That took more time than expected. The most suitable was sailing with the evening tide on Saturday but all the berths were taken. If I cared to come back in the morning the clerk thought there might be a cancellation. No point in going out to Gore House with this uncertain news, so I decided to wait till the next day and went back to Abel Yard. The next thing was to deliver the message to the valet, Bruno Franchetti. By that time, Tabby had decided to reappear. She had her own way of reporting for duty. Among her urchin friends, she wore a tattered shawl belted up for a skirt or even breeches like a boy. When she chose to be my apprentice again, she'd put on the grey dress I'd bought her, with shoes that were scuffed but serviceable and hair pinned up in a way that would be just about respectable in a maid of a none-too-critical household. I accepted her appearance without comment and told her the address of the place near Hatton Garden which was the *poste restante* of the Italian valet. She thought about it for no more than half a minute then started walking. Her sense of direction was one of the amazing things about Tabby. She couldn't read or write. If she'd bumped into her own mother in the byways around Shepherd's Market, they wouldn't have recognized each other; they'd parted company about the time when children in more conventional families were being taken out of nappies and put into pinafores. Her father wasn't even a distant memory. She'd fought dogs in the gutter for ham bones and slept in every doorway from Mayfair to Haymarket. But all this, along with a quick ear for names, had given her a map in her mind of London that a cab driver couldn't equal. She started walking and I fell in alongside her. The way we went, along back alleys and side streets, may have been the most direct but had another aim as well: to avoid patrolling policemen. Tabby and her urchins feared them as mice fear a cat, and had a mouse's ability to sniff them from a long way off. Our destination turned out to be a narrow side street between Hatton Garden and Leather Lane. By then, we were in Italy. One of the things I love about London is that in a mile or so you can walk through most of the countries in Europe. Refugees from various revolutions and failed coups flock here like dispossessed pigeons and settle on their own ledges. Soho, for instance, is as French as Paris, with old aristocrats who escaped the guillotine rubbing shoulders with failed revolutionaries in cafes where good coffee soothes the pain of exile. Hatton Garden is the perch for the refugees from the various Italian statelets, dreaming and scheming under grey London skies for the day when Italy will be united from the Alps to Sicily. They cluster in tall lodging houses with cards in their windows offering, in Italian, rooms or beds for compatriots from different regions – Piedmont, Tuscany, Rome, Naples. On the ground floors small shops as dim as caves spill on to the pavement with sacks folded back to show dozens of varieties of dried beans, brown, white, green or speckled, with thick limbs of sausages dangling from hooks above them. In between the shops and lodging houses, every fourth or fifth house seems to be involved in the making of barrel organs. We passed one grinding away on a street corner surrounded by children who looked too poor to put even a farthing into the cap held out by a monkey in a red fez. The organ grinder was more than half asleep, turning the handle automatically as if it would, in time, generate enough clock-work energy to get him to the West End, where pickings were better. Some of the children ran up to us, begging or trying to sell strings of beads or plaster saints that they produced from ragged pockets. Tabby batted them away with a nonchalance I couldn't have managed. Women gathered in small groups outside the shops, mostly swathed in black, but some of the men swaggered as if they'd just come down from the mountains, in wide trousers, soft leather boots and cummerbunds that would surely have had

23

swords and pistols in them in their home lands. We passed the steps of a small church with its doors wide open and a smell of incense wafting out, then two houses further on we found the address we wanted. It was a house in mid-terrace, two storeys high with a shop on the ground floor, but this shop was a cut above the others, having windows with glass in and no frieze of sausages. A neatly printed sign in one of the top window frames read, in Italian and English, *Mutual Aid Society*. More notices, mostly handwritten in Italian, covered so many of the other frames that they almost cancelled out the advantage of having windows at all. Some of them were people looking for rooms to share but most advertised meetings with speakers newly arrived from Italy or, in one case, a charity bazaar for the distressed families of men imprisoned for the cause. It all had a familiar look to me because the various houses where my father had lived usually played host to at least one campaigner for an oppressed cause, usually foreign. Rescuing Italy from under the boot of Austria was one of them. Tabby gazed at them with her impartial hostility for the written word in any form. The door stood hospitably open, so I walked in. Tabby stayed on the pavement. The room had the same chaotic worthy-cause look as the window. It was large, probably taking up most of the ground floor and divided by what had been the shop counter, now occupied by an old hand-printing press, piles of leaflets and empty wine bottles crusted with candle wax. The furniture amounted to no more than a few hard-looking chairs and a large table, equally cluttered. On the far side, a curtain covered a doorway that might lead to a storeroom. A flight of wooden steps led up to a landing with another curtain across it. An elderly man sat at the table writing. He was grey haired, with a gentle, scholarly face, as if he should have been teaching Dante at a Tuscan university, but for all I knew he might have been a retired revolutionary fighter. He wished me good morning in Italian but courteously switched to English when my first few words betrayed that it wasn't my native language. I explained that I'd been asked to deliver a note and gave it to him. I thought he looked as if the name meant something to him, but he gave a non-committal nod.

'Do you know him?' I said.

'I hope we'll be able to find him.'

'We need to get the message to him urgently.' But I had no right to insist. Judging by the name, Bruno's origins were Italian and places like this would protect a compatriot's identity. I rejoined Tabby and we began walking back towards Hatton Garden.

'Somebody's watching us,' she said.

I laughed. 'More like several dozen.' In the little streets, where any stranger was an event and possibly a threat, of course we'd be watched. There had been faces at the windows of tenement houses; women chatting on the church steps had paused and followed us with their eyes as we passed; hopeful children were still trailing us.

'Nah, I mean watched like it's important.'

'Who and how long?' Her instincts were sharper

than mine and I felt that quivery feeling in the back that comes from having eyes on you.

'Dunno. Whoever it is, they were watching when you went into that shop, but it might have been before that.'

'And still watching?'

'Yes.'

It was tempting but useless to stop and look around. If somebody really were watching us and Tabby hadn't identified him already, then he was good at his work. Later, when we were going along Holborn, I said: 'Still there?' She shook her head. We reached home without incident and she disappeared, probably back to her gang in the mews.

I hardly had time to take off my cloak and bonnet before somebody knocked on the door of our main staircase. I looked out of my study window on a glossy top hat and a grey-gloved hand that was raised to the door knocker.

'Hello. May I help you?'

He looked up at me and swept off his hat. His hair was dark and curling, handsome face clean-shaven, expression amiable but anxious. You never forget the face of a man you once suspected of murder.

'Miles Brinkburn.'

'Miss Lane, I'm sorry to call without invitation. If it's inconvenient, say the word and I'll go away.'

But he must have known that the word wouldn't be said to one of his family. 'Come up,' I said. 'The other door.'

I should have invited him up to the parlour, with Mrs Martley as chaperone, but things had happened between us that were well beyond convention. In spite of that, when I'd got him seated in my office, the conversation was as correct as a copy book. He asked after my health and my business. Both good, I told him. I asked after his wife. Rosa was down in the country, he said, in blooming health. An adjustment of his fine eyebrows and the hint of a smile conveyed that she was expecting. He asked after Amos Legge and Tabby, or rather 'that girl of yours'. I asked after his brother, now Lord Brinkburn since the unregretted death of their father. Stephen was well, he said. Had I heard he was getting married? I said I'd heard and was sure they'd be very happy. All the time, my heart was pounding like a road mender's hammer and I wanted to yell out to him to be done with all this and say what he'd come for. At last he did, although in a form that an outsider might have taken for just another family inquiry.

'Have you heard from Robert at all?' The slightest of shifts in his position, the shade of a change in his voice, showed we'd got there. I tried to keep my tone conversational.

'I had a letter from him in Bern, about two months ago. I think he was intending to cross into Italy.'

The look he gave me was not far from pleading. He was too gentlemanly to trespass on delicate ground. After all, there had never been a formal engagement between me and his half-brother Robert Carmichael. Not even an informal one, come to that. The situation between us must have been pretty clear to his half-brothers, who weren't fools, but I doubted if they'd discussed it.

'I expect you've heard more recently,' I said.

The reply mattered. If Robert had written to his brothers and not to me, that carried its own message. At the start of his travels, I'd had letters from him almost every week, often more than that, from every place he'd stopped at for more than a day or two. Sometimes they were pages long, vivid descriptions of the places he'd seen and people he met, sometimes no more than hasty notes, but always with some odd saying or unexpected sight. In one of his longer letters he'd said that nothing properly existed for him until he'd had a chance to share it with me.

'Only a note to Stephen saying he'd arrived in Bern,' Miles said. 'It was dated six weeks ago but for some reason Stephen only received it last week.'

'My last was from Bern too, before I went to the country.' Quite a long one, as it happened.

'The fact is, we're becoming a little worried,' Miles said. 'I know a lot can happen to delay mail from abroad, but he's usually such a regular correspondent. We were hoping you might know more about his plans.'

'They were uncertain,' I said. 'No fault of his. It was the man he's travelling with, Henry O'Leary. I think I'd better show you the letter Robert wrote to me from Switzerland.'

I went across to my desk for it. I hoped it didn't show the signs of being much read and I took

28

out the last page, which was meant only for my eyes, before I gave it to Miles. It was one of the longer letters and it took some time to read. In spite of his worry, he couldn't help smiling at some of the things in it.

You may remember that this whole project began because Henry had been rejected by the love of his life in Ireland and it was either foreign travel or drowning himself with his broken heart in a convenient lake. I was properly sympathetic but what I failed to realize was that Henry's heart is an organ which repairs itself with a speed that might fascinate the medical profession. We'd hardly landed in France when the man who'd never look at another woman again had to be extricated from a fight in a hotel restaurant for doing just that in front of a bad-tempered husband. We had to leave Paris prematurely because of a more serious involvement with a young woman at the opera who turned out to have a jealous statesman for a protector. His heart was broken all over again beside Lake Geneva and carried in pieces to Bern, where it has performed another of its miraculous regenerations, in time to be thrown at the feet of a lady from Vienna with a brother who is already fingering a metaphorical sword hilt. I only hope it remains metaphorical. I haven't mentioned this to you so far because it's Henry's business after all, but to be honest

29

I'm growing tired of having our travel arrangements dictated by his unpredictable needs to either stay or flee. As you know, our plan was to cross into Italy, travel the length of the country to Brindisi and take a ship from there to Athens. Henry is now suggesting that we go overland all the way, taking in Vienna en route, as eccentric a route to Greece as can be imagined, unless he encounters some Chinese belle and wants to go via Peking. I've told him roundly that if we can't come to an agreement by this time next week I shall take myself off on my own. So I shall spend the next few days studying maps and timetables and considering my plans. As soon as anything is settled, I shall let you know.

Miles looked up from the letter. 'And this was the last you heard from him?'

'Yes. I don't even know if he and Henry went their separate ways.'

'They did.' Miles sounded grim. 'Henry O'Leary is back in London. I saw him yesterday.'

'So what's happened to Robert?'

'O'Leary doesn't know. They agreed to separate in Bern, just as Robert thought they might in this letter. O'Leary stayed in Bern for a few days, then gave up any idea of travelling further and came home. From what Robert says, we can guess there's yet another woman involved. He's been back in London for two or three weeks and seems in no hurry to go home to Ireland.'

30

'Does he know about Robert's plans?'

'I didn't have time to ask him. He was with another man and they were hurrying somewhere. Stephen sent a note to his club inviting him to dinner tonight. He's accepted, so I hope we'll find out more.'

'Will you tell me if you find out anything?'

'Better than that. If you're free, you're invited. It will be mostly a family affair, just Stephen's fiancée and her aunt besides ourselves.'

'Are you sure Stephen wants me there?'

'Stephen suggested it. He said with your brain, you'd probably get more sense out of O'Leary than we would. We can't tackle him about it over dinner, but we'll make sure there's a chance afterwards.'

I was being invited as an investigator, not as a prospective member of the family. So be it. I accepted the invitation and Miles said Stephen would send the carriage for me at seven. When he'd gone, I put the letter away in the drawer. I was tempted to re-read that last page but decided against it on the grounds that it might not apply any more. I tried to distract myself by deciding what to wear and settled for the forget-me-not blue, with the darker blue silk stripe and fringed pelerine – nothing too elaborate for a family dinner, or a business occasion.

As it happened, the social part of the evening was more entertaining than expected. Stephen Brinkburn's fiancée, Julia, was pretty and well connected but a pleasant down-to-earth girl for all that. Through the meal, she and Stephen kept exchanging those meant-to-be-secret glances of two people so close that the rest of the world is only a distraction. She was chaperoned by her aunt, a good-humoured lady with musical tastes. But the main source of entertainment at the meal was Henry O'Leary. He was seated on my left, with Miles on my right. I'd never met him before, though it felt as if I had because of Robert's letters. He was close to the boundary that divides men into handsome and altogether too handsome, but just on the right side of it. His hair was dark and curly, his eyes brown and sparkling. He had a way of looking at you when you were speaking as if you were the most interesting thing in the world and when he spoke, in his soft Irish accent, you couldn't help smiling. He had a fund of stories, mostly against himself, of amateur plays, family visits, steeple-chases. Some of them concerned his travels with Robert through France. Naturally there was nothing about his succession of heartbreaks, just anecdotes about inns good and bad, unreliable guides, meals exotic or inedible. I was on the alert for any indication of disagreement between himself and Robert, but there was none. In most of the stories, Robert was the calm and far-seeing one, rescuing O'Leary from various scrapes. Stephen and Miles were content to leave most of the talking to him. As agreed, we said nothing about the main business over dinner. The gentlemen didn't sit long over their port, because Julia and her aunt had relatives to enter-tain so left early. They lived just a few streets away and while Stephen escorted them home in the carriage, Miles, Henry O'Leary and I sat in the drawing room, drank coffee and discussed horses. When Stephen came back the atmosphere changed. He refused coffee and sat down in a chair opposite O'Leary.

'When exactly did you and Robert part company?' he said.

O'Leary seemed surprised, both by the tone and the question. 'In Switzerland. Didn't he tell you? I wanted to visit Vienna and he didn't. All perfectly friendly. I hope you don't think I abandoned him.'

'We don't know what to think,' Stephen said.

For the first time, O'Leary looked less than cheerful. 'Did I offend him after all? When you invited me, I hoped he might be here tonight and we could compare travel stories.'

'As far as we know, he's still in Switzerland or Italy,' Miles said.

O'Leary frowned and seemed about to say something, but stopped because Stephen was asking a question.

'Did he give you any idea of what he intended to do?'

'We didn't discuss it very much.'

I thought that wasn't surprising. Judging by Robert's letter, O'Leary's mind had been elsewhere most of the time.

'He'd been taking an interest in the Swiss canton system, goodness knows why, but then he's interested in politics.' He spoke as it if were something harmless but eccentric, like breeding guinea pigs. 'It was just the same with him in

33

Paris, talking to all sorts of people. He'd met some Italians there and they'd given him letters of introduction to people in Turin. I think that was why he was keen to press on.'

'I hope he hasn't got mixed up with anything in north Italy,' Stephen said. I knew what he meant. The Piedmont area around Turin was one of the latest places where the Italians had been rising up against the Austrians.

'Like Lord Byron fighting for the freedom of Greece, you mean,' said O'Leary cheerfully. Then he looked at our faces and realized it wasn't the happiest of comparisons.

'Lord Byron died in Greece,' said Stephen.

He and Miles looked at each other. 'I suppose it's in our minds that he might have been kidnapped and held hostage to raise money,' Stephen said. 'I've had no letters demanding money, but if . . .'

'Well, if he had got himself kidnapped he must have managed to get away pretty quickly,' O'Leary said. The inappropriate cheerfulness of his tone struck me before his meaning.

'Get away?'

'Well, from what I heard he didn't have a gang of black-bearded ruffians surrounding him when he got off the boat at Dover.'

'Dover?'

'Off a boat?'

'When?'

The three of us fired off our questions at once. O'Leary blinked.

'Didn't you know?'

Through gritted teeth, Stephen spoke for all of

34

us. 'Would you kindly tell us what you're talking about?'

'Why is that so surprising? Of course he came back by boat. He could hardly have swum all the way.' O'Leary was puzzled now, becoming annoyed.

'Came back where?' Stephen said.

'Here, of course. London. You mean to say you didn't know?'

Miles clutched his forehead. Stephen spoke very calmly.

'Are you telling us that Robert is back in London?'

'He must be, mustn't he? It's two weeks ago that my friend saw him coming ashore in Dover. Surely the first thing he'd do is let you know he's back.'

Everybody went quiet. O'Leary looked at Stephen's expression and Miles's bent head and at last realized that something was badly wrong.

'No, he hasn't let us know,' Stephen said after a while. 'As far as we knew, he was still somewhere on the continent.'

'Can you please tell us what you know?' I said. 'Who is your friend who's supposed to have seen him?'

O'Leary was serious now. 'The friend's named Charteris. He and I were at Trinity together and we happened to meet in my club. He'd met Robert when we were planning the journey and didn't know we'd gone our separate ways. He said he was surprised he hadn't seen me at Dover with Robert.'

'And that was two weeks ago?'

'Yes. So I explained about coming back earlier. I asked him if he was sure it was Carmichael he'd seen getting off the boat at Dover and he said he was quite sure. He'd even spoken to him, though not for long. It had been rather a rough crossing and Carmichael said one of the people he was with was ill and he was hurrying to get a coach before they were all taken.'

'People he was with?'

'Two people. My friend happened to see them later. Carmichael had got his coach and was hurrying them over to it. The man looked steady enough, but the woman was leaning on Carmichael's arm. I suppose she was the one who'd been ill on the crossing.'

'Did your friend recognize them?'

'No.'

'What did they look like?'

'He only had a back view of the man, nothing remarkable that he could remember. The woman was wrapped up in a cloak with a hood, but the hood fell back when they were helping her into the coach. Pale face, dark hair. Charteris didn't pay much attention. He was too busy looking for the porter with his luggage.'

So many questions I should have asked, but the one on my mind was too humiliating to speak. Then Miles asked it instead.

'A young woman?'

O'Leary only nodded, but something about his expression answered another question too: young and pretty.

'So is that why he hasn't let us know he's back?' Miles said to Stephen.

36

I looked at Stephen's face, then looked away. Something had changed. Although all three of the men were sitting just where they had been all through the conversation, it felt as if they'd moved closer to each other and further from me. A man comes back from his travels with a woman he can't introduce to his family. Regrettable, but these things happen. Men may talk about them, but not before ladies.

Not much more was said, I think, or nothing to the purpose. Soon after that O'Leary got up to make his farewells, subdued now. I wondered if Robert had talked to him about me, if he knew what there'd been between us. I thought not. Robert didn't open his heart easily. O'Leary looked me in the eye, said how much he'd enjoyed the evening and that he hoped we'd meet again. When he'd gone, the three of us stayed on our feet.

'I'll see Miss Lane home,' Miles said.

Stephen nodded. I guessed that when Miles got back, the brothers would have their discussion. They were relieved that Robert was alive, that was clear, but painfully embarrassed. At least Miles didn't try to get away from the subject as we went home in the family coach.

'You don't think O'Leary's friend could have been mistaken?'

'Not possibly,' I said. 'He actually spoke to Robert.'

'We can't even be sure he's in London,' Miles said. 'He could have gone anywhere in the country.'

The carriage stopped outside Abel Yard and Miles walked with me to the foot of my staircase.

'I'll let you know when we find out anything, Miss Lane.'

So it was the brothers' business to find out now, not mine. Still, he meant well. I thanked him and went slowly upstairs.

THREE

On Thursday afternoon I was back at Gore House with the news that there had indeed been a cancellation and my invalid brother could set out two days from now in a comfortable berth on the evening tide. It had to wait because Lady Blessington was entertaining company, with a gaggle of wits, poets and critics competing to outdo each other over the teacups. She looked tired, only half her attention on them, and I guessed the burden of her secret guest was weighing heavily. It was six o'clock before the last of them left – still quoting from his latest political satire as he went – and we were alone together. She was delighted to hear about the ship, summoned D'Orsay and Mr Lesparre, who'd been keeping out of the way upstairs while there were visitors, and we settled down to planning details. In case somebody was spying on the house, simply driving up seemed to her too risky. Instead D'Orsay would hire a closed carriage and he, Lesparre and the valet would leave the house early on Saturday morning, Lesparre sitting well back in the seat with the curtain drawn. D'Orsay would pay a breakfast call on a friend in Mayfair, not far from where I lived, and leave Mr Lesparre and his valet there when he went. Amos and I would drive to the address in the livery stable's plain carriage, collect Lesparre and valet, then all speed to Gravesend. Lesparre asked if I'd delivered his message for Bruno and seemed concerned that there had been no assurance that it would be passed on. He hoped the valet would report for duty that evening or Friday morning at the latest. From Lady Blessington's expression, she was determined that Lesparre should travel, valet or no valet. Apart from that, Lesparre raised no objections to the plan and thanked us all, but he still seemed to me less than enthusiastic. He was carrying a leather wallet on a strap over his shoulder, the kind government messengers use.

'The documents?' I said.

He nodded. 'Whenever there are visitors, I keep them by me. Who knows when I might have to leave suddenly.' Lady Blessington looked offended at this implied criticism of his safety under her roof, but D'Orsay was sympathetic.

'You must keep them safe at all costs.' He turned to me. 'Mr Lesparre even sleeps with them under his pillow. Very properly. A lot depends on them.'

We'd got on to the subject of other luggage – very little, thank goodness – when pandemonium broke out: shouts from the garden, then a bell clanging and a man crying, 'Fire.' A footman came into the library at a run.

'Ma'am, there's a fire in the kitchens.'

Just a moment's shock then she was in control of the situation. Various indoor servants had joined the footman at the library door, waiting for orders, and she sent them running. Had the

40

gardeners gone to fetch the fire cart? Yes. Then all the male indoor servants were to go and help, filling buckets from the pool in the garden. But remember that the poor carp must not be left high and dry. They were to be fished out in nets and put in bowls of water well away from the fire. Where was the poodle? There under the table. Two of the maids were to take him and the greyhound into the orchard and keep them there. If the fire got near the aviaries, they were to be opened so that the birds could fly. Were all the kitchen staff out? Well, go and see at once. D'Orsay was hustled out with the rest, leaving only the two of us and Mr Lesparre. He was on his feet by then, satchel clutched to his side. 'Must I go up to the loft?'

'No, not with a fire in the house, although I hope it will stay in the kitchen. You'd better go up to Alfred's study. We'll let you know if you need to move.'

By then, the smell of burning was leaching into the flower-scented air of the library. I followed her along a corridor and through a door to the back courtyard behind the kitchens. No flames were visible, but clouds of black smoke were rising, along with white columns of steam where the bucket carriers were doing their work, at least as much white as black, suggesting that the fire was coming under control. As we watched, a clangour of bells and shouts came from the direction of the main gates and the drive – probably the insurance company's fire wagon arriving, as usual for them, too late to be much use. Just as well Lady Blessington had made her own

41

arrangements. They made a great business of earning their money by organizing their own bucket chain, but mostly got in the way of the staff. Within half an hour of their arrival the fire was out with nothing left of it but the smell and clouds of smuts. With her usual presence of mind, Lady Blessington ordered the firemen to empty the water left in their tank into the pond, so that the carp could go back. The dogs were brought back from the orchard, the housekeeper instructed to issue beer to staff and firemen alike and the cook to serve dinner as near the usual hour as possible, although cold cuts since the kitchen was clearly out of operation.

As it turned out, the fire had been less damaging than had seemed likely. It had started not in the kitchen itself, but in a pile of empty vegetable baskets and wooden trugs left outside the scullery door. The flames had burned the door frame and blackened the walls of the scullery, but the gardeners and indoor servants had managed to douse them before they got any further. A few injuries had been suffered. A scullery maid had bravely but unwisely tried to tackle the blaze on her own and scorched her arm. She was soothed, bandaged and sent to bed. A groom who'd sprained his ankle tripping over a bucket was also bandaged and given a glass of whisky to ease the pain. There were various other minor burns and bruises, but the word had got round that Lady Blessington intended to add an extra day to everyone's wages so the male servants who stood around in the dusk outside the back door were a cheerful crowd, enjoying their beer and embroidering stories about their actions and the incompetence of the insurance men. In the lamplight spilling out from the scullery they looked like miners who'd just come up from underground, faces blackened from smoke so that their eyeballs showed very white, clothes covered with ash and smuts, boots singed and ash encrusted. When I went back inside the house I found Count D'Orsay, who had been more effective than I expected in firefighting, looking at the smuts and scorches on his linen like Saint Sebastian counting the arrows. He was deep in discussion with Lady Blessington, and as I moved towards them I caught a few words: '. . . anybody with a grudge.'

'But there's nobody,' she protested. She turned to me. 'Alfred thinks the fire was started deliberately.'

'Not a doubt of it,' he said. 'How else would it have happened? There were burning scraps of newspaper flying around. Why should anybody leave newspapers outside a scullery? They were used to start the fire.' He looked down unhappily at his kid gloves, beyond saving. 'I'm not a fit sight for company. You will excuse me if I go and change.' He hurried indoors.

'Do you think he's right?' I said.

'I don't know. He suggested it might have been a dismissed servant or a tradesman with a grudge. But we haven't had to dismiss anyone for a year or more and the tradesmen's bills are paid.'

'Somebody would have to know that there were baskets and things outside the scullery,' I said.

'It could have been an accident. If a gardener came carrying a basket of vegetables with a pipe in his mouth . . .' She was trying to convince herself. 'Besides, if somebody wanted to start a fire deliberately, wouldn't he have done it where it would cause more damage? A fire near the kitchens was bound to be spotted quickly, with so many people preparing dinner.'

'Could it have been anything to do with Mr Lesparre?' I said.

She stared at me, alarmed. 'Why in the world do you think that?'

'Suppose somebody suspected he was hiding here and wanted to flush him out. With most fires, the whole household would rush outside.'

'But it was never that serious and we would never have been so stupid as to let him be seen.'

'A warning, then. Somebody letting you know that if you go on sheltering him worse things will happen?'

Her two soft chins went firm as granite. 'If that's so, they've picked the wrong woman. And if that's the worst they can do, we don't need to worry.' She took out her watch. 'Lord, how the time has gone. I must change for dinner. You'll stay here tonight? There are still things we must settle.'

I pointed out that my only clothes were the riding habit I stood up in, now smelling of smoke as well as of Rancie, but she said it didn't matter because the meal would be informal.

Dinner turned out to be a superior form of cold cuts – trout with cucumber, chicken in aspic, rare beef with horseradish, plus excellent champagne. We were four at the table because it was safe for Mr Lesparre to come down from his bedroom. As Lady Blessington pointed out, the fire gave her a good excuse for turning away callers. The conversation hopped easily from French to English and was entertaining as it always was with D'Orsay present, gossip occasionally malicious, but usually against people who deserved it, and always funny. Lesparre contributed the occasional anecdote from Paris, neat and to the point. I began to warm to him more, yet had the feeling that he wasn't letting down his guard in spite of the wine and good food. Not surprising perhaps in a failed conspirator who was no longer young. We all did our best and yet I sensed an atmosphere, with people a little too ready to fill conversational gaps, voices a shade too high and bright. It might have been because of the fire, but I sensed that D'Orsay as well as Lady Blessington would be glad to see the last of their guest. Then, over late raspberries and more champagne, talk turned serious because D'Orsay raised the question of the Boulogne raid. I was surprised when he did because it could hardly have been welcome to Lesparre and D'Orsay's politeness was a byword. It struck me later that, with Lesparre due to leave the day after next, he thought there might not be other opportunities. If my guess was right and he and Lady Blessington had invested more in the attempt than they cared to admit, they might reasonably want to know what had gone wrong. Lesparre took it well, though the social temperature of the room dropped by several degrees. He explained that for one thing the weather was against them, wind from the wrong quarter and waves higher than a steamer built for going up and down the Thames was used to encountering. A lot of their men were seasick and their arrival at Boulogne was delayed by almost a full day.

'Did that make such a difference?' D'Orsay asked.

'In itself, no. But the plan depended on the commanding officer of the garrison being away for several days. We knew he would be. His second in command was totally on the prince's side and he and his men would have come over to us. But the commanding officer returned early and the garrison rallied to him.'

'Was that simply bad luck?' D'Orsay asked.

Lesparre gave him a hard look. 'I think you know it wasn't. You've heard things said?'

D'Orsay returned the look. 'That the commanding officer had been warned? You had a traitor in the ranks?'

Lesparre nodded, drained his champagne glass and put it down too heavily. The silence they'd been trying to avoid all through the meal came over the table, broken eventually by Lady Blessington.

'If you put fifty men and guns aboard a steamer, somebody's going to ask questions. And I'm afraid the prince himself wasn't always the most discreet of men, not to speak of all those French agents spying on him.'

'It was worse than that.' D'Orsay was

contradicting her for once. 'From what I heard, the commanding officer knew just the moment to return, when it was too late for the prince to turn back. Wasn't that the case, Lesparre?'

He sighed. 'Just so.'

This time, it didn't need Lady Blessington to break the silence. It was done by the entrance of a footman.

'Ma'am, there are two persons at the back door who wish to speak to you.'

Lady Blessington looked annoyed. 'I told you, I'm not receiving callers this evening.'

'They're police officers, ma'am.'

Mr Lesparre stood up, overturning his chair.

'Tell them they must come back in the morning,' Lady Blessington said.

'They say it's about a thief, ma'am.'

'Thief?' Instinctively, she clasped the pearl and diamond bracelet round her wrist with her free hand, as if worried it would fly away.

'I think you should see them, Marguerite,' D'Orsay said.

'But . . .' She gestured towards Mr Lesparre. 'There isn't time to . . .'

'Take your time letting them in, keep them talking in the servants' part of the house and Lesparre can go up the main stairs.' D'Orsay was the man of action again.

She nodded and spoke to the footman. 'Stedge, tell the butler he's to let them into the house-keeper's room but not to hurry about it, then take Mr Lesparre upstairs. Alfred you'd better stay with me.'

* * *

47

I suppose I should have stayed with her too, but she was more than equal to dealing with policemen and I was curious to see Mr Lesparre put into his hiding place, so I fell in behind Mr Lesparre as he followed Stedge up the main staircase. On the first landing we took a smart right turn, through the doorway that led to the servants' part of the house. Stedge had brought a candle in a holder with him, necessary because there were no lights burning on the back landing and the small window showed only darkness outside. But Mr Lesparre seemed accustomed to dim light as he followed the footman up another far less grand flight. From there, a small flight of steps led up to a final half-landing of bare planks. The only things on it were a long pole with a hook on the end and a wooden ladder fastened to the wall. Stedge set his candle down on the floor and the movement sent our long shadows wavering over the walls that boxed us in. Ten feet or so above our heads was a loft hatch of unpainted pine boards, about five feet square. Stedge took the pole in his hand, mounted halfway up the ladder and leaned across to hook the pole through the iron ring in the hatch cover. He pulled on the pole and the hatch cover slid sideways on wooden runners as smoothly as a drawer in a dressing table, all with a lack of concern that suggested it was no more than a footman's normal duties. In Lady Blessington's household the staff prob-ably grew accustomed to anything. When the hatch was open Stedge climbed the final rungs and eased himself through the black space into the loft. Mr Lesparre and I, down on the landing,

48

listened to his steps moving cautiously overhead. As I looked at Lesparre in the dim light I saw strain on his face and thought what an ordeal these gymnastics must be for a man no longer young. I couldn't help feeling sorry for the turn his life had taken. If things had gone right, he might have been dining with the prince at the Tuileries by now instead of going through all this. A flint lighter scraped and a soft light spread down through the loft hatch. Then Stedge's cheerful voice: 'All ready, sir. Coming down now.'

His shoes and stockinged calves hung down from the hatch and found their foothold on the ladder. He climbed down beside us and Mr Lesparre took his place on the ladder. I noticed the satchel with the papers was still on his shoulder. When he'd gone up the first few rungs of the ladder he unhitched it and threw it up ahead of him. He made a neater job than I'd expected of getting through the hatch into the loft. We waited for a while, then Stedge called up: 'Everything to your satisfaction, sir?'

'Yes, thank you.'

'I'll close you up then, sir.' Stedge went through the procedure in reverse, using the pole to push the hatch back in place. He came down the ladder, replaced the pole and I followed him down the back stairs. On the landing of the main bedroom floor he started opening the door that would take me back to the family side of house.

'How often does that have to happen?' I said.

'Three or four occasions since the gentleman got here, ma'am.'

49

'It must be quite hard for him.'

'Not as bad as you might think, ma'am. Her Ladyship's had the loft made quite comfortable, even put a camp bed up there for him.'

'How long does he have to stay up there?'

'Depends what's happening downstairs. No more than an hour or two, usually.'

'It must be lonely, shut up there on his own.'

'He could always come down if he wanted to, he's not locked in, but he's got his reasons I dare say. To be honest, ma'am, we get used to it.'

'Used to what?' I wondered if Lady Blessington were in the habit of sheltering foreign refugees and it was common knowledge among the servants.

'Duns, ma'am. Cunning as foxes and once they hit you with their bit of paper you're properly done for.' He grinned at his own pun. 'So it makes sense for him to stay up there until Her Ladyship lets him know it's safe to come down.'

Lady Blessington had been clever. In her world, there were always people on the run from debt collectors – D'Orsay himself one of the prime examples in the past – going to any lengths to stop them delivering their writs. It would explain many little eccentricities like guests hiding in lofts. I asked how they let him know when it was safe to come down.

'I give him four knocks ma'am, like this.' He demonstrated on the doorframe: two quick knocks, then two more widely spaced. 'He knows to stand clear then and let me open the hatch.'

'Always you?'

'Yes, ma'am.'

* * *

50

He opened the door inviting me to go through, but I remembered I was supposed to be joining Lady Blessington and the policemen in the housekeeper's room, so I followed him down to the ground floor. By then, quite a party had gathered. Lady Blessington was sitting at a chair by the big wooden table, with the housekeeper's basket of things that needed mending at one end of it. D'Orsay was standing beside her, with two police constables, one middle-aged and one younger, standing at the other end of the table by the mending basket, top hats under their arms, and a tall middle-aged woman in a black dress – presumably the housekeeper – beside them.

Lady Blessington turned to me. 'Would you believe it, Miss Lane? These officers say a boy called at the police office with a message that there'd been a fire and a robbery.'

'It's frequently the *modus operandi* of the more ingenious gangs,' the older constable said. 'They start a small fire to distract the occupants while an accomplice does his work inside the house.'

'But I wasn't told anything about a robbery,' Lady Blessington said. She looked at the housekeeper. 'Were you?' The housekeeper shook her head.

'The watch officer said a boy came running with the message that Lady Blessington wanted somebody there at once because a man had been seen climbing down out of a window.' The older constable was doing all the talking, the younger one standing like a waxwork.

'When was this?'

'About seven o'clock.'

'In that case, it took you long enough to get here.'

'We came as soon as we could. There was a runaway horse in the Kensington Road that occupied most of our men.'

'I assure you, I sent no such message. All we've had here is the fire and that was out long ago. I'm afraid you've been troubled for nothing.'

'Since we're here, Your Ladyship, wouldn't it be as well to check there's nothing missing? We've had jewellery stolen from houses near here not long since.'

I could see Lady Blessington struggling to come to a decision. On one hand she wanted the police off the premises as soon as possible. On the other, a concerned householder with nothing to hide would naturally check her jewel boxes.

'Very well.' She turned to the housekeeper. 'Mrs Neal, would you kindly ask Cicely to come to us, then make inquiries among all the staff and find out if any of them saw anything out of the way. And ask them if they know anything about a message to the police.'

The maid Cicely appeared almost immediately and we all went up in procession to Lady Blessington's bedroom. She kept us standing there while she and Cicely went through to the dressing room. From the sounds, they were checking the safe where serious jewels were kept. 'Nothing gone,' she said when they came out. 'The safe hasn't been touched.'

Cicely went over to the dressing table and started opening drawers and moving aside a large and untidy assortment of bottles and jars on the top of it. 'I can't find your lapis lazuli pendant, ma'am, or your garnet bracelet.'

'Weren't they in the safe?' D'Orsay asked.

Lady Blessington looked pitying at his male ignorance. 'We keep only the important pieces in the safe. The everyday ones stay on the dressing-table drawers or on the top. Are you sure they're not there, Cicely? I can't remember when I last wore them.'

'The bracelet with your plum velvet and the pendant with your blue silk,' Cicely said. 'I put them in the box in the top right-hand drawer as usual. They're not there now.'

'You've probably just taken them off and left them somewhere,' D'Orsay said. 'You know you do have a habit of mislaying bits of jewellery. Remember when we found the earring on the dog's collar?' I couldn't decide whether he was really bored or sounding it for the benefit of the police. Certainly by Lady Blessington's standards a couple of trinkets with semi-precious stones wouldn't provoke excitement.

The older constable stepped forward, smug with justification. 'Since the pieces are missing, may I suggest a search of the house to see if anything else has been taken? Also, there's a chance that an accomplice may still be hiding.'

'He'd have to be a very stupid accomplice in that case,' she said. 'A whole regiment of thieves could have marched out with all the fuss about the fire going on.'

She made a good point, I thought. If the messenger had reached the police office around seven he must have left Gore House while the fire was still burning. But the police constable would not be deflected from his duty and possibly simply curiosity about the famous Gore House and its inhabitants. She sighed.

'Very well, I'll send a footman to show you round. Please get it over with as soon as you can. We've had more than enough disruption for one day. Cicely, please ring for Stedge.' She was keeping her head well, I thought. Stedge would head them away from any curiosity about the loft. Unseen by the policemen, she caught my eye and blew out her cheeks in relief that Lesparre was safely stowed away.

We left the policemen in the bedroom, with Cicely to keep an eye on them, and went downstairs to the housekeeper's room where Mrs Neal was waiting. Lady Blessington asked if any of the staff had seen anything or sent for the police.

'Ronson, ma'am.'

'Oh dear.' An exasperated sigh from Lady Blessington.

'Saw something or sent for the police?' D'Orsay said.

'Both, sir, only he's not quite sure what he did see.'

Lady Blessington sank down in a chair. 'We'd better have him in.'

'You're tired,' D'Orsay said. 'Won't it wait till morning?'

'If he really did see something I suppose we should find out while the police are still here. Please send him in, Mrs Neal.'

'He's dirty, ma'am.'

'Just send him in.' She explained while we were waiting, 'Ronson gets very confused sometimes. Nervous too, but he means well.'

One of her lame dogs, I thought. She was charitable in adding to her dependants, human or animal. Ronson was a man of average height, in his early thirties, dark hair cut short and sleeked down, pale face with eyes that moved quickly around without settling on anything. He was nervous, as Lady Blessington had said, but intelligent looking. He was dressed as an under-servant in black trousers and white shirt, with a green baize apron from waist to knees. At least the shirt had probably once been white, but now it was dark grey and his apron was covered in black smears and so crumpled that it might have been used for cleaning boots. His face was smeared black too but it looked as if he'd made some attempt to clean it, probably with spittle – no great improvement as it showed red splotches under the dirt. His arrival brought a strong whiff of soot and smoke and something more unpleasant underneath it: vomit and dried sweat.

'You should have washed,' I heard the house-keeper saying to him, low voiced.

'There's no water left in the well,' he told her, bending his head. From his voice he was a Londoner, with some education. Being an under-servant at his age suggested bad luck or bad conduct somewhere in his career.

'Ronson was fighting the fire with the rest of them.' The housekeeper apologized for him. 'He was sick from swallowing the smoke.'

55

'Then we shan't keep him longer than we can help,' Lady Blessington said gently.

'You think you saw somebody coming out of a window, Ronson?'

'Yes, ma'am.' He kept his eyes and his voice low.

'When was this?'

'About the time the fire engine got here, ma'am.'

'And you didn't say anything to anybody?'

'They were all busy with the fire, ma'am. I didn't know who to tell so I saw a boy standing there – one of the garden boys I think it might have been – and said he should run and get a policeman.'

'Why didn't you come and tell me?' D'Orsay said.

'I couldn't find you, sir.'

'What did the man look like?' Lady Blessington's tone was kinder than D'Orsay's.

'Big. Quite big. He was wearing black I think, but I couldn't see well because of the smoke in my eyes.'

'What room did he come out of?'

'One of the bedrooms, ma'am – the family bedrooms, not the servants'.'

'Could it have been from my bedroom?'

'I don't know which one's your bedroom, ma'am.' D'Orsay looked annoyed at that but it seemed credible to me. A male lower servant would have no reason to know about bedrooms.

'I suppose you'll have to tell the police about it when they've finished searching,' Lady Blessington said. 'Mrs Neal, do you think you could find some water somewhere to get him clean, or cleaner at any rate? Then give him some broth to settle his stomach. Alfred, would you please go and see how they're getting on upstairs.'

It was a good hour before he joined us in the small drawing room.

'All done?' she asked him.

He nodded. 'They're talking to Ronson now, not that they'll get much sense from him. Then Stedge will show them out.'

'He kept them away from the loft?'

'Yes, they were mostly interested in the main bedrooms where jewellery and valuables might be. I can't find any sign of anything else missing.'

'Well done you and Stedge.' She lay back in her chair and closed her eyes. 'If anything else happens today, please don't tell me.'

D'Orsay had unlocked the tantalus on the sideboard and was pouring brandy – three glasses, I was glad to see. 'That Ronson fellow is useless. He must have been seeing things. You're sure the pendant and bracelet have really gone, Marguerite?'

'After all this, I'm not sure of anything. Cicely says so and she knows where I put things better than I do.'

She looked so weary I didn't want to add to her worries, but something was bothering me. 'It wasn't a very ambitious robbery, was it? Somebody goes to all the trouble of starting the fire so that he can get into the house, then he takes two not very valuable pieces of jewellery and draws

57

attention to himself by jumping out of an upstairs window when he could have just walked out.'

Lady Blessington opened her eyes and looked at me sadly. 'Is this leading to Mr Lesparre again?'

'Possibly. The fire failed because your people acted quickly and brought it under control, so somebody had to think of another way to flush him out. If so, they didn't waste time.'

'If you're right and if they've done all this, then they must want Lesparre and those papers very badly.' Lady Blessington spoke slowly. D'Orsay's face was grim.

'Yes,' I said.

She sighed. 'One doesn't like to sound inhospitable, but the sooner that gentleman's out of the house, the better. At least the day after tomorrow he'll be on his way, thanks to you, Miss Lane.'

'Tomorrow now, not the day after,' D'Orsay said, looking at the gilt clock on the mantelpiece. It was nearly two o'clock in the morning.

'Should we bring Mr Lesparre down?' Lady Blessington made the suggestion half-heartedly.

D'Orsay shook his head. 'He's perfectly all right up there and he should be asleep by now. We'll bring him down for breakfast.'

Lady Blessington herself showed me to a guest room a few doors along from her own and brought me a nightdress. Cicely had been allowed to go to bed hours before. Could I possibly manage with only cold water on the wash stand? She could have hot water brought up, but . . . I said hastily that cold would do very well, knowing

58

that the alternative would be summoning the housekeeper to tell the chambermaid, who'd have to pass it on to the scullery maid, who'd probably have to stir up the kitchen fire and send the boy out with the coal bucket. It had been a long day for us but an even longer one for the staff, and faint sounds of clanking and scrubbing were still coming up from the kitchen. As I sank into a goose-feather mattress as soft as a summer cloud, I hoped that Mr Lesparre might be even half as comfortable on his camp bed two floors above, then I drifted into a dreamless sleep.

FOUR

I woke at daylight, far too early for breakfast, put on my riding habit and went quietly downstairs in stockinged feet. The front door was bolted, so I went through the kitchen, getting a surprised look from the lad attending to the fire in the cooking range, and sat on the step outside to put on my boots. It looked like being a fine day, with the sky clearing from grey to pale blue and the dew heavy. I walked on paths between espaliered fruit trees through the vegetable garden towards the stables and picked an apple for Rancie. She was looking out over the door to her loose box in the stable yard and welcomed me with that loose-lipped burring sound, less urgent than a whinny, seeming not at all put out by her new surroundings. I bit the apple into halves and gave them to her, with the morning bustle of the stable yard round us. I'd known the grooms and lads would be up at first light.

'Everything all right, ma'am?' It was the head groom. I'd met him before, a big friendly man with an Irish accent. He was more than ready to talk about the events of the day before and pleased with the efforts of his men in tackling the fire.

'Then there was a robbery too,' I said.

'So we heard, and the police here. Was there much taken?'

'Nothing important, as far as we can tell. Did

any of your men see anybody coming out of the window?'

He shook his head. 'Too busy with the fire. As we heard it, one of the maids found them in a bedroom, screamed blue murder and they jumped out of the window and ran off.'

Since this was clearly wrong in at least two respects, rumour was already taking over from the little we had in the way of fact. We talked horses for a while then I started back for the house, but made a detour on the way to the flower borders. Ronson would presumably have been with the other firefighters in a bucket chain from one of the garden ponds to the kitchen door, which would have given him a view of the back of the house. The borders were closely planted with chrysanthemums and sedums, all in bloom. A fairly large man jumping down from a bedroom would have made a considerable hole but there was no sign that anything larger than a hedgehog had passed that way. Apart from the loss of Lady Blessington's trinkets, the only evidence of the burglar came from one glimpse on the part of a man who was otherwise occupied, sick from inhaling smoke and probably of an excitable temperament. I went back to the house, hungry for breakfast. D'Orsay was already in the dining room, wearing a waistcoat patterned in peacock feathers and sipping black coffee. He wished me good morning and said I was up early. I returned the sentiment.

'I'll admit I didn't sleep well,' he said.

I asked him if Lesparre's valet had arrived as requested. No sign of him, he said. Sometime later Lady Blessington arrived in a dressing gown of green and gold merino, looking as if she hadn't slept well either. D'Orsay seemed surprised to see her and I guessed she usually breakfasted upstairs in her room. The giant poodle followed her and before she'd attend to anything else she poured a bowl of warm milk for it and put it down on the floor, then sank down in a chair while D'Orsay brought her coffee with plenty of cream and sugar. I drank coffee, ate toast and coddled eggs and decided it was time to come to business. I was conscious that I hadn't changed my clothes or had a proper wash since yesterday and knew that Mrs Martley would be worrying.

'We should have a talk with Mr Lesparre before I go about the arrangements for tomorrow. If there are French agents so determined to get to him, we can't afford any mistakes. I'll try and find out what's happened to the valet, but if he's not here early tomorrow, we'll have to go without him.' Privately, I'd decided to have a council of war with Amos to review our plans for getting to Gravesend.

'Yes, of course we must talk to Lesparre. It's high time we brought him down for breakfast anyway. He must be awake by now.' She rang the bell for the maid and sent her to fetch Stedge. He arrived looking as neat as ever, shoes shined and wig newly powdered, though he'd probably had less sleep than any of us. 'My compliments to Mr Lesparre and ask him to join us for breakfast.'

* * *

62

D'Orsay decided to go with him. I followed them up the main staircase to the first landing, then through the door to the back stairs. The morning bustle of the kitchen, pans clanking and voices giving orders, sounded below us. When we got to the top landing the footman took the pole from the wall and knocked on the hatch, two quick knocks then two more widely spaced. No answer, except I thought there was a faint stirring from above.

'He must still be asleep,' D'Orsay said, sounding impatient. He called up: 'Lesparre, wake up. It's quite safe to come down.'

No answer. D'Orsay nodded to Stedge, who picked up the pole, climbed halfway up the ladder and leaned out to hook the ring on the hatch. He pulled and nothing happened, the hatch remaining firmly in place.

'Seems to have got jammed, sir.'

D'Orsay clicked his tongue, anxious to get on with the arrangements for seeing Lesparre on his way as soon as possible. Responding to his impatience, Stedge moved down a step, took a firm grip on the pole with both hands and put all his weight on it. Even then, instead of sliding back smoothly as it had done the night before, the hatch juddered and moved reluctantly. Then it gave suddenly. Stedge dropped the pole and screamed, alarming in itself from a footman trained to silence but understandable because a dark shape had come hurtling down from the loft, knocking him off the ladder so that he landed in a heap on the boards, then screamed again as something landed on top of him. Or not quite landed because it was supported by a rope. It hung about two feet above the landing like a giant black skittle ball, butting against D'Orsay, feet just touching Stedge's hunched back. A smell of excrement filled the air. Stedge blundered to his feet, falling into me.

'A knife,' D'Orsay said. 'Fetch a knife.'

Stedge got himself upright and put his arms round the man's knees, trying to support his weight. But it was too late for that. Once the tension of the rope had been taken the head lolled sideways to the shoulder like some engorged fruit on a broken tree. His arms were pinioned behind him with a thin twist of rope. His eyes were protruding and there seemed to be a terrible grey grin on his face, then I realized it was a dirty rag gagging him. In spite of that, he was recognizably my temporary brother, Mr Lesparre. D'Orsay looked at me over the bent head of Stedge and his burden, face as pale as a flounder's belly.

'Yes,' I said. 'A knife, yes.'

Useless of course, but I ran downstairs and startled the cook by grabbing the one she was using to chop carrots. No point in hiding that something was dreadfully wrong. On the way back up, I went into one of the servants' dormitories and grabbed a sheet off a bed. On the landing, Stedge had been sick but was still managing to hold the body. D'Orsay sawed through the rope, managing well enough for a man whose greatest exertion was usually picking up a paint brush. He cut through the thin rope binding Lesparre's wrists and the back of the gag too, though it was obviously no help. Perhaps, like me, he'd been struck by the obscenity of that grey grin. Then the three of us bundled Lesparre in the sheet. His left arm flopped out and I noticed, as you notice small things when something awful is happening, that the signet ring with the phoenix and laurel wreath was gone from his little finger and the knuckle was bleeding.

'Wait on the next landing,' D'Orsay told the footman. 'Stop anybody from coming up.' Then he and I went down together to break the news to Lady Blessington.

FIVE

'Miss Lane, what in the world are we going to do?' The news had been broken. She looked shaken and older, the sunlight through the window of the breakfast room emphasizing the lines round her eyes and mouth. I daresay I looked as strained and knew I smelled bad. I envied D'Orsay, who'd gone to bathe and change as soon as he knew she wasn't going to faint or have hysterics. Another footman had been sent upstairs to relieve Stedge.

'We'll have to tell the police,' I said.

'Tell them what? I don't trust the police. After this, I don't trust anybody. Can't we just . . . dispose of the poor man ourselves? Decently, I mean. A quiet burial?'

'What do you suggest? A grave in the garden?' For an awful moment I thought she was going to leap at the idea, but she sighed and took the point.

'One can't, I suppose. But if we tell the police then the whole business will have to come out.'

'Nobody will think the worse of you for trying to protect a friend's friend.'

'I don't care a fig for what anybody thinks of me. They've been gossiping about me for thirty years. It's the prince I'm thinking about. And those papers.'

'Mr Lesparre took them up with him to the attic, in that satchel.'

'But they won't be there now, will they? I suppose whoever killed him will have taken them. Or perhaps they forced him to hand them over and he hanged himself because he knew he'd failed the prince.'

'No.' So far we'd spared her the worst details, but she had to know. 'He couldn't have done it himself. Somebody had left him bound and gagged, standing on the trapdoor with a noose round his neck and the rope tied to a beam in the loft. He'd have died as soon as the trap was opened.'

'So he'd have known . . . he must have heard you and Alfred down there and . . .'

'Yes.' I thought of the small sound I'd heard from the loft and D'Orsay's guess that Lesparre was still in bed. I didn't want to think of the desperation of his last seconds. There was a decanter of brandy on the sideboard. Rather than bother with finding glasses I poured a generous measure for each of us into our coffee cups.

'How did they get in?' she said.

'I don't know. Is there any other way into the loft?' She didn't know. I suppose it was too much to expect it. 'We need to go there for a look before the police arrive,' I said. 'For one thing, we must see if the papers are still there, though I don't suppose they will be. But we'll have to do it quickly. The longer we put off sending for the police, the more suspicious it will look.'

D'Orsay returned, in fresh clothes and smelling sweetly of Floris's bay water. He supported me

67

in saying that we must tell the police. 'The question is how much we tell them.'

'As little as possible,' Lady Blessington said promptly. The brandy had brought some colour back to her cheeks. 'We can say we've never met the man before and perhaps it was a falling out among burglars. That wretched business yesterday will be to our advantage.'

'As long as the servants don't talk,' D'Orsay said.

'They won't. They're totally loyal.' She spoke like the head of a fighting clan.

'They will,' I said. 'It doesn't matter how loyal they are. They might not mean harm, but servants have friends and families and they're bound to talk about something like this. I think we'll have to admit that he was a friend staying with you.'

'But can we keep the prince out of it?' she said.

'With luck, yes. Do the servants know about the connection between Lesparre and the prince?'

'No. We have so many people here there's no reason why they should remember one in particular.'

So we concocted our story, such as it was. Mr Lesparre was an acquaintance of D'Orsay's from France, fallen on hard times and lodging with them temporarily. Given the political turmoil in France, that would be quite credible. We could let it be known that he had been cast down and depressed and, without actually saying so, imply that he had killed himself. I was doubtful about that, thinking that there must be marks on his wrists from struggling to release them, but the other two passed over that with the speed of people practised in ignoring inconvenient details. Lady Blessington was actually cheered up by the plotting, but then she was a novelist after all. A boy would be sent to the nearest police office to report the death, but only after we'd had time to look in the attic. D'Orsay and I did that together – he stoic about the ruin of another pair of trousers, I thankful that my riding costume had skirts narrow enough to negotiate the hatch into the loft. It was a bad few moments, edging past Lesparre's sheeted body in the muck and slime of the half-landing to get to the ladder. We took up a candle lamp borrowed from the kitchen. By its light, I could see that Lady Blessington had made the part of the loft nearest the hatch as comfortable as possible for her guest, with a canvas camp bed and chair and a table with an oil lamp and flint lighter. There were no signs of a struggle. The lamp was empty, with the wick burned right down, and the glass chimney cold. Lesparre had waited for death in the dark. The loft was about the size of a large parlour, closed off with brick walls on two sides and stout boarding on the others, a barn-like ceiling stretching up into shadows. I guessed that in a place the size of Gore House there would be other lofts with their own entrances, but if so there seemed no way through to them.

'Here it is.' A triumphant cry from D'Orsay. He held up the leather satchel. 'It was just on the floor here.' He was holding the courier's satchel by its strap and the heavy swing of it showed it was full – the last thing I'd expected. I was about to suggest we should take it downstairs to look at it, but he opened it at once, plunged his hand in and brought out a wodge of papers. 'Oh.'

I went across for a look. He was holding a handful of folded newspaper pages.

'Is that all, nothing inside them?'

He brought out handful after handful with the same result, letting them fall to the loft floor – only newspapers, nothing else. 'So whoever killed him did take the letters, as we thought.'

I wondered why, in that case, the person should have taken trouble to pad out the satchel and whether a murderer brought wads of newspapers with him as a matter of course. D'Orsay let the satchel drop, dejected. The only other things we could find were a pair of monogrammed velvet slippers that D'Orsay had given Lesparre for wearing in the loft, so that he could move quietly. The thought of that small comfort in such an uncomfortable situation for Lesparre brought a sudden rush of sadness for him and a life that had gone so terribly wrong. I thought that if it hadn't been for loyalty to the Napoleon family he would have been a comfortable gentleman on his ancestral acres. We left the cut rope dangling down through the open loft hatch exactly as it was. D'Orsay said he'd send men up to move the body to an unused room then ask the house-keeper to clear up the mess, but I thought it should stay there until the police arrived and he agreed.

The two constables, neither of them the same as the day before, and then a sergeant were efficient,

70

but properly respectful to Her Ladyship. After they'd been upstairs to see the body, I stayed with Lady Blessington and D'Orsay while she explained to them about her unfortunate and nervous guest. She was sorry that she knew so little about his family in France, except she gathered they had estates near Bordeaux. The police didn't seem suspicious that she should give house room to a mere acquaintance and probably considered it of a piece with her unconventional reputation. The sergeant asked who'd discovered the body. We'd decided in advance that I should be kept out of it. D'Orsay gave an adequate account of being concerned when Lesparre failed to come down to breakfast and was not in his room. He and the footman had searched the house and found him hanging from a loft beam on the top landing, obviously dead. Stedge was called and backed up D'Orsay's account, having been primed in advance. He said as little as possible, which was only natural in a footman, and if the sergeant caught a whiff of gin on his breath, that was understandable in the circumstances. After hearing him out, the sergeant said they didn't need to trouble Her Ladyship any more for the present, but she'd be hearing from the coroner's officer when the time and place of the inquest were fixed. Count D'Orsay and the footman might be called on to give evidence. When they'd left, Lady Blessington breathed a great sigh of relief.

'Thank you, Miss Lane. I don't know what we'd have done without you.'

'I don't know that I've been much use at all.'

71

I was weary with strain and shock that hadn't quite hit me when there was so much to settle. All I wanted to do was ride home, bathe and change. Lady Blessington said a bath and clean clothes could be provided there, but I wanted to get away from Gore House for a while. I promised I'd be back. Rather than trouble the staff I let myself out of a side door and walked towards the stables. The smell of fire still hung over the kitchen courtyard and my feet scrunched on scorched wood. A small black wagon drawn by a tired-looking hack was standing in the yard, with a police constable who looked as tired as the horse holding the door open. Two more constables came out of the kitchen doorway carrying a bundle wrapped in a grey blanket, with the sergeant behind them. They slid it on to a bench in the wagon, carefully enough but with no reverence. A few hours ago, that bundle had stood in the dark, hearing voices below, knowing what would happen and powerless to do anything about it. I would come back later because I'd promised I would, but more than that I wanted to know who could do that to a man, and why.

On Saturday afternoon Amos and I rode out to Gore House together. I knew he'd have been worried when I wasn't there for our usual early morning ride on Friday, so the first thing I'd done, after I'd bathed, changed and dodged questions from Mrs Martley, had been to walk across the park to see him. As usual, just being in his company had been calming, sitting in the orderly tack room with stable sounds for a background and his voice with its Herefordshire accent that always made me think of quiet rivers and willow trees. His first question, once he'd calmed me down, had been whether I needed to have any more to do with it.

'I'm afraid so. I can't just desert Lady Blessington – and besides, I want to know.'

He hadn't asked me any more questions then, beyond whether I wanted him to go back to Gore House with me. I jumped at the idea, though I knew it would cost him money in lost tips and in persuading other grooms to take on his duties of riding out with the gentry, not to speak of the disappointment to fashionable lady riders. Our ride out to Kensington the next day, with me in a calmer frame of mind, gave us the chance to talk over what had happened.

'You say there wasn't any other way in or out of that loft.'

'Not as far as I could see. But that wasn't what we were looking for at the time.'

'From what you say, once they'd got him tied up and standing on that hatch, they couldn't have used it to get themselves out, so there must have been some other way.'

'They?'

'Don't you reckon it would take more than one?'

'I don't know. He wasn't young and didn't look very strong. Somebody might have crept up on him when he was asleep.' It still hurt to think of it, Lesparre going up so trustingly into the loft, settling on his camp bed. I thought of our casual

73

decision to leave him there till morning and whether it had killed him.

'In that case, they'd have had to open the hatch – and you'd think that would have woken him – or get in some other way.' It helped that Amos was sticking to the practicalities.

'We should speak to the servants,' I said. 'Their dormitories are just under the loft. They must have seen or heard something.'

'Won't the police have done that?'

'I don't know. But they don't always ask the right questions.'

When we got to Kensington Lady Blessington was deep in a business discussion with a publisher. Even murder, fire and theft couldn't be allowed to interrupt business for long, but she gave instructions to the housekeeper to provide coffee then let us go where we wanted and speak to whoever we wanted. She took me aside. 'My dear, please don't disturb the servants more than necessary. It's been a difficult time for them.' Since Amos would not have been invited into a drawing room we took our coffee together in the housekeeper's room, where his height and good looks obviously caused a flutter among the housemaids coming and going. Afterwards we made our way up the back stairs, on to the half-landing below the loft. The floor-boards had been mopped and scoured, with a faint smell of carbolic still lingering. Apart from that there was no sign of what had happened. The loft hatch was closed, the hooked pole back on the wall. Amos listened while I described exactly what had happened as dispassionately as I could manage.

'The man was unlucky that Stedge gave such a pull on the hatch,' I said. 'If they'd done it gently, they might have saved him.'

Amos doubted it. 'Once he was falling, he was falling. Somebody would have to get the length of the rope just right though, to break his neck. The question is whether there's another way in or out.'

He'd given up trying to persuade me to let him search the loft on his own. I was wearing old skirts to my riding habit, not full, with my sleekest petticoat underneath. I gave him my little burglar's lantern and a flint lighter to put in his pocket. He took the pole, climbed the first few steps on the ladder and drew the hatch open. It moved as easily as when we'd put Lesparre into the loft. Amos swung himself up, then knelt and reached an arm down to where I was standing on the middle step. I took his hand and he pulled me up as easily as an angler hooking a trout. It was dim in the loft with what light there was coming up through the hatch. We lit the lantern and started investigating. The camp bed, chair and table were still there but the rope that had hanged Lesparre had gone. I didn't know if the police had taken it away or the servants had tidied it. Amos looked up at the crossbeam above the hatch, raising our lantern.

'You can see where they knotted it, where there's no dust. He'd have to climb up to it, or stand on somebody's shoulders.'

* * *

75

The satchel that Lesparre had guarded so carefully was still where D'Orsay had let it fall, with the folded-up newspapers strewn beside it. I took some of them over to the lamp. They were from *The Times*, the dates mid-August, two weeks or so ago. Since nobody else wanted them I put them back in the satchel to take down with me. Meanwhile Amos had been looking for other ways to get in and out of the loft. We trained the thin beam from the lantern upwards, looking for evidence that somebody had come in through the roof, but could see no sign that the tiles had been disturbed. The bricks in the walls were uniformly dusty and cobwebbed, the timbers on the other two sides solid and well jointed, with nothing to show that anybody had forced a way through. It took us an hour or more to find what we were looking for and by then the lamp was burning low. A brick chimney stack, so massive that it must be an outlet for half a dozen flues combined, stood out from the wall of the loft furthest from the hatch. In the dim light, we almost missed seeing a metal plate in the side of it, about three foot square. It had obviously been put there to help chimney sweeps and their boys – easier and more humane to get up into the loft and push a brush down than to force a boy upwards. It was held in place by large screws at the four corners. Amos touched one and sniffed his fingers.

'Oiled recently.'

I held the lamp close while he undid the screws with his pocket knife and lifted off the metal plate. We were looking down into sooty blackness. I think Amos might have tried climbing down it, but it was obvious his shoulders wouldn't go. Mine would have, but lowering myself into that close dark was something I couldn't face unless I had to.

'There'd have been a lot of soot, wherever he came out of the chimney,' I said.

The lamp guttered out and the darkness closed in on us. We inched our way back to hatch. Amos went through first, took the lamp from me, stood on the steps to guide me down then pulled the hatch cover shut.

'You couldn't get that plate off from inside the chimney,' Amos said. 'Not unless you'd already been up in the loft and loosened the screws so that they were only just holding it.'

'And you'd have to know the house very well,' I said.

We brushed our clothes off and went down-stairs. Amos went to speak to the outdoor staff. I found Mrs Neal, the housekeeper, and asked her about falls of soot down chimneys.

'Quite often,' she said. 'We have a lot of trouble with pigeons.'

'Where was the most recent?'

She didn't have to think about it. 'The old nursery. It's a room we use for storing furniture mostly so we only clean it every now and then. One of the maids had occasion to go in and there was soot over everything.'

'So that was yesterday?' I said.

She looked surprised. 'No, before that, days before. We found it last Monday. I remember that because Monday's washing day and we had enough on our hands without soot. It could have happened several days before that.'

In that case, at least four days before the murder, probably more. It made no sense. 'I suppose it's all been cleaned by now.'

'Yes, it took us the best part of the day. We had to leave the window open for days to air it. You know how a soot smell hangs on.'

I suggested that we should go up and see, hoping for something that might make sense of it. We went up the back stairs and through the servants' door to a second floor of bedrooms, most of them for servants. The carpet was only a well-worn strip along the middle of bare floor-boards, doorways not scalloped and gilded as they were on the main bedroom floor. Mrs Neal led the way along the corridor to the far end, walking fast.

'The three end rooms were the nursery and nursemaids' accommodation, but there are no children in the household.' She paused with her hand on a door knob. 'We cleaned it thoroughly after the soot fall. But there's nothing to see inside now.' She turned the knob, opened the door and then stood frozen on the threshold. 'Oh.'

The room looked as if soot demons had been rioting inside it. The polished floor and rugs were clotted with soot, the chairs, mirrors and other bits of unwanted furniture piled round the walls smudged with greasy black, the smell of it strong enough to set Mrs Neal coughing, probably because her mouth had fallen open in surprise. 'Not again,' she said once she'd caught her breath. 'Not again.'

We went into the room. Near the fireplace, where the soot was thickest, there were footprints, too confused to see if they were one person's or more. As I looked at them she was casting round the room.

'Dratted pigeons,' she said.

'There wasn't one,' I said. 'Somebody came down the chimney.' Perhaps I shouldn't have said it, but her obvious astonishment convinced me that she wasn't part of whatever had been happening. She stared. 'But why?' Then, 'Oh, do you think . . .?'

'Were there any sooty footprints along the corridor?'

We went outside to look. They weren't obvious, but there were regular traces of soot on the bare boards to one side of the carpet strip as if somebody had tried to avoid leaving tracks. They went past the servants' rooms to the door that opened on to the back stair landing, and there we lost them.

'We'd have noticed if it hadn't been for all the other upsets.' Mrs Neal was distressed at what she saw as the failure of her housekeeping arrangements.

'When the police were searching, did they go in that room?'

'I don't know.'

Either they hadn't bothered or they'd taken it for an ordinary soot fall. But then, they hadn't seen the plate on the chimney breast.

'Don't tell the servants about this,' I said. 'I'll report it to Lady Blessington.' We went down the stairs and through to her own room in the servants' quarters. 'What made you think it was pigeons the first time it happened? It's usually jackdaws in chimneys.'

'Because we've been having trouble with them anyway. One of them flew straight from the garden through the window into Lady Blessington's bedroom last week and broke the glass. The smell was awful too.'

'Smell?' I didn't know why the pigeons bothered me, but they did.

'We had to burn pastilles to sweeten the room. Dirty birds they are.'

I left it and went on to the more general question of the staff. She echoed her employer's words: they were loyal and trustworthy and in most cases had been with Lady Blessington for years.

'There was a man applying to be a footman,' I said.

'He didn't suit and we didn't need one. In any case, I didn't take to him. He wasn't precisely impertinent, but seemed as if he might be, given occasion.'

'Foreign?'

'Yes. Adequate English, but foreign.'

She was doing her best to be helpful and suggested that I could use her room to talk to the staff. Whom did I wish to talk to first?

I'd intended to work my way methodically down the list, hoping for some crumb that the police had missed, but the discovery of the hatch and the soot fall changed things. Somebody had come down the chimney and out into the grate of the old nursery between the time when Lesparre was put up there after dinner on Thursday and his death at breakfast time on Friday. I thought back to Thursday night. We'd dined quite late, then sat a long time discussing Boulogne. It was probably well after nine before the police arrived. I thought of the walk up the back stairs to the loft and Stedge's query: *Everything to your satisfaction, sir?* Lesparre had answered yes, from above. He'd hardly have done so if there had been an assassin already waiting for him, but then the loft was dark. Put the time, say, at half past nine. In the next twelve hours Lesparre had been overpowered, bound and gagged and left standing on the hatch with a noose round his neck while the man – or men – responsible wriggled down the chimney.

'Who sleeps in the rooms nearest the loft hatch?'

'The men. The maids have their own room on the second floor. Stedge, the other footman and the under-footman have one room, the four other indoor men the other, apart from the boot boy who sleeps in the kitchen.'

I opted for Stedge first. He arrived, as immaculate as ever. I offered him a chair but he wouldn't take it and remained standing to attention throughout our talk. I decided to tell him about the chimney and the soot, guessing that the whole household would know soon in any case.

'So he was waiting up there all the time, ma'am?' Interesting that was the option he favoured. There was a mind behind those professionally blank eyes.

'Or went up the chimney after we'd put Mr Lesparre in the loft. What time did you get to bed on Thursday night?'

'Late, ma'am, very late. Nearly three o'clock. What with the fire, then the police, then having to clear up everything after Her Ladyship had gone to bed and a bite to eat ourselves, it was the latest for a long time.'

'Was that true of all the staff?'

'Yes, ma'am.'

'Before you went to sleep, did you hear any noise from the loft?'

'I was asleep before my head hit the pillow. Reckon we all were.' His face was impassive as ever, but there was something near a laugh in his voice. By that hour of the morning, the servants would have been up and working for around twenty-one hours.

'But you'd have heard if there'd been a struggle up in the loft?'

'Yes, we're so close you hear rats scuttling across the floorboards. If the gentleman had called for help, I'd have been up there.'

'And none of the other men heard anything?'

'None of them.'

So by three in the morning Lesparre was already standing on the hatch, only a few feet above the sleeping servants, but helpless. 'Would all the servants have known that Mr Lesparre was in the loft?'

'Well, they would and they wouldn't.' Then, in reply to my questioning look, 'There are things you're supposed to know, so you do, and other things you're not supposed to, so you don't.'

I took it for a yes. 'Did the police go into the old nursery when they were searching?'

'No. It was mostly the family bedrooms they were interested in. I told them there was nothing upstairs worth stealing. They'd had enough anyway, once they realized how big the place is.'

'By the by, has Mr Lesparre's valet arrived yet?'

'No, ma'am. Nasty shock for him when he does.'

I asked him to send me, in turn, all the other servants who'd been sleeping in the two rooms nearest the loft, six altogether, and one by one they arrived in various shades of nervousness. One of them was Ronson, still pale and sickly looking but cleaned up and smelling of nothing worse than metal polish. The answer in all cases was the same: they'd gone to their beds exhausted around three o'clock and heard nothing but each other's snoring. The first of them had been stirring again well before daylight, to get down to their duties by half past six. A lucky few, including one footman and the kitchen porter, had lounged in their beds until seven and still heard nothing.

By now I needed a stroll in the gardens to clear my head. My feet took me to the stable block, where I found Amos smoking his pipe and yarning with the groom. It was a modest establishment, Lady Blessington keeping only a light one-horse whiskey, a saddle horse for Count D'Orsay and a pony for mowing the grass. Amos raised a hand to the groom, tapped out his pipe and came over to talk to me.

'Nothing much to the purpose,' he said. 'The gardener and his wife sleep over the stable. They didn't hear anybody coming or going the night it happened.'

'Amos, did you ever hear of a pigeon flying into a window and breaking it?'

He frowned. 'You sure it was a pigeon?'

'Yes – anybody would recognize a pigeon, wouldn't they?' As I told him the housekeeper's story, the frown stayed on his face.

'Not like any pigeon I ever heard of. I saw it happen with a sparrowhawk once, swooping down fast on a little bird, slap into a window and broke its neck. But even then it didn't bust through into the room, just cracked the pane and fell down dead outside. And your sparrowhawk's a powerful bird going as fast as a race horse when it's diving on something. Pigeons don't fly like that.'

'Do they smell especially bad?'

'Only if you're standing under a roost of them. No worse than any other bird otherwise.'

'A pigeon that smelled bad enough to stink a room out came hurtling through Lady Blessington's bedroom window.'

'What became of the pigeon?' Amos said.

I had to go back to the housekeeper to find that out, while Amos waited in the stable yard. The poor woman was so resigned to inexplicable things by now that she answered without asking why I needed to know. Household sweepings went into a bin in the backyard of the kitchen. Every Friday the bin would be taken by one of the gardeners and emptied on to the bonfire pile, to be burned with the next lot of garden waste. I hurried back to Amos and we questioned the gardener. The bonfire heap was on a waste patch near the outside wall, alongside the compost heaps. He planned to set fire to it as soon as it had dried out. Hadn't lit it for a month and hadn't needed to. The household waste would be emptied on anywhere, no particular plan. Amos and I found the bonfire, piled high with broken bits of wood and garden waste. Here and there a scurf of dust and paper showed where household rubbish had been thrown.

'I'll do it,' Amos said. 'You're not dressed for it.'

But I took a long stick off the pile and helped, raking out the promising areas. We turned up quantities of old rags, hairballs, bits of broken china and enough dust to set us both sneezing. In the end, Amos found it wrapped up in a piece of newspaper, probably as the maids had handled it. The maggots inside it had hatched, grown wings and flown away long since, leaving only a cage of light bone half covered with dulled feathers and a sharp skeleton head and beak.

'Heavy for a dead pigeon,' Amos said, weighing it in his hand. He parted the breast bones gently and showed me what was inside – a stone about the size of a hen's egg. 'Died of trying to swallow it, would you think?'

'Glued?'

He poked at the stone and it shifted only a little. 'Hard to tell. Could be from how it rotted. On the other hand, if you took a dead pigeon, gutted it and let it dry off, poured in some carpenter's glue, it might do the job.'

Especially if you relied on squeamish housemaids, not wanting to look at or handle the bird more than they could help. Somebody had taken a great deal of trouble, but then that was the problem with this case. Somebody was taking a great deal of trouble and I couldn't see why.

'The point was breaking a window,' I said. 'That particular window. The window would need repairing and they might have to bring in a man to do it.'

'Tibble,' the housekeeper said. 'Odd-job man for years, used to work here all the time but only comes in as needed now, lives in the cottages at the back. We had him in to repair it the day after. We thought he might not be able to do it because he'd hurt his hand, but he brought in a lad to help him and managed perfectly well.'

'A lad?'

'A relative of his, I believe. I told him we wouldn't pay extra for a one-man job, but he said that was all right, the lad needed the experience.'

'Is Tibble working today?'

'No. He sent a message to say the hand had gone septic, so he hasn't been in for a week or more. We have a few jobs mounting up for him, so we hope he'll be back soon.'

I went back to Amos, standing by the bonfire with his pipe going and the pigeon at his feet.

'Do we want to keep it?'

'I don't think so. It may be evidence of something, but it's a long way down the chain.'

86

He pushed it back into the bonfire with his toe. 'Reckon we ought to talk to this Tibble?'

I said yes, probably at some time, but my attention wasn't on Amos because I was looking at something his toe had displaced. It looked like a bundle of sooty rags rolled together and I'd have taken that as only natural in a house that had recently suffered a fire, except there was a man's shoe in the bundle. I rolled it out with my stick. A pair of men's shoes, or rather the cloddish boot-shoe hybrid called high-lows in scuffed and sooty brown leather, a man's flannel shirt and a pair of old corduroy trousers, both soot-smothered, and a filthy grey flannel muffler. Amos bent to spread them out.

'Looks like a man came down a chimney in these.'

'And went away naked?'

'If he planned well ahead, he'd have brought something to change into.'

There were no labels in the clothes, nothing in the bundle that couldn't have been bought for pennies in any old clothes shop. Amos went back to the stables for an empty feed sack and we bundled it up to take with us. Back at the house, Lady Blessington insisted I should stay for lunch and I accepted, knowing Amos would charm whatever he needed to eat and drink from the kitchen maids. Over the meal I told Lady Blessington and D'Orsay what we'd found out, ending with the clothes on the bonfire pile. He was the more startled of the two.

'Now there's the oddest thing.' He turned to Lady Blessington. 'I wasn't going to mention it to you because it seemed petty with all these other things, but some of my clothes have disappeared.'

'When?' I said.

'I don't know. My valet found out this morning when he was tidying my dressing room.'

'Are you sure? You have so many clothes.' Lady Blessington was paying him out for the jewellery.

He frowned. 'He's quite sure. A jacket, a plain shirt, an overcoat and quite a good pair of shoes.'

'Any soot in your dressing room?'

He stared at me. 'Soot, why should there be? Oh, I see.'

'Yes. If the person who came down the chimney took your clothes to change into, ready for when he needed them . . .' I didn't have to emphasize the point that this would need some familiarity with the house. Lady Blessington was unusually quiet for the rest of the meal.

By the time Amos and I left about an hour later there had still been nothing heard from the police and no information about when the inquest would be, which was puzzling because they were supposed to take place as soon after death as possible, preferably the next day. I said I'd do what I could to find out. Amos and I rode back slowly and I told him about the theft of D'Orsay's clothes.

'Fits then, doesn't it?' he said. 'He steals them, leaves them ready in the room where he knows he's going to come down, changes and walks out

88

down the back stairs all clean and tidy, then out by the garden gate.'

'Pausing to push his old clothes into the bonfire pile as he goes. Only one thing about that bothers me. Why the sooty footprints along the corridor?'

Amos checked his horse as it considered shying at a handcart loaded with pots and pans. 'See what you mean. He goes to all that trouble to get clean clothes and doesn't change into the shoes.'

'I'd like to know where the valet is,' I said.

'You're thinking he might have something to do with it?'

'Perhaps, but I don't see why. Lesparre obviously felt warmly towards him and said how loyal he was. He'd proved it too, going with him on that Boulogne business and helping him escape. We don't know if he got Lesparre's message to meet him and he might not know he's dead.'

'We could do with a ferret,' Amos said.

'To flush him out?'

'I mean, find out what his interests are. Everybody has something he can't keep away from. There was a man who owed this cousin of mine ten pounds. Everywhere my cousin looked for him – home, market, public – he wouldn't be there. So I said to my cousin, what he had to do was think of something the man couldn't stay away from, and it was ferrets. Whatever it was – rabbiting with a few bets on, racing along drainpipes, a good one up for sale – he'd be there. So we got a friend of ours who bred ferrets to put it about that he had a specially good young jill to sell and he'd be there in the public on such and such a night with her in his pocket, taking bids. And sure enough, there's the man my cousin hadn't been able to get sight of for six months, pocket full of coin to bid for the jill. So we had him and my cousin had his money.'

'We know practically nothing about him and the Italian place doesn't trust strangers. I don't know where to start looking.'

When we parted at Abel Yard, with Amos leading Rancie back across the park with him, we still hadn't come up with an answer.

SIX

On Sunday I went to see my old friend in Fleet Street, Jimmy Cuffs. Jimmy earned a very modest living reporting coroner's courts. If there were any justice he'd have been enjoying an easy life as a classics professor at Oxford or Cambridge because he was one of most learned men I'd ever met, but a height of less than five feet and a limp from a club foot meant the world had never valued him as it should. If he ever felt resentment about that, he declaimed it late at night in ancient Greek to the lamp posts in Fleet Street after the Cheshire Cheese had closed.

The only likely inquest he could find was one on a male deceased, name unknown, set for ten thirty on Monday morning in the back room of a public house in Kensington, not far from Gore House. It puzzled me because the police had been told Mr Lesparre's name, but I decided to attend. Jimmy Cuffs might not have bothered with yet another of London's inquests on unknown males, but my interest alerted him. When I arrived at the dingy little room on Monday morning he was sitting in the front row. I slid as unobtrusively as I could into a seat in the back row, along with the assorted ghouls, male and female, who always infest inquests. The jurors were filing back from viewing the body. The sergeant who'd been called after it was found was sitting at the front, between another police officer and a man who looked like a doctor. Nobody from Gore House was present. The police sergeant was the first witness called. In a monotone, he described how he'd been called to Gore House on the morning of Friday 4 September and found the body of the deceased on an upper landing with a rope round his neck. The coroner asked him the name of the deceased. Identification is after all the first business of an inquest and here the proceedings struck a rock.

'I was informed that the deceased was known by the name of Lesparre. He was said to be a French gentleman.' The sergeant said it as if he wanted to keep both statements as far from him as possible, like a lady handling something noxious with tongs. The coroner couldn't miss it.

'You doubt that, Sergeant?'

'We have reason to think the name may be an alias, sir.' Not exactly sensation in court, but a stirring of interest. Jimmy Cuffs was sitting up straight and writing.

'If so, what is his real name?' the coroner asked.

'Investigations are proceeding, sir.'

'He died on Friday. You've had three days already.'

'Yes, sir.'

'So the police expect me to adjourn the inquest while they find out the man's name?' The sergeant looked straight ahead and didn't reply. The coroner sighed. 'You may stand down. Since the doctor is here we might as well take his evidence. If you're ready, sir.'

The doctor's evidence was at least precise as

far as it went. The deceased had died as a result of hanging, the cervical vertebrae exhibiting the classic hangman's fracture. Death would have been instantaneous. The doctor could form no opinion as to whether the hanging had been self-inflicted. At this, I must have made some movement because the man next to me was staring. It was just possible that the doctor might have missed marks left by the gag and the rag itself could have been lost in moving Lesparre's body, but I couldn't believe there had been no marks on the wrists. It looked as if Lady Blessington's and D'Orsay's trust in luck had been justified. The doctor didn't have the air of a liar, nor did any of them, but it was all so totally wrong that I felt more angry than relieved, sorry that I'd had any part in this. The coroner knew something was wrong too. His annoyance seemed genuine and I guessed he'd have something to say to the sergeant and the coroner's officer in private. Meanwhile, without identification, he had no choice.

'I adjourn the inquest *sine die* for further investigation by the metropolitan police. And in case you're wondering, Sergeant, that does not mean all the time in the world. I shall be expecting daily reports on progress.'

He dismissed the jurors, who looked surprised and disappointed at this abrupt ending. Even after the coroner had left they lingered in the hall, asking each other what had happened. There was nobody else to ask because the police officers had disappeared almost as smartly as the coroner.

Jimmy Cuffs turned round and caught my eye. I went over and greeted him. We walked out together.

'Can you tell me what's happening, Miss Lane?' He sounded almost as angry as the coroner.

'I wish I could.'

'Is your friend Lady Blessington using her influence to pervert the course of justice?' He was angry with me as well.

'I don't think she has that sort of influence.'

The noise he made was surprisingly vulgar by his standards. 'You might be surprised. Something's happening. The coroner's officer bolted like a rabbit into his hole and wouldn't talk to me. We're usually quite good friends. So were you there on Her Ladyship's behalf?'

'Yes, I suppose I was.' I couldn't lie to Jimmy Cuffs. The question was how much I should tell him. 'In fact, I was there when the body was discovered.'

He stopped walking and stared at me. 'So you should have been called at the inquest.'

'Probably, yes.'

'No probably about it. Who else was there? Lady Blessington?'

'No.'

'The son-in-law then.' Some contempt in his voice. I didn't answer. He started walking again, fast in spite of his club foot. 'When you say you were there when it happened, you mean you found him hanging?'

'Not exactly, no.'

'I'd have thought it was something about which you could be exact.'

94

So, rightly or wrongly, I told him. I cared enough about Jimmy Cuffs not to want to live with his bad opinion of me. He heard me through without saying anything till the end.

'So he was murdered?'

'Yes.'

'And the police know that?'

'I think they must do.'

'What about the name?'

'He was introduced to me as Monsieur Lesparre and that's the name Lady Blessington knew him by. I suppose it might be a *nom de guerre*.'

We walked on in silence for a while, until he spoke again in that beautiful deep voice that was so at odds with his appearance. 'Miss Lane, I'm afraid you've got yourself into something pretty deep. Walk away is my advice.'

'I'm not sure that I can. You won't write about this, will you?'

He shook his head. 'If even half of my suspicions are right, I don't suppose I'd be allowed to in any case.'

'Miss Lane, Jimmy.' A voice from behind us, almost breathless. I turned and saw a tall man in his early thirties, clean-shaven, carefully dressed with a well-cut coat that emphasized a slim waist, hair brown and short, nose long, eyes grey and watchful. I'd noticed him from the back, sitting in the second row at the inquest and thought he might be a lawyer. Seen from the front, there was something familiar about him.

'Miss Lane, it's a pleasure to see you again. Jimmy, you never told me you were acquainted with the famous Miss Lane.'

He spoke to Jimmy like an old friend. I looked at him, trying to remember where we'd met before. Then it hit me and I realized what a mistake I'd made in being at the inquest.

'Constable Bevan.'

'Sergeant Bevan, as of last month,' Jimmy said, seeming not at all put out to see him.

'I see he still holds the same views on police uniform.' I remembered them from the case that had brought us together over a year ago.

'That it's unfair that police officers must stand out like palm trees in stovepipe hats while criminals change like chameleons? Yes, we've discussed the subject over our cups,' Jimmy said.

Sergeant Bevan was smiling but his eyes were hard. 'I believe my views are gaining ground. But in fact, I'm not on duty. I came here merely out of curiosity. Is that the case with you, Miss Lane?'

I didn't reply, willing him to go away.

'So is this a case of yours?' Jimmy said to Bevan.

'Oh no. Just passing by.' We all three knew he was lying, yet when we'd met on the other case I'd quite liked the man and thought he was honest. We came to the omnibus stop for the journey back to town and the omnibus was in sight. Jimmy and I stopped. Sergeant Bevan stopped too.

'So will you be writing a report on this, Jimmy?'

'Nothing to report.' The omnibus stopped and we climbed on board. Sergeant Bevan raised a hand in farewell as we clopped and clattered away. We didn't respond.

'Bevan's one of the new men,' Jimmy Cuffs said. 'Secret work, lurking and listening rather than pounding pavements. He specializes in foreign politicals. Whatever this is, it goes up a long way.'

We parted in Fleet Street. I called on a sick friend on the way home and it was mid-afternoon before I got back to Abel Yard. Mrs Martley said two gentlemen had called wanting to see me and would be back later. She sounded as if she approved of them. When she didn't she had a way of saying *gentleman*, letting me know that in her opinion the person was anything but. I tidied up the office and waited, wondering what to say if they proved to be new clients. 'I'm sorry, I'm not taking on any more cases. I shall be travelling abroad for some time and I don't know when I'll be back.' I tried it over in my mind: olive trees shifting from green to silver in the breeze off the Mediterranean, palm trees against the sunset and the smell of Bombay spices. I was half in a dream when a knock came on the door. I looked out of the window and saw an upturned face, brown hair and watchful eyes. Beside him, the crown of a hat. The other gentleman wasn't looking up.

'Sergeant Bevan again.'

I didn't try to sound welcoming, but he smiled just the same. 'Good afternoon, Miss Lane. I apologize for disturbing you, but I wonder if we might talk.'

Had I ever told him where I lived? I was on the point of telling him to go away but decided to play him instead. The game would be to find out more from him than he did from me.

'Come up,' I said. 'The door's on the latch.'

They walked in, Sergeant Bevan first. The man behind him was somebody I hadn't seen before, in his late forties, plainly dressed, top hat in hand. He looked like a man left out in the rain, shoulders hunched as if walking against a perpetual drizzle, brown hair thinly distributed over a shiny pate like water trails. But when he raised his head and looked at me, the small dark eyes on either side of his beak of a nose gave quite another impression. In winter, when the sky is too troubled and cloudy for flight, you sometimes see buzzards perched on fence posts, looking for prey down in a ditch, and the contrast between the high-flying power of the bird and its present low circumstances is both sad and sinister.

'Miss Lane, may I introduce Mr Slater,' Sergeant Bevan said. He seemed ill at ease. Mr Slater's gloved hand floated towards mine and barely touched it. Even under a glove, the fingers were thin. The small eyes looked briefly into mine then drifted away. No explanation of who Mr Slater might be. I drew up chairs for them and sat down opposite at the table.

'If you'd like tea I'll ask my housekeeper to bring it,' I said. 'But I don't suppose tea is what you came for.'

'Please don't trouble your housekeeper,' Sergeant Bevan said.

'So what did you come for?'

'To see if you'd answer a question you didn't answer this morning. Was it just curiosity that took you to the inquest?'

Mr Slater just sat there, looking down at his hands.

'You know very well that it wasn't,' I said.

'Oh?'

'Any more than on your part. I don't suppose you spend your spare time attending inquests. You were sent there because the police are interested in Lady Blessington's household. So you'll know already that I'm a friend of Lady Blessington and that I was visiting her when all this happened.'

'Quite a coincidence,' Bevan said.

'One of many. Like a fire happening to break out. Like a burglary that might not have happened. You'll know the police were called to Lady Blessington's on Thursday night as well as Friday morning.'

No sound or movement from Mr Slater. The sergeant had a decision to make. He could say he didn't understand what I was talking about, in which case our conversation would come to a quick end, or he could accept what I said, hoping to draw me into giving something away. I watched carefully, to see if he would wait for some kind of signal from the other man. He didn't hesitate, showing they'd planned tactics in advance.

'And why should anybody invent a non-existent burglary?'

'You might know more about that than I do, depending on how closely the police are working with agents of the French government.'

His face showed pained surprise. 'You're suggesting that the Metropolitan Constabulary has acted less than honestly?'

'I'm suggesting it's been a party to concealing

99

things from a coroner to an extent that probably amounts to perjury and perverting the course of justice.'

'And why would we do that, Miss Lane?'

'Possibly because a person at a very high level, probably in the Foreign Office, thinks Lady Blessington knows something that would cause political embarrassment. Whether he's right or wrong about that, I don't know.'

'Did Lady Blessington know that man was in the loft?'

I looked him in the eye, hoping my face was giving away as little as his. 'She was as shocked as anybody when he was found hanged.'

'Does she know who he is?'

'She knew him as Monsieur Lesparre. Do you know more?'

Before he could answer, Mr Slater spoke at last. His voice was lower and more resonant than I'd have expected from his hunched build, with a slightly hollow sound as if he carried his own echo in his chest. 'Perhaps the sergeant will permit me to answer for him. In these times it's not easy to be a policeman. This country has a reputation for welcoming all sorts of political men who've made their own countries too dangerous for them. They come here, where they can say anything they like, write anything they like. A man may publish something in London that makes men kill other men several hundred miles away and we can do nothing about it. He may plot to overthrow another country's govern-ment without hindrance from us. But if some sneak thief filches a few shillings from that same man's pocket, the constabulary are called in to protect his rights and put the thief in prison. Those are the circumstances in which the sergeant and his colleagues are forced to work.'

It wasn't an answer to my question and I knew I wasn't going to get one. 'This country has always had a reputation for welcoming refugees,' I said.

'Peaceful refugees, yes. But the hospitality we give them doesn't confer the right to engage in plots, whether against this government or others.'

The eyes were beginning to mesmerize me, so rather than be a vole in a ditch I turned back to Sergeant Bevan. 'If you hoped I might help you find out the identity of Mr Lesparre – if he has another identity – I'm afraid you're wasting your time. I know very little about him.'

'Time is never wasted with you, Miss Lane. I'm sorry you couldn't help us. We'll probably never know who he was, or why he was killed. But some cases are like that, aren't they? If anything occurs to you, I hope you'll let us know. You could leave a message for me at any police office.'

That sounded like the end of it. I stood up to open the door and the sergeant stood too, but the other man stayed in his seat. Sergeant Bevan looked puzzled at the delay.

'Tell me, Miss Lane, have you seen your travelling friend since he got back?' Slater's voice was lighter now, trying to make the question casual.

'Travelling friend?'

'Mr Carmichael. I believe he's a friend of yours.'

I couldn't hide the shock of hearing Robert's name. Sergeant Bevan seemed surprised too. 'I didn't know he was back in the country,' I said and wondered why I was lying.

'Really?' He didn't believe me. 'Well, if you do happen to meet him, you might give him a warning. He's made some dangerous friends.'

'Or do you mean dangerous enemies?' I said, looking him in the face.

'I'm sure he has no enemies – unless he's brought them back with him. Some travellers collect strange souvenirs.'

There were a dozen things I wanted to ask him, but I knew I'd be wasting my time, even gratifying a cruelty I sensed in him. He was like an experimenter, sucking air from a creature under a bell jar to see it struggle for breath. Perhaps Sergeant Bevan sensed it too because he looked uneasy, but he said nothing. Slater wished me good afternoon and stood up. I followed them downstairs. Slater put on his hat, raised it in my direction but without looking at me and walked slowly through the gateway into the mews. Sergeant Bevan gave me a rueful look, spread his palms out in what might have been a gesture of apology then fell in behind him.

'What are they doing here then?' asked Tabby, from the alcove under the stairs.

'Tabby, can you follow them? If they part, follow the older one. Find out where he works or lives. Don't let him see you.'

'They raw lobsters?' Meaning police in their

102

blue jackets as opposed to the red boiled lobster of soldiers.

'The younger one is. The older one might be. Don't let him see you.'

The warning was hardly necessary. Nobody was better at melting into London crowds than Tabby. She asked no more questions, just nodded and went. I knew it wouldn't matter how long or how far it took her. If Slater had work or lodgings anywhere in the city, she'd find him and perhaps he'd lead me to Robert. Though it looked as if Robert didn't want to be found, especially not by me.

SEVEN

Tabby was back in the morning, just after daylight. Her penetrating whistle, learned from the stable lads in the mews, woke me from a half-sleep. I brought her up to the parlour. This would usually have guaranteed a day of sniffs and pointed silences from Mrs Martley, because she persisted in regarding Tabby as guttersnipe rather than apprentice, but my housekeeper's snores were audible from a floor up and she'd be out of the world for an hour or more. Tabby's dress was spattered with mud and muck for at least a foot above the hem, her hair flopping down, face pale and dark rings round her eyes.

'Have you been out all night?' I asked.

She nodded. 'He walks, most of the night.'

'On his own?'

'Yes. Started around Hatton Garden, where I went with you, then right out to Cheapside, down Newgate and back along Holborn.'

'Just walking?'

'Nah, talking to people as well. Three different publics he went into, two in Holborn and one near St Paul's, sort of a hole in the wall that one was, not a proper public. Didn't stay longer than it would take him to swallow one drink, then out again.'

'Did he talk to many people?'

'All the time. I didn't follow him into the

104

publics in case he started noticing me but I looked in and every time he was sitting in a corner talking to a man, different man every time of course, heads down as if they didn't want to be noticed.'

'Any particular sort of man?'

'No. One had grey hair, another one was young with a beard. In the St Paul's place it was a man who'd come out from behind the bar. I couldn't see for sure, but I think he gave that one some money. Might have done with the others, but I couldn't see.'

'Did he only talk to people in public houses?'

'A couple of times people came out of doorways as if they'd been waiting for him and they'd talk a bit, too quiet for me to hear anything, not long though, then he'd be walking again. One funny thing – you said he might be a raw lobster.'

'Something to do with the police at any rate.'

'Well, when he was walking up a street and there were two of the raws on their beat, he ducked into an alleyway as if he didn't want them to see him.'

'Was he walking all night?'

'Pretty near. Sometime after it struck three he had a cup of coffee at the stand in Holborn the cab drivers use, then he went home. He's in Lisle Street, just off Leicester Fields, the Princes Street end of it. Looks like a lodging house but not the rough kind, as far as I could make out in the dark. There are no lights on inside and he lets himself in with a key. Sometime after that, there's a light of the candle in a top room. It stays lit for some time, then goes out.'

'So he's spying,' I said. The pattern of a man

out trawling for information was as clear as a constellation in a frosty sky. Mr Slater had been doing the rounds of his paid informants. From the fact that his long walk had started and ended close to an area where Italian refugees congregated and the speech he'd delivered to me the day before, it was easy to guess his target. The surprise was that he should be doing it himself rather than leaving it to underlings. He was undoubtedly from the gentleman class, a long way from the need to live in a lodging house and walk the streets at night. Only a man determined to the point of fanaticism would do that. And this man was making inquiries about Robert Carmichael. I dragged my mind back to what Tabby was telling me.

'I thought I'd better watch for a bit in case he came out again. He didn't. There was an empty house nearly opposite. I made myself comfortable on the doorstep.'

Conscience hit me, which it should have done earlier. The pity of it was Tabby wasn't being sarcastic when she said she'd made herself comfortable on a doorstep. She'd slept in worse places. But the mention of Robert had made me so greedy to find out anything that I'd set her on the trail without thinking. How was one girl, even one as tough and resourceful as Tabby, supposed to keep track of a man all the time, especially one of such wandering habits? I stirred up the fire, added the few coals that were in the bucket and put on the kettle. Tabby dozed in the chair as I waited for it to boil. When she woke I gave her tea, strong and sugary the way she liked it, bread with plenty of butter and thick slices of ham.

'You've done well, Tabby. The question is what do we do now we know where he lives? He may be some kind of threat to a friend of mine.' Friend at least, surely I could still say that. 'I want to know anything I can about him – where he goes, who he speaks to, all day and every day.'

'So I've got to keep following him?'

'You can't do it all. You have to sleep sometimes. I can't do it because he'd be looking out for me. Is there anybody among the boys we could trust?'

The boys in Adam's Mews outside our gates, ages somewhere between nine and seventeen or so, formed a loose gang, with Tabby as its only female member and probably leader, though the politics of it were a mystery to me. They slept in the straw of the stables and earned a bare living holding horses, running errands and occasionally pickpocketing, though they had to be careful not to trespass on other gangs' territory.

'Plush'd do all right,' Tabby said, after pausing to think. 'Cobblers too, if he keeps off the beer.'

Plush I knew about. He was her chief lieutenant, a fierce scrapper against other gangs, with a face that would frighten babies, constantly smoking scavenged tobacco in an old clay pipe. But, with his friends, he was a gentle and obliging character. Cobblers I knew little about, beyond the fact that he had dark bristly hair and had acquired the nickname, shortened from 'cobblers' ruin', because he never wore boots.

107

'It will be difficult,' I warned her. 'He's clever. He'll notice them if they're too obvious.' I hoped Mr Slater's interests didn't include a detailed knowledge of street urchins.

'Do I tell them he might be a raw lobster in ordinary clothes?'

'Yes, you'll need to. If he goes into Scotland Yard or any government building, tell them to keep their distance and only start following him when he comes out.'

'They'll keep their distance all right. When do I tell them to start?'

'Get some sleep first. Then tell them where he lives and get them to keep watch from early tomorrow morning. Let me know every day what's happening.'

I took ten shillings in small change from the petty cash box and gave it to Tabby for expenses. She disappeared into the mews and I was turning to go upstairs when Amos Legge came through the gateway, riding a blue roan cob and leading Rancie. I'd forgotten all about my morning ride with Amos yesterday and today, which just showed the poor state of my mind.

'Amos, I'm sorry. You came yesterday?'

He nodded, not perturbed. 'I guessed you were at work on something. Are we riding?'

'Yes, if you can wait while I change.'

I fumbled with hooks and buttons, angry with myself for discourtesy to Amos, all the worse because he was so slow to take offence. When I came down he'd dismounted and was talking to Mr Grindley by the gate about a possible customer for the roan. He never missed the chance to do a deal. He helped me mount and we rode across the road to the park, a little later than usual. The fashionable world was stirring, young men cantering up and down to show off new jackets or horses, a few carriages on early visits. We said nothing for a while. I knew Amos was owed an explanation for my thoughtlessness, but it was hard to give. He liked Robert Carmichael and, without making a great parade of it, had gone out of his way to find opportunities for us to walk and ride together. If he thought Robert were in difficulties, he'd do anything to help him. If on the other hand he thought Robert had done something to hurt me, then God help Mr Carmichael. We cantered along the Row, with the roan showing a fair turn of speed for his build. As we walked back, I told him about the inquest.

'Somebody high up's going out of his way to keep Gore House out of it, and I don't think it's from kindness to Lady Blessington.'

'Why then?'

'It's in my mind that Lesparre might have been planted to spy on her and D'Orsay because of the Prince Louis business.'

Amos raised a hand to an acquaintance cantering past, probably one of his horse customers. 'Struck me that way too. This Frenchman arrives at her house out of the blue, asking for help when before that he's just visited for a cup of tea.'

'Yes. If you wanted to plant a spy in her household, appealing to her generosity would be a good way of doing it.'

'So whose spy is he, French or English?'

'I don't know. It might be the French, trying to collect more evidence for the prince's trial, or our own people worried about those papers he was carrying. They might be embarrassing if they show somebody close to the government was giving encouragement to the prince.'

'And now they've gone, we don't know where, except it's likely whoever strung up the Frenchman took them away with him,' Amos said. 'It's a wretched way to kill a man. Even with murderers, they don't keep them standing around waiting on the trap.' Then, after a pause for what must have been some grim memory: 'Not unless the hangman's not up to his job, at any rate.'

'So was the valet helping him spy? It sounds as if they were close to each other.'

'But then he goes off and leaves him.'

'With Lesparre's encouragement. We need to find him. In common humanity we should let him know Lesparre's dead.'

We rode on, Amos deep in thought. After a while, he came out with the results of it. 'I've been thinking about that pigeon.' It was typical of his stubbornness that he would chew away at a bothersome detail. I'd almost forgotten it in the press of other things.

'I don't see that it can have anything to do with the killing. It happened days before. It might be just some boy playing a prank.'

'A lot of trouble for a boy to go to. I think we ought to have a word with that handyman, Tibble.'

'If you like. I should go out to Kensington anyway to tell Lady Blessington about the inquest.'

Amos was busy that afternoon with new horses to try, so we agreed we'd ride to Gore House in the morning. We parted by the round reservoir near Grosvenor Gate. As we were saying our goodbyes, a movement caught the corner of my eye. Why it should have, I don't know. By this time there were dozens of horses, carriages and pedestrians moving up and down the park in the autumn sunshine, groups of people pausing to chat by the reservoir. A man moving into the shadow by a tree should have been nothing special and I might have been mistaken entirely because when I turned my head for a proper look, there was nothing.

'Something up?' Amos said, catching my alarm.

'No, nothing.'

'Tomorrow morning, then.'

I hoped he couldn't sense the way my heart was racing, because I was ashamed to find my nerves in such a state that the half-sight of an anonymous man in the park could shake them. I rode on for a hundred yards or so before looking behind me. Nobody was following me. I'd been imagining things. I was of only minor signifi-cance in whatever was going on. Mr Slater – if it had been Mr Slater in the park – surely had better things to do than spy on me.

EIGHT

When I got to Gore House on Wednesday afternoon Lady Blessington was the nearest I'd ever
seen her to frantic. She hurried out of the library
to meet me.

'What's happening? Is there to be an inquest?
Nobody's telling us anything. Alfred's dreadfully
concerned. Coffee, or would you prefer sherry?
I don't even know what time it is.'

I settled for coffee. We drank it in the library
and I told her about the inquest.

'But that's absurd. Of course the police know
who he was. We told them.'

'The police think Lesparre's a *nom de guerre*,'
I said.

'Well, it might have been for all I know. Alfred
and I have been discussing it. I asked him how
much he actually knew about the poor man.'

'And how much did he know?'

'Well, not a great deal when it came to it.'

Which pretty well confirmed my view of Count
D'Orsay, though I tried not to let it show. 'He
did remember meeting Lesparre in the prince's
company?'

'Vaguely, yes, but with quite a few other people.
Of course, there always was quite a gathering
around Prince Louis and it was changing all the
time depending on who was in town. The prince
knew he had *carte blanche* to bring any of his

112

friends to my soirees. Lesparre wouldn't have needed a particular invitation.'

'But you didn't talk about his background?'

'My dear, would you? You don't start quizzing a person about his family history the moment he's introduced to you. Besides, there were so many of them and I daresay I picked up at once that he wasn't going to be especially entertaining, which he wasn't. Alfred spoke to him more than I did.'

'And gathered much about him?'

She shook her head. 'As far as I remember, Alfred said he had family estates near Bordeaux and his grandfather had been guillotined in the revolution, but then so many of them were. He seemed very attached to the prince.'

'Did the prince regard him as a close friend?'

'No. He certainly wasn't one of the inner circle. But poor Louis is always charming to everybody.'

It struck me that poor Louis would now be exercising his charm on his gaolers and possibly in the near future on a firing squad. 'So you'd seen this man perhaps twice before he turned up at your gates with his valet and this story about escaping from Boulogne with the papers?'

She poured more coffee. 'My dear, you're leading up to something, aren't you?'

'Has it struck you that he might have been a spy?'

She took it more calmly than I expected. 'Yes. In fact, I discussed it with Alfred. He won't have it, of course. Men are so tribal, don't you find? If a man wears the right clothes, moves in the right places, is seen with the right people, then there can't be anything wrong with him. And of course they do hate admitting they might have been deceived.'

'Did you get as far as deciding which side he might be spying for?'

'Oh, the French government, wouldn't you say? They'd love to find any proof that our Foreign Office had been encouraging poor Prince Louis to do what he did, especially if Palmerston himself were involved. And of course, he and the prince did meet here now and again.'

'Palmerston and Prince Louis talked to each other?'

'Of course they did. There'd be little point in a salon where people didn't. But if you're going to ask me whether Prince Louis mentioned that he intended to invade France and Palmerston wished him luck, I've no notion. Not likely, I'd say, though with Pam you never know.'

'You said Lesparre was carrying papers and some people might be embarrassed by what was in them. That was what he told you?'

'Yes.'

'Did you ask him who might be embarrassed?'

'Naturally I was dying to, but it would have been rude to pry.'

At least she'd never have to make a living as a private investigator. 'And you never actually saw the papers? I suppose Count D'Orsay told you there were only old newspapers in that satchel.'

'Yes. I imagine whoever killed him took them away. Wouldn't that have been the point? I'm so angry I can hardly think straight. One way or another, our hospitality has been violated. If he was a spy, somebody was imposing on us and I want to know who sent him. If he was what he claimed to be, then he's been murdered in the cruelest way I can imagine when he was a guest under my roof, and I want to know who did it and why. And I don't trust the police any further than I could throw that table. So what are we going to do about it?' Her outburst made me realize that her overwrought air came from suppressed anger rather than nerves. In her style, she was a fighter.

'I need to find the valet Bruno too. I suppose nobody's sent to tell him.'

'We couldn't. I didn't make a note of the address on that letter you delivered.'

'How long did the valet stay here with Lesparre? Did he know about the hiding place in the loft?'

'Three days, and yes. We were planning it, making sure Lesparre had a reasonably comfortable place to hide if he had to.'

'Didn't you think it odd that the valet didn't stay here with him?'

'The whole thing was odd. If I thought about it at all, I supposed there were still some secrets Alfred and I didn't know about and the valet had been sent to deal with them.'

'In three days here he could have found out quite a lot about your household. What was he like?'

'Mrs Neal and Alfred's valet had more to do with him than I did. Neat, quiet, respectful – what

115

you'd expect in a valet. You're not thinking he had something to do with this?'

'It has to be somebody who knew the house.'

'But why would he do it – rescue Lesparre in Boulogne and come all the way to London with him and kill him?'

'Possibly because somebody was paying him. When you think about it, isn't it suspicious that he and Lesparre escaped from Boulogne when everybody else was captured?'

'I don't know what to think, and that's the truth.'

I asked her to excuse me, intending to join Amos at the stables.

'Before you go, there's somebody I'd be glad if you'd speak to first,' she said. 'I'm sure you'll think it's a plot, but I assure you it isn't. He happened to be visiting in any case to talk about a book he's writing, but when you were announced I banished him to the drawing room. He says you were so angry with him the last time you met that he's quite scared to face you.'

My heart sank. 'Mr Disraeli?'

She nodded. 'Oh dear, the expression on your face. What has he done?'

The answer, though I didn't tell her, was that he'd tried to recruit me to spy on people the government thought of as radical troublemakers and I thought of as friends.

'Whatever it was, he's terribly contrite,' she said. 'He said there was obviously a misunderstanding and it was probably his fault, and he would like to set matters right with you.' I wanted to refuse, but her hand was on my arm, her eyes looking into mine with just that hint of humour along with concern that made her so hard to resist. 'My dear, as far as I'm concerned you can scorch him again if he deserves it, but at least let the poor man speak to you. Meanwhile, I'll go and find Alfred and ask him if he can remember any more about the valet.'

So I gave in. She rang for a footman and I followed him to the small drawing room. When the door opened, Disraeli was sitting on a sofa reading a book. He was on his feet immediately, smiling as if my arrival had made his day complete.

'Miss Lane, what a very pleasant surprise.'

He was dressed quite quietly for an afternoon visit, a gold chain round his neck with what looked like an ancient seal hanging from it, only three rings on his fingers, waistcoat of copper and burgundy damask. I held on to my bad temper, resisting the lift of spirits I'd so often felt in his presence.

'Hardly a surprise,' I said.

'Truly, I didn't know you'd be visiting. I've been hoping to see you for weeks to set matters right between us, but nobody seemed to know where you were.'

'In the country. Saving a political agitator from being hanged.'

'I'm sure he deserved it. Saving, I mean. You thought I meant the reverse, didn't you? I'm sorry you have such a low opinion of me.' He was quoting back at me part of something I'd said when we quarrelled. And yes, he had put me off

117

balance, making me mistake his meaning. Worse, his smile was so open and friendly that I could feel myself wanting to respond to it. 'Lady Blessington tells me that you've very kindly been supporting her through this bad business. She says she doesn't know what she'd do without you.'

'Lady Blessington has many friends.' I was trying hard to keep things formal, but could hear my voice softening.

'But not many so resourceful. She's keeping a brave face on it, as ever, but it is worrying her very much.'

He sounded sincere and I'd no doubt that he was, at least as far as Lady Blessington was concerned. But he was a politician with every breath he took and was skilfully moving the conversation on from our disagreement to a subject he hoped I couldn't resist.

'I hope you've been able to advise her,' I said.

'Probably less effectively than you.' Humility was rare with him. He must be trying very hard to win me over.

'I doubt that,' I said. 'After all, you're in a much better position to know what worries government ministers. At least, that was the impression I had the last time we met.' It was a mistake to battle with him and I knew it as soon as I'd spoken, but scornful silence has never been my forte. He looked hurt.

'May we forget that unfortunate conversation? It seems I offended you, and I'm sorry. We might at least declare a truce for the sake of helping a mutual friend.'

Had he and Lady Blessington discussed his approach in advance? I could hardly fight against both of them.

'Truce?' he invited.

'Truce, then,' I said, not very graciously. 'So what *is* worrying the foreign office? And please don't give me that quizzical look. Somebody's been interfering with an inquest. Either the coroner had his instructions or the police have been complicit in hiding things from him.'

He sighed. 'The fact is I simply don't know what's happening.' This was something new. Mr Disraeli's whole career was based on knowing what was happening. Although he was still only an MP, with the longed-for ministerial post not achieved, he had a reputation that went far beyond the House of Commons for knowing the people who mattered and the details of any great event, at home or abroad. He might sometimes exaggerate the extent of his knowledge, but I'd seen enough examples of it to know much was well based.

'Do you think the Foreign Secretary gave any encouragement to Louis Napoleon?'

'I don't know. He wouldn't have been doing his job if he hadn't kept on cordial terms with him. Louis was still a player in the game until he threw it all away in this crude attempt at Boulogne. The man's uncontrollable. He nearly managed to drown my wife and me on a river picnic by rowing us straight into a mudbank out of sheer over-confidence in himself. She was furious. If he'd had the patience to bide his time, with France so unstable, there was always a

119

chance that the Napoleon name would work magic.'

'Would Palmerston have put anything in writing to him?'

'Good heavens, no. I'm no admirer of our dear foreign secretary, but he's not a complete fool.'

'I suppose Lady Blessington's told you about those papers he was carrying. Have you any idea what they might be?'

'A bluff, possibly. If the prince's supporters can make Louis Philippe's government believe they've still got cards to play it might make them think twice about bringing him to trial.'

'If it's a bluff, somebody took it seriously.' In spite of the truce, I sensed he was keeping something from me. 'You really have no idea?'

'I'll make inquiries, if you like – delicately, of course.'

'Of course. Tell me, did you meet Lesparre here or anywhere else before the Boulogne business?'

'Not that I can remember.'

'Does it seem odd to you that he should come to Lady Blessington for help on such slight acquaintance?'

He gave me one of those droll looks from under his eyelids. 'Are you and I thinking the same thing?'

'Probably. Just how deeply was Count D'Orsay involved in the Boulogne business?'

He said nothing but his hand with its heavy rings rose horizontally to the level of his cravat: up to his neck.

'Does Lady Blessington know that?'

A shake of the head.

'So if Louis Philippe's government were looking for more evidence for the trial . . .?'

I waited and eventually he finished the sentence: 'They might have thought it worthwhile to introduce a spy under his roof, yes.'

'Which doesn't explain why somebody took a lot of trouble to kill him and take the papers,' I said. 'Unless D'Orsay . . .'

He laughed. 'Can you imagine D'Orsay doing anything half so crude? Oriental poison in a Venetian wine glass, perhaps. Deadly scuffles in lofts, no.'

'And D'Orsay doesn't have the kind of friends who can influence an inquest,' I said. 'Which brings us back to somebody at a high level in our own government. If Lesparre really did have important papers, what were they and who would be embarrassed by them? As I said, you're better placed to find out about that than I am.' We'd come full circle. I sensed that his eagerness to talk to me had more to do with getting information than giving it. I might have said so, but the door opened and Lady Blessington walked in, followed by Count D'Orsay. She looked at our faces. 'So you two are reconciled. I'm very glad.'

'Entirely,' said Disraeli.

I said nothing. She sank down into an armchair and signed to me to sit down opposite her.

'I've been talking to Alfred. He really can't remember much about Bruno.'

Count D'Orsay's Apollonian forehead was wrinkled with the effort of trying. Knowledge of acquaintances' valets was a lot to expect. 'I didn't see very much of him,' he said. 'When they arrived, it struck me that he seemed a little more familiar in his manner with Lesparre than was quite appropriate, but then the two of them had been through a lot together.'

'Did Bruno speak English?'

'Yes, very well.'

'Was it Lesparre's suggestion that he should go and stay with his Italian friends?'

'I think it was agreed between them. A man hardly needs a valet when all he has are a suit of borrowed clothes and three shirts.'

'Would he go up and see Lesparre in the loft?'

'As far as I remember, there were no alarms while he was here, but he'd naturally have helped set everything up. It's a valet's business to see that his gentleman's made as comfortable as possible in all circumstances.'

'What did Bruno look like?'

'Below average height, neat in appearance, very short glossy brown hair, like a cap. In his early thirties, probably. Moved well, as if he'd been trained as a fencer or dancing master. Appearance spoilt by a nasty wound across his left cheek, like a sword cut, but Lesparre said he'd fallen against something when they were escaping from the steamer. It will leave a scar.' He ran his fingers over his own smooth cheek in sympathy.

'You could draw him for Miss Lane,' Lady Blessington said. 'You know how good you are at likenesses.'

I thought of Amos and his ferrets. 'Can you remember anything at all about him that might help us find him, what he likes or where he might go?'

More brow wrinkling. 'Clothes. Of course that's most of a valet's work, but I think he liked good clothes for himself. When he and Lesparre arrived here they had nothing but what they stood up in and a couple of spare shirts. Their shoes were falling to pieces, especially the valet's. I suppose they'd had to do a lot of walking. I gave Lesparre the run of my spare wardrobes and when I came back, both he and the valet had kitted themselves out. I meant it for Lesparre, of course, but I didn't grudge the valet. He'd chosen a pretty good pair of my shoes, nearly new. Sheer vanity because they were obviously two sizes too small for him and the seams would be splitting in no time. I don't suppose that helps at all.'

I thought not, but didn't say so. We left him and Disraeli together. As Lady Blessington and I left I noticed Ronson in the corridor with a box of new candles to replace the ones that had burned low in their sconces. He kept his face turned away from us, as any servant would in a task meant to be invisible to the gentry, but I noticed that he looked cleaner and calmer.

'I'm so glad that you and Mr Disraeli are reconciled,' Lady Blessington said. 'I do hate it when my friends are at odds.'

Were we reconciled? It would have been cruel to disappoint her, but I still thought Disraeli was keeping something from me, and I resented it.

NINE

Amos, waiting for me in the stable yard, had already got directions to Tibble's cottage. We went out of the back gate from the garden on to a field of thin grass dotted with dry thistles and anthills and a few cows grazing. A footpath led diagonally across it to a row of four raw brick-built cottages, not old but already looking decrepit, with roofs sagging and low sooty chimney pots. A woman bringing in clothes from a line outside the end house told us that Tibble's was the one next door.

'He's not in, though, only her.'

She turned out to be Tibble's daughter, a woman in her twenties but already weary-looking, heavily pregnant and a toddler pulling at her skirts.

'Neither of them's in. My husband's at work and Dad's gone to see a man about a dog.'

'Dog?' I said, as Amos and I walked away.

He laughed. 'Usually means public house. There was a way she said it, though, as if she didn't like it.'

He was looking away across the next field. Small groups of men were straggling along a footpath, some with dogs at heel, others carrying bags and baskets. The sun, low in the sky, stretched their long shadows over the grass. They might have been going for an evening picnic, except it didn't seem cheerful and there were no

124

women. A barn, black against the sky, looked to be where they were heading.

'I think I know what they're at,' Amos said. 'Why don't you go back to the house and wait?'

'No.'

He shrugged. We waited by a gate while another dozen or so men took the path across the field then, when it looked as if there were no more coming, we walked in the same direction. The light had almost gone by the time we got to the barn, but lamplight showed through the cracks between its boards. A low murmur of men's voices was coming from inside. Other men stood in small groups by the open door, heads together. They were mostly the labouring sort in caps and heavy jackets, with a few sportsman types in boots and breeches. Inside, a voice raised above the rest, loud and gruff.

'Ready, gentlemen. All on.' The men at the door filed into the barn.

'I'll go in,' Amos said. 'You'd best wait outside.'

This time I agreed with him. I'd guessed what was happening, even before we heard a cock crowing inside, and I didn't like it. I waited in the dark by the barn wall and listened. First an intense silence, then murmurings, swelling into shouts of encouragement, an occasional stomach-deep collective groan, a dog yapping, soon silenced. Then cheers and groans together and the gruff voice again: 'Game to the Shark.' A man came out of the barn, carrying a cockerel by the legs. One of its wings was still flapping, but feebly, and even from where I was standing I could smell the bird's blood. The man wrung

125

its neck with a quick, practised movement, not even looking at it, and threw it away into some bushes. Two lurchers bounded after it and the air filled with yipping and growling as they fought over the body. Soon afterwards Amos came out.

'It's going to be a while. Three more pairs to go after this.'

'I should have got a description of the man Tibble.'

'He's in there all right. I got somebody to point him out. Small man, fiftyish. He didn't look happy when the Shark won, so I reckon he dropped a bit of money on it. You still want to wait? I can walk you back, if you like.'

Stubbornly, I said I'd wait. Amos went back inside and I sat down on a log of wood, trying not to think too much about the noises from inside the barn. Amos came and found me while the last fight was going on.

'Our man's still unhappy, reckon he backed the wrong'un every time. Unless he picks up on this one, he won't be in the best of moods. I'll go back in there and stick close to him when they all come out and try and get him away from the others.'

Amos did it neatly. After a final burst of cheers and groans the men filed out and disappeared into the dark. Tibble was one of the last out. Even in silhouette from the lamplit doorway there was a disconsolate look about him, shoulders hunched, head down. He was trailing behind a group of men, and gave a flinch of surprise when Amos

126

came up beside him. The size and solidity of Amos made Tibble look even smaller than he was. I waited until they were well clear of the barn then moved in beside them. Tibble hardly noticed at first. He was explaining to Amos an infallible system for winning money at cock fighting. It seemed to have all the complication of astronomy without the excitement.

'But it didn't work, did it?' Amos said.

'It would if you gave it long enough.' Tibble's voice was high and eager, an optimist against desperate odds.

'So that's why you needed the money?' I said.

He jumped a good foot off the ground then came to a standstill. I suppose up to then, if he'd noticed me at all, he'd assumed I was another man from the audience. I followed up, before he could recover. 'You must be pretty badly in debt to try that trick with the pigeon.'

I couldn't see his features in the dark, but his eyes had gone so wide that the whites of them shone. 'What . . .?' We waited, but he couldn't say another word.

'Was the pigeon your own idea, or the man who gave you the money?' I said. 'Clever, in any case.'

'Does Her Ladyship know? Did she send you?' The words came out slurred, his whole body stiff with shock. Then, 'Who are you?' I could feel his fear. I was no more than a shape come out of the darkness, hardly human.

'Never mind that. How much did he give you?'

'Seven pounds.'

'A lot of money.'

'Five he offered. I got him up to seven. It was risking my job, I told him.'

'What's his name?'

'I don't know. Honest to God, I never knew his name.'

'How did he find you?'

'Followed me home, he must have. I don't know how else.'

'When was this?'

'Thursday before last.'

'So he followed you home and offered you money to get him into Lady Blessington's bedroom. Did he say why?'

'I asked him that.' Tibble was speaking more fluently now. There were just the three of us, standing among the cows and thistles in the dark, as odd an interrogation as I'd ever known. 'He said he just wanted to breathe the same air she breathed.'

A chuckle from Amos, soon suppressed. 'He what?' I said.

'As Her Ladyship. Just wanted to breathe the same air as where she slept.'

'This man, what was he like?'

'Dressed like a stable lad, but well spoken.'

'Old?'

'Young. Not much more than a boy.'

Dumbfounding. Lady Blessington might have been one of the great beauties of her day, but that was a generation ago. 'Didn't that seem odd to you?'

A stirring in the darkness might have been a shrug. 'Quality, playing games. You never know what they'll do.'

'So he struck you as quality?'

'Yes.'

'And the pigeon, your idea or his?'

'Mine, that was. What he wanted was any way to get into her bedroom.'

'How did you let him know when you'd done it?'

'He came to my house, early next morning. The first morning I hadn't done it and he got impatient, the second one I had, so in we went.'

'The Saturday?'

'Yes.'

'What did he do while you were repairing the window?'

'Breathed, I suppose, like he wanted.'

'Anything else?'

'Walked around. I wasn't watching him much. All I wanted was to get the job done and get him out.'

'Did he get the chance to take jewellery from her dressing table?'

'Nothing to do with me what he did. I didn't see him take nothing.'

'While you were working, did he leave you and go to any other parts of the house?'

A pause. 'He might have gone out to the corridor for a while.'

'How long?'

'Not long.'

'Did the police question you?'

'No. When I heard they were up at the house I thought I'd better lie low for a day or two. Not that I'd had anything to do with any of it, but the other thing might have come out.'

'Have you seen this young man since?'

I expected a no, but got silence as he made up his mind. 'This morning. Early this morning. He was there in my yard when I went to let out the hens.'

'What did he want?'

'To get into the house again. Not her bedroom this time, just into the servants' quarters and be left there.'

'To breathe again?'

'I didn't ask. He seemed different this time, more like giving orders than asking me, but as if his nerves were on edge. I said no, it was too much of a risk after the trouble there'd been, though I didn't tell him about the dead man. He said it was worth another seven pounds to me. I tried to put him off. I said I needed time to make up my mind but he said he'd be there anyhow. If I'd been lucky tonight I could forget all about meeting him, but I wasn't.'

'So you have an arrangement to meet him. When and where?'

'Midnight, outside the door into the back of her garden.'

'Any signal?'

'I'm supposed to wait inside the door. He'll knock and I let him in.'

'You won't be there,' I said.

'But the money . . .'

'Forget about that. Promise you won't meet this man and I'll promise not to tell Lady Blessington about the trick with the pigeon.'

He really had no choice. Afterwards Amos, who could be quite soft-hearted at times, said he felt

130

almost sorry for the man because he'd got in deep with his gambling. I remembered the dying cockerel and felt no sympathy for him. Not much more was said as we walked towards the group of cottages. When we got there Tibble wished us a dejected goodnight and went inside. We walked carefully in the dark among the cows and thistles and in at the back gate of Gore House.

'So we're here till midnight,' Amos said. He'd taken it for granted, rightly, that we'd keep Tibble's appointment for him. 'It's not long after ten o'clock now. We might as well make ourselves comfortable in the stables.'

While he checked that our horses had enough hay and water I went to beg some refreshments from the housekeeper. Lady Blessington would willingly have entertained me inside, but I had my word to Tibble to keep so didn't want to speak to her until we knew more. Stedge found me in the housekeeper's room and gave me D'Orsay's sketch of the valet, carefully done up in a cardboard portfolio. It seemed better than D'Orsay's usual efforts. A neat man, as he'd said – round face, round eyes, cap of hair and the unreadable expression of the perfect valet, the wound represented by one long slash of charcoal. I returned to the stables with the drawing and a basket of bread, cheese and a bottle of wine to find Amos waiting on a bench outside the tack room. When I shivered in the cool autumn air he found a horse rug to put round me. We shared the food and wine.

'So was his young man the valet?' Amos said.

'It sounds as if it might have been. Tibble said

the man was quality, but to him a valet would be. But why would he have to use such a roundabout way of getting back in the house? He could have walked in and the other servants would have assumed he'd come to see Lesparre.'

'Somebody was ready to spend quite a bit of money.'

I thought of Slater. He certainly couldn't be described as a young man, but he'd probably have men and money at command. 'The time fits. The first soot fall in the old nursery was found on Monday, but it could have happened before that, on the Saturday. The man could have left Tibble working on the window, got into the loft and loosened those screws on the chimney plate. He might have been out of the room for much longer than Tibble admits.'

'But then if he'd put the plate back he couldn't have come down the chimney,' Amos said. 'He'd have needed somebody inside helping him.'

'Then why come down the chimney in any case? Unless he was making sure that it could be done.'

'My money's on the valet,' Amos said. 'I reckon he and Tibble's man are one and the same.'

'I'll take you for half a sovereign that they're not.' Though I wasn't sure why. 'Anyway, we'll soon know.'

A clock somewhere struck eleven, then the half hour.

'Better not keep him waiting,' Amos said.

We packed the remains of the picnic, folded the horse rug and walked quietly to the door into the garden. The man was late. It must have been quarter of an hour or so after midnight before the knocks came, three of them, light and quick on the outside of the door. Amos and I had planned it. I'd open the door because I was nearer Tibble's build and hope that the man would walk in, unsuspecting. Once he was inside, Amos would slam the door shut and hold our man if he looked like running away. It worked like a charm, most of it. I opened the door. The figure outside was about my height, wrapped in a cloak with a hood drawn up over his face. He came in without saying anything, walking quickly, then stopped, sensing something wrong. The door slammed behind him. He gasped and turned to run. I grabbed his cloak, feeling the rush of Amos coming past me like a man chasing the greased pig at a country fair. His attack swept the man off his feet and he fell with Amos's weight on top of him, giving a hooting gasp as the breath went out of him. So far as planned, but then things started to unravel. First an exclamation of surprise from Amos, then he'd pushed himself up on his knees, taking the weight off our captive. After a few more gasps, the figure on the ground started struggling upright and found its voice.

'What are you doing? Who are you? How dare you?' But not a man's voice, not even a boy's – quite definitely a woman's.

'Well, that's upset the apple cart,' Amos said.

TEN

She was on her feet, making for the garden door. I got there first and stood with my back to it.

'We want to talk to you,' I said. 'Either that or we're handing you straight over to the police.'

We were practically touching. I could feel her breath on my face, though her own was no more than a pale blur in the dark. Anger burned off her, clear as flame.

'You have no right.' Her voice was low but clear. She had the slightest of accents, but I couldn't place it in the few words we'd spoken.

'Anybody has a right to arrest a thief.'

I should have saved my breath because she turned and broke away, into the darkness of the garden. I went after her.

'Amos.' For once, he was not much use. He'd have tackled a seven-foot assassin cheerfully but the discovery that he'd felled a woman had unnerved him. A sound of swishing foliage and cracking sticks suggested that she'd charged through a flower border, the dahlias probably. I went in the same direction, tripping and sliding over grass and plants. She was setting a good pace and I thought I was losing her, until a thump, a crashing of flowerpots and a gasp of pain came from up ahead. I suppose a gardener had left a wheelbarrow of pots out because I ran into the upturned wheel of it, with pot shards crackling

134

under foot. She was struggling up again, but with difficulty. I took her arm to help her and held on to it.

'If we go on like this, we're going to wake the whole house,' I said. 'Is that what you want?'

'Who are you?' Her question was less angry this time, more curious. She might be in pain, holding her free arm across her chest.

'I'm a friend of Lady Blessington. What were you doing in her house?'

'She shouldn't be sheltering a traitor.' She spoke the last word like a curse, operatically.

'Are we talking about Lesparre?'

'What do you know about him?'

'I'm not going to answer any of your questions until you've answered some of mine.'

'Is he still in that house?'

I wondered if we were going to spend all night deadlocked among broken flowerpots. Luckily Amos's footsteps sounded at long last, coming along the gravel path. 'There are the two of us,' I said to her. 'You can't get away.' She didn't know that Amos was temporarily a broken reed and clasped her arm more tightly to her chest, probably expecting to be skittled again. 'We'll go back to the stables,' I said to Amos. 'We can talk there.'

He led the way and we followed, with me still holding the woman by her uninjured arm. Where the path was too narrow I let her go ahead and followed close behind, but she made no more attempts to escape. When we got to the stable yard Amos held the door of the hay store open and she walked calmly into the sweet-smelling darkness.

'I'll find some light,' he said. 'You all right with her?'

'Yes,' I said, but she answered 'Yes' at the same time, as if I were the threat and Amos her protection. Whatever or whoever she was, she thought quickly. He came back with a candle, lit it from the flint in his pocket and set it upright on a beam well away from the hay.

'Did I hurt you, miss?' He plumped up hay into a seat for her.

'It wasn't you, it was the wheelbarrow,' I said, fearful that he'd dissolve into apologies when I needed him. Her face was still no more than a blur in the darkness.

A smell of sweat and the sharp tang of rosemary from stumbling over a bush was coming off her. I daresay my smell was much the same. As the light from the candle spread the first thing that struck me were her great dark eyes. Perhaps they looked even larger and deeper than they were because of the angle of the light, the pupils wide and black from being in the dark. Her cheekbones were high and sharp, black hair twisted up under the man's cap she'd managed to keep on her head through it all, with a few damp tendrils escaping. She wore breeches, boots and a man's riding coat. She was beautiful. Goodness knows how Tibble could have mistaken her for a lad. Perhaps, in his need for money, he'd wilfully ignored the evidence or just considered it another example of the peculiar behaviour of the quality. Amos took a bandage out of his pocket, meant for a horse but mercifully clean.

'Let's see that wrist, shall we, miss?'

It looked puffy. She held her arm out to him and he bandaged it with great care, making the small soothing sounds that he might to a horse. All the time she stared into my face as if trying to make a decision. I held her look and tried to give nothing away. Amos tied off the bandage and went to put her hand carefully down in her lap, then was embarrassed again because of the breeches. She sensed this and almost smiled, then was serious as a statue again. I told her my name and asked hers.

'Eleonore.' Just the one word, no surname. The accent was French.

'So what are you doing here?'

'You said the name Lesparre. Are you friends of his?'

It was more of an accusation than a question, but I noticed she put it in the present tense. I followed the example.

'Not especially. You say he's a traitor. Who to?'

'The man who should be emperor of France. Prince Louis Napoleon Bonaparte.' She said the name like a herald announcing a title, her great eyes intent on mine.

'Lesparre told Lady Blessington he was with the prince and managed to escape.'

'She's a fool if she believed him. He's the reason the attempt failed. He warned the garrison in advance. If it hadn't been for him, the prince would be in Paris by now, not in prison. Some of us suspected him, even before we sailed. But the prince is too trusting, too open-hearted.'

'So he's a traitor. What do you want with him?'

'To kill him. After we've put him on trial.'

'We?'

'Those of us who care about France.'

'And if he's guilty, who carries out the sentence?'

'I shall, if necessary.' This time she spoke without drama, as of a distasteful but necessary piece of work, like clearing a drain. Amos moved uneasily on his heap of hay and caught my eye. His expression asked what kind of creature it was that we'd caught and what were we going to do with it. 'So you can tell your friend Lady Blessington what she's got under her roof,' she said. 'Now, if you like.'

'So that you can assassinate him? No, I don't think so.' I didn't believe that had been her intention, not on this visit at any rate. If she'd been carrying a knife or gun she'd have probably used them on us. 'You've proof he's a traitor?'

'Proof of my own ears and eyes. I was at Boulogne, dressed as I am now. The prince would not have allowed me to go, but I stowed away. I saw it all. We'd chosen a day when we knew that the commander of the troops at the Boulogne garrison was away. He was not sympathetic to the prince but his deputy was of our party. But somebody got word to the commander. He hurried back and found the soldiers cheering the prince, shouting *Vive l'Empereur* and getting ready to march on Paris. He surrounded them with his own men, threatened to fire and everything was over. The prince wanted to kill himself there and

138

then on the field of battle but his friends persuaded him to preserve himself for another attempt. It will happen. They can't keep the eagle in a cage.' You could almost hear the drums and 'La Marseillaise'.

'You were in the garrison itself?' I said, half envying her the adventure.

She looked down. 'No. The prince insisted I must stay on the ship.'

'With Lesparre?'

'Yes. There we were, just a few of us, waiting for news. We heard the cheers for the prince from the garrison, but then the shots and the shouting. We knew something was wrong. Some of the men came running back to the ship but the French soldiers followed and arrested them. They searched the ship. By then, I had changed into women's clothes I had brought with me, just a confused and frightened woman. They let me go.'

'And Lesparre?'

'He was simply allowed to walk off, through the police and soldiers and nobody made any attempt to arrest him. That was when I knew. It was Lesparre who betrayed the prince.'

'If you're so sure of that, why not just go to Lady Blessington and Count D'Orsay and tell them? They're good friends of the prince.'

'Friends in prosperity aren't always friends in distress. You can tell them for me, see what they say.'

'I'm certainly not going to burst in on them with this story in the middle of the night. You can come home with me and we'll discuss it in the morning.' I'd decided while we'd been talking. I'd no intention of letting her go but it would have been awkward to keep her by force, particularly since Amos would be no help. She nodded, looking weary. I supposed she'd keyed herself up to whatever she'd planned to do that night and was feeling the draining of energy that comes when things aren't as straightforward as they seemed.

'I'll go and tack up the horses,' Amos said.

He left the candle with us, relying on himself to saddle and bridle two horses in a strange stable in the dark. I'd have liked to help him, but didn't trust Eleonore not to run away. She lay back on the hay, eyes closed, but I was pretty sure she wasn't sleeping. The candle was nearly burned out when two sets of hooves sounded outside. I carried it in one hand and gave the other to her to help her over the shifting hay. Amos was holding the reins of Rancie and the big cob from his livery stables. I took the picture of the valet with me in its portfolio and managed to lash it to my saddle with a piece of string I'd found.

'I'll put you up first then get up in front, miss,' he said to her, preparing to lift her up on to the cob's back. She moved away. 'Don't worry, I'll be careful of your hand.'

'You think I'm going to ride behind you?' All of her arrogance was coming back.

'That was the general idea,' Amos said. Then, to me, unhappily, 'Tell her I don't go around knocking ladies over.'

That wasn't the problem, as it turned out. Eleonore, in her man's gear, flatly refused to ride

140

pillion behind him 'like a farm woman going to market' as she put it. I pointed out that at about two o'clock in the morning, pitch dark, there was nobody to see, but it made no difference. She looked longingly at Rancie who, even by candle-light, showed like the thoroughbred she was, but I had no intention of letting Eleonore on her back. In the end, Amos said she could ride the cob and he'd walk leading it, so that's what happened. The road back from Kensington to Hyde Park seemed a long way in the dark and knowing Amos was plodding so patiently and that he'd have to be at work in a few hours I could cheer-fully have strangled her. Our hooves clattered along the cobblestones in Adam's Mews and into Abel Yard as the workhouse clock was striking three. Amos helped Eleonore off the cob, then me off Rancie.

'I'll bed her down here, if you like. You'll maybe be wanting to go back to Gore House first thing in the morning,' he said. I nodded and thanked him. Just occasionally, rather than send Rancie back across the park to his livery stables, we'd make her comfortable in an empty stall next to the cow sheds at the end of the yard. I stuffed a hay net while he spread straw and filled a bucket from the pump by lamplight. Eleonore sat on the mounting block and watched. 'Sure you're safe alone with that one?' he said.

'I think so. She needs our help, so I don't suppose she'll knife me.'

'Are you going to tell her he's dead?'

'Probably yes, when I've got more out of her. Of course, she may not need telling.'

141

'I reckon she's not pretending about that. She thinks he's still alive.'

'I wouldn't depend on it.'

He vaulted on to the cob's back and rode off with a cheerful, 'Goodnight, ladies.'

Eleonore didn't reply. I tucked the portfolio with D'Orsay's sketch of the valet under my arm and led the way upstairs to the parlour. While I lit the lamp and coaxed the fire back to life she draped herself across an armchair, trousered legs hitched over the arm of it, and watched from half-shut eyes.

'Madeira?' She accepted a glass in her good hand as if doing me a favour. I swung the kettle on its trivet over the fire and settled with my own glass in the opposite armchair. I tried to guess her age. A few years older than I was, possibly even in her thirties. But then she was tired and in pain, though hiding it well. 'So you're a friend of Prince Louis?' I said.

'A friend and a soldier.'

'Soldier?'

'My father was an officer in the emperor's imperial guard. Before he marched away to his last battle I swore to him that whatever happened I'd be loyal to the emperor.'

'And that loyalty transfers to Prince Louis?'

'The prince is a fighter for freedom everywhere, like his uncle.' She glared at me as if Waterloo had been my fault. 'So, have I answered the question you wanted to ask me?'

'What question?'

'Whether the prince and I are lovers. That's usually what women want to know. Love, love,

love.' She sang the words sarcastically, in a fine contralto voice. Her glass was already empty. I refilled it.

'Not this woman,' I said (though I'd have liked to know). 'What would you have done in Lady Blessington's house tonight if you'd got in there.'

'I've told you that – look for a traitor.'

'What made you think he was at Gore House?'

'We have friends in many places.' Quite likely, I thought, and Lady Blessington's home was, after all, one of the great gossip centres of London. Short of standing on a pedestal in Whitehall, there weren't many worse places for a man to hide.

'Your people had tried before, hadn't they? There was a foreigner looking for a footman's post. But that didn't work so you decided to get in yourself. Seven pounds was a lot to pay. Did you get your money's worth?' The look of surprise on her face was gone in the blink of an eye.

'What do you think?'

'I think you did. You had time to go up the back stairs to the loft and unscrew that plate in the chimney. Then you had a rake around inside the chimney to clear it for the next time.' I'd realized that she could hardly have come down the chimney and reappear to Tibble covered in soot, but simply raking around might account for the first mess in the old nursery. One detail bothered me even as I spoke: how would she have known to take up an oil can to loosen the screws?

She was staring as if I were some unlikely creature in a zoo. 'Could you kindly tell me what

143

you're talking about. Are you mistaking me for a chimney sweep?'

'You left Tibble repairing the window and went out for a look around.'

'Yes. If it interests you, I went along the corridor and found the door to the servants' stairs. I'd have liked to do more but there wasn't time. And I can assure you I was not poking around in any chimneys. Soot is terribly bad for the voice.'

'So what were you doing?'

'Reconnoitering, of course. I wanted to know where they were hiding Lesparre and how we'd get him out. It was obvious I'd have to make another visit when there was more time.'

'Like tonight?'

'Like tonight.'

'Was it you who stole the bracelet and pendant?'

'These, you mean?' Her voice was contemptuous. She slid a hand into her breeches pocket and dropped a bracelet with red stones and a blue pendant on the table beside her. 'I was going to put them back tonight. You can give them to her next time you see her.'

'Why did you take them?'

'An impulse. I thought I might get one of our people to say he'd found them and take them back to her.'

'As another way of getting in to Gore House? You could have done that by walking up to her front door by daylight. So what did you intend to do there tonight?'

She didn't answer. I thought I knew, though. Lady Blessington asleep, her maid gone and the

144

lamp turned out. This woman appearing from the wardrobe or under the bed, hand over mouth before she could scream. I smiled, thinking it wouldn't have worked: Lady Blessington would have bit her to the bone and cracked her over the head with a water carafe. She caught the smile.

'You think this is a joke?'

'Far from it.' I thought of the black shape falling from the hatch, the smell. Lesparre was, in their eyes, a traitor already condemned. So had some of her friends trussed him up to wait for a mock trial before the hatch was released? If so, why hadn't they told her? The kettle boiled. I made tea but she wafted her glass for more Madeira so I filled it up again.

'Lesparre talked about papers,' I said. 'He told Lady Blessington he was carrying some that might save the prince's life.'

'Believe me, whatever he was carrying, he wasn't intending any good to the prince. Are there papers?'

'Lesparre wouldn't be parted from a satchel of them.' I was fishing and she was definitely interested, though wary.

'He has them now?'

'I don't know.' At some point she'd have to learn that Lesparre was dead – always supposing she didn't know it already – but I wanted to get what I could from her first. I'd given her something new to think about and watched her eyes rove round the room as she did it, taking in what seemed to me the comfortable disorder of the place, the glowing fire, scattered books and newspapers, the cat that had given her breeches a cautious sniff then taken up residence on my lap. Suddenly she was tense, sitting up straight and focusing on something.

'What's that?'

I'd put the portfolio with D'Orsay's drawing open on the table. She was on her feet before I could say anything, picking it up. The movement was so sudden that the cat jumped down, startled. Then she froze, looking down at it.

'What's that doing here?'

'Lesparre's valet. But of course you'd know him from Boulogne. Is it a good likeness?'

She took her time, staring down at it. 'Not particularly, no. But why are you interested in Lesparre's valet?'

'I want to find him. Do you know where he is?'

She shook her head. I'd expected more questions but tiredness and probably the pain from her wrist seemed to be catching up with her. She sat down and closed her eyes. 'So, will you permit me to go now?' Energy was visibly draining away from her.

'Go where, and at this time of night?' No answer. 'I suggest you stay here, and in the morning we'll both go and speak to Lady Blessington. You can try and convince her that Lesparre is a spy. Why not do it the direct way?' I was aware that I was being anything but direct myself but I didn't want to lose sight of her. Even with her hurt wrist, I was by no means sure I could stop her if it came to a physical struggle.

'Very well, I'll trust you,' she said, as if making a great concession, eyes open now. She trusted

146

me as much as a jeweller trusts a jackdaw. So I'd gained my point and landed myself with the problem of where to put her. My bed upstairs was big enough for two of us but for all I knew she might have a knife in her pocket after all. Any other visitor could have had the chaise longue in my study, but I'd have had to sleep on the floor or the landing outside.

'We'll stay in the parlour,' I said. 'You can have the sofa.' She took off her boots and stretched out on it like an old campaigner and I took the armchair by the fire. I didn't expect to sleep but must have dozed because when a noise downstairs woke me the fire had burned low and daylight was coming in through the gap between the curtains. Eleonore was asleep, or pretending to be. The noise again, the sharp rattle of gravel against the window. Only Tabby's aim was that accurate. I drew back the curtains and saw her white face looking up from the yard. She signalled to me urgently to come down. I put on my shoes and went, taking the precaution of bolting the door at the bottom of the staircase from outside.

'Cobblers,' she said. 'He's hurt. He might be dead by now.'

'Where?'

'Off Hatton Garden. Plush and I found him. Plush is with him.'

I was still fuddled from the happenings of the night and wondered what they'd been doing so far from their usual area until I remembered about following Slater. By then, we were out of the yard and walking fast. The morning was grey and drizzling but there was no question of going

147

back for my cloak, not with that clenched look on Tabby's face. We made our way eastwards, by alleys and shortcuts she knew, through the backstage area of a city that was still heaving itself awake, night soil wagons creaking along behind raw-boned horses, beggars in doorways rolling themselves tighter in their bundles of rags to put off the moment of being fully awake, night watchmen walking home muscular dogs that were threats on four legs.

'How did it happen?' I asked.

'Don't know.' She resented the waste of breath, so I didn't ask again.

As we turned into Hatton Garden, I began to have a suspicion where we were heading. It was too early for the barrel organ to be out and shutters were still down on most of the shops, yellowed blinds blanking the windows of grey lodging houses. We turned into the familiar narrow street and she made for the church. A flight of three steps led down from its shallow portico to the pavement. Plush was sitting on the bottom step, with Cobblers slumped against him, face buried into his shoulder, bare feet splayed apart on the pavement. An elderly woman in black was standing beside them, holding a glass of water.

Plush looked up at us, his face crunched up with anxiety. 'What's she saying?'

The woman was speaking Italian. 'That we should get him to hospital,' I translated. It seemed like a good idea to me. St Bartholomew's was only a short cab drive away. But when I said the word Tabby looked shocked and Cobblers gave a groan and his feet writhed, trying to propel him upright.

'People die in hospitals,' Plush explained and Tabby nodded.

'What's wrong with him?'

'Head mostly.' Gently, for a lad whose hands looked harder than horses' hooves, Plush raised Cobbler's head. The left side of his face was totally clotted in a mask of partly dried blood, the eyelid closed and gummed down. More blood dripped off his chin on to the grey knitted comforter he wore tucked into his jacket instead of a shirt, making it look like red chain armour. His right eye was open, but only just, the flesh round it red and swollen. I made myself look closely and realized that most of the blood was coming from a wound on his forehead, a triangular flap of skin hanging down. No sign of a broken skull at any rate. I went up a step to look at his head from the back. A lump was forming above his right ear suggesting he'd been coshed there.

'What else?' I said to Plush.

'His knees. He says they kicked them.'

'Anywhere else?'

'All over.'

I knew he should be in hospital, but it was no use trying to get him there against the opposition of the three of them, even with Cobblers helpless. Hospitals meant people in authority and they were the enemy. I crouched on the steps while the woman persuaded Cobblers to drink some water.

'Very well, I'll get a cab and we'll take him home. Wait here.' Then, thinking about it: 'Unless the people who did this to him are likely to come back.'

'If they do, you'd better bring a coffin cart for them along with the cab,' Plush said. He looked as if he meant it and so did Tabby. It wasn't reassuring but I walked quickly back to Hatton Garden and then to Holborn and managed to flag down a cab. The driver up on the box was happy enough to take a lady to Park Lane, less so when he found out that the journey would be via Hatton Garden. When we turned into the small street and he saw the situation, unease turned into downright rebellion. Get fleas and blood in his cab and he'd have to wash it out and be off the road for days, probably need new upholstery. Judging from the cracked state of the seat inside, it was well overdue for that anyway, but I didn't argue, just stood there on the pavement, keeping tight hold of the rein of his horse that was in no hurry to move anyway, and held up two sovereigns in my palm. Incidents on past cases had taught me never to travel without a war purse.

'One of these now, the other when you get us home.' It was gross overpayment, even if the cab would need washing. Even so, it might not have convinced him except that Tabby was holding firmly to the rein on the other side and the Italian woman had gathered a squad of friends, possibly from inside the church, who seemed to have enrolled themselves as Cobblers's guardian angels. Some huddled round Plush, who'd managed to get Cobblers on his feet, and helped

150

to propel the two of them towards the cab while others stood across the street so that the driver couldn't move without mowing them down, all this with a chorus of voices in operatic-sounding Italian that burst round the man like a thunderstorm. He watched, beaten, while we manoeuvred Cobblers inside. A cab will only take two people, side by side, so when he wasn't looking I tried to give Tabby the remains of my war purse so that she and Plush could find another cab. She waved it aside.

'We'll be there before you will.' Given their knowledge of the back streets, and the pressure of other traffic once the cab had turned into Holborn, she was probably right. Throughout the long journey, Cobblers leaned against me. I think he was conscious most of the time because sometimes when the cab lurched badly he swore in a harsh, concentrated way that was probably his substitute for groaning. He was still bleeding, but not quite so badly. Most of it was mopped up by an old shawl one of the women had tucked round him. I didn't ask questions because he was too ill for that. Perhaps he'd said something to Tabby and Plush. If so, they'd tell me in time. The priority was trying to keep Cobblers alive. Then, whether he was alive or dead, they'd want revenge on whoever had done this to him. I thought about this, then corrected it in my own mind: *we'd* want revenge.

151

ELEVEN

Tabby and Plush were in the yard waiting for us. The first thing that happened after we got Cobblers upstairs and into my bed was a blazing row with Mrs Martley. She met me in the parlour, face full of disaster.

'Your ragamuffin girl has gone upstairs, bold as brass.'

'Along with two ragamuffin lads, if that's what you want to call them. One's in my bed. I'm sending Tabby for the doctor.' If I'd invited the Four Horsemen of the Apocalypse into the house it wouldn't have shocked her so much. At least, being scriptural, they could have claimed some respectability. I let her rant on for a while about vermin, disease and having to burn bedding until tiredness and shock took away my patience. I told her she could burn every thread of bedding and the bed along with it if she liked, but only after Cobblers had recovered, if he did. Until then I expected her to nurse him and feed him, with Tabby's help, and if she didn't like it she could pack her bags and go. I didn't care for what I was saying because I knew very well that she had nowhere else to go and her possessions would fit into one carpet bag. I'd always paid the rent, fuel and food bills and given her a few shillings in her pocket when there was money to spare and mostly put up with being ordered around and criticized with sniffs and pointed silences. But we'd been through a lot together and there was a good heart underneath it. More to the point, she'd once earned her living as a midwife and was as skilled as any chemist in the properties of herbs. If anybody could save Cobblers, she could. The doctor, who knew our household, confirmed that judgement when he'd examined the patient. In his opinion young Mr Cobblers, as he put it, was suffering from loss of blood and severe bruising, and possibly several cracked ribs. But he was a tough subject and, as far as he could tell, no other bones had been broken and as long as infection didn't set in, there was little that wouldn't heal with a few weeks' rest and careful nursing. By that time Mrs Martley was standing by the bed in a clean apron – in the doctor's honour and not to please me – and nodding. She still wasn't talking to me, but accepted money to go out and buy band-ages, steak for beef tea and whatever herbs she needed. Cobblers fell asleep and seemed to be breathing normally so I took Tabby and Plush downstairs.

'So what happened?' I said. 'Was it the man Slater?'

'Dunno,' Tabby said. 'He was like it when we got there. He must have been there some time from the blood on the pavement.'

'Where was he? On the church steps?'

'Nah, we got him to the steps. When we found him he was in front of that house further up.'

'That house?'

'The one you and me went to together.' The

Italian mutual aid office, where I'd delivered the message for Lesparre's valet.

'How did you know he was there?'

'We didn't. We'd gone looking for him because he wasn't outside the man's house where he should've been.' It took a while to sort out what she meant, because I hadn't paid enough attention to their plans for trailing Slater and left it to Tabby to organize the details. She'd done it with her usual efficiency. The arrangement was that Cobblers would follow him through the night hours then sleep in a doorway opposite his lodgings in Lisle Street. Around sunrise, Tabby and Plush would arrive to take over the day shift when Slater left his lodgings and went wherever he was going. They'd arrived to find no sign of Cobblers and had started inquiries around the street. Although the two of them were well away from their usual territory, there seemed to be a freemasonry among the street gangs that might help in times of trouble, as long as it wasn't to their disadvantage. Through that network, they'd heard about an injured man off Hatton Garden. 'They said he was dead at first, then we got there and he wasn't quite.'

'Did he say anything about what happened?'

'Three or four of them set on him. He'd never seen them before.'

'Did they say why?'

'Never said a word the whole time, he says.'

'What was he doing outside the house?'

'Following the man Slater.'

'Had he gone inside the house?'

154

'Cobblers didn't know. It was dark, he was following him and he just disappeared.'

'So Slater had left his lodgings before daylight?'

'Must have, or Cobblers would have stayed where he was.'

'And he wasn't one of the men who attacked Cobblers?'

'I told you, he'd never seen them before.'

We'd get no further until Cobblers recovered enough to tell us more, perhaps not even then. I made them cups of tea – ignoring Plush's suggestion for a spot of gin in it – and cut hunks of bread and butter. They took it down to the yard to eat, Plush being as respectful as Mrs Martley of the sanctity of the parlour. I took my tea up to sit beside Cobblers's bed. He hadn't stirred. Blood was clotting on the bandage the doctor had wrapped round his head. The guilty, weary feeling that comes over you after you have lost your temper weighed me down like a dirty blanket. However good the motive, I'd shame-lessly bullied Mrs Martley, who was only trying to do what she thought best for me. Worse, I might have killed Cobblers. Until today, he'd been just one of Tabby's gang, a boy I knew well enough by sight to say hello to when I walked or rode through the mews. Now he was injured because of my greed to know something that had nothing to do with his life and should never have mattered to him. With luck and good nursing he wasn't going to die, but his injuries could stay with him for life. He had no home, no family, no money but the few pennies he

155

might earn running errands or begging. A bed in clean straw was luxury for him. His only asset was his physical toughness, and a decision of mine might have robbed him of that forever. My mind shuttled between him and Mrs Martley, uncomfortable with either. The conversation with Mrs Martley kept running through my head and I realized there had been something about it that worried me, quite apart from my harshness. Something she'd said – but then once I'd started she hadn't had a chance to say much at all. Something she didn't say then, some protest that should have been made, but wasn't. Then it came to me. She'd made no trouble at all about the presence of an unexpected guest, even worse than unexpected: a woman in man's dress. Surely, as well as objecting to Tabby's presence in the house, she should at least have mentioned the visitor in the parlour. The reason was obvious – as far as she was concerned, no visitor was there. Sometime between when Tabby had called me out while it was still dark and when Mrs Martley had got up, probably a couple of hours later, Eleonore had disappeared. I got up and went downstairs. Only an empty Madeira glass on the table and a dent in the sofa cushion showed that anyone had been there at all. One possibility was that she'd discovered the small door that led through to my study and decided the chaise longue there was a more comfortable place to spend the night. No sign of her there, but one odd thing. I kept a small bowl of apples on the table and two of them had gone. So she'd found her way to my study – not an easy thing unless you knew the odd arrangement of my lodgings – and been hungry. No apple cores though. Once in the study, she could have got out if she wanted to. I'd bolted the main staircase door, but not the other one that led directly to the study. It turned out that she'd taken something with her besides apples. When I went back to the parlour, D'Orsay's sketch of the valet had gone from the table. I ran down to the yard, hoping to find somebody who'd seen her go. Mr Grindley, the carriage mender, was in his workshop by the gate, firing up his forge. I had a job to hear what he was saying above the roar of the flames and the bellows his apprentice was pumping and even then couldn't believe it.

'Young fellow rode out just after it got light. I thought it was Mr Legge come to take her back to the stables, but it wasn't him so he must have sent a lad.'

'Take her back?' Once I'd understood what he was saying I rushed down the yard to the stall where we'd left Rancie. Empty, apart from scuffed straw and a pile of droppings. Her saddle was still on the rail, but the bridle had gone from its hook. My howl of grief and rage brought Tabby and Mr Grindley running. We all of us rushed into the mews, trying to find anybody who'd seen her go. All the grooms and lads there knew Rancie and some of them had seen her, being ridden at walking pace along the mews in the first light, and thought nothing of it. Like Mr Grindley, they'd assumed that she was being taken back to the livery stables. I tried to get a description of the rider. Young lad, they thought, slim built but too tall for a jockey. It hadn't surprised them that he was riding her bareback, as it would be preferable to a side saddle for most men. Sat easily, they said, obviously good with horses. When I heard that, I could have howled again at Rancie's treason. Why hadn't she bucked the woman off, reared up, screamed a protest at being taken away from me? Her mouth was delicate, she needed soft, calm hands, an easy balance. The idea that this creature from nowhere, this possible murderess, had the ability to ride her so easily went to my heart with a sharp blade of envy. Back in the yard, I sat down on the mounting block, rocking backwards and forwards from rage and grief, hands over my face. In the blackness, I thought how I'd loved two things, a man and a horse, and they'd both been taken away from me. Worse, they'd chosen to go away. How long I was like that, I don't know. What brought me back to something like my senses was an arm round me, a smell of pipe tobacco and sweet hay from a jacket sleeve, a voice murmuring calming syllables in a soft Herefordshire accent. Amos Legge. Tabby was standing at a distance. I suppose she'd been afraid of coming near me in a state she'd never seen me in before, but Amos was responding as he would to any distressed creature.

'Don't you worry. She's done the stupidest thing she ever did in her life, taking that horse. We'll have her.' As I opened my eyes and started coming back to my senses, he explained. 'A good-looking horse like that with just a lad-seeming on her, she'll stand out like a flamingo in a duck pond. It's only a few hours she's been gone. Unless she's grown wings and flown, I'll find her. That woman too, and you can do what you like with her.'

He'd calmed me enough to start thinking. I told him about the missing sketch of the valet. 'She recognized him, I'm sure of that, though she pretended she didn't. She took the sketch because she doesn't want us to find him.'

'And she doesn't know the man Lesparre's dead?'

'No, but she wants him dead. But then I don't know what to believe. There's not a single thing about her that's true, but whatever's happening, she's at the centre of it.'

Now I was calmer, Amos said he'd go and start the hunt for Rancie. I knew his network of grooms, ostlers, boys, farriers and drivers extended over the whole city, the whole country even, but when I thought of a single thorough-bred mare in all the confusion of London, even that didn't seem enough. When he'd gone, Tabby came to join me, still nervous as if I were a hissing firework that might go off unexpectedly.

'Plush is going back there. I should go with him.'

I didn't have to ask where. So far they hadn't been involved in the events at Gore House but now that following Slater had proved so dangerous and Eleonore had come on the scene, Tabby needed to know something of what was happening.

She listened and showed some ghoulish interest in Lesparre's hanging. But Gore House was a long way from her scheme of things and her friend mattered more.

'I wish you wouldn't go back there,' I said. 'Do you want to get yourself half killed as well?' She scuffed her boot toe in the straw and muck of the yard and wouldn't meet my eye but I knew I might as well argue with the mounting block. 'If you two are going, I'm going with you.' We should all have been bone-tired but were too strung up to rest. I went upstairs to find Cobblers still asleep and Mrs Martley chopping steak for beef tea. Something herbal and bitter smelling was infusing on a saucepan at the fire. She'd do her duty at least. Tabby and Plush were waiting in the yard and without anything more being said, we set off towards Hatton Garden again, not quite so hurriedly this time but with a purposeful look about the two of them that didn't allow for talking. By this time the whole of the Italian quarter was so crowded that we had to push our way through groups of women with shopping baskets blocking the pavement as they stopped to exchange news about villages at home, the children trying to sell us things, the men from the mountains. The street with the mutual aid office was crowded too, with women and a few men going in and out of the church. I got into conversation in Italian with a couple of the women and asked if there had been a disturbance on the street the night before. No, they'd heard no disturbance. No, they knew nothing about a boy being hurt.

'We could repeat that with everybody in the street,' I told Tabby and Plush. 'Nobody will have seen or heard anything.'

'Can't expect it,' Tabby said.

We walked the few dozen yards from the church to the Italian office. Nothing new there, the same cards and posters in the windows, the same air of a good cause on hard times. Tabby was staring at something on the pavement. She caught my eye and nodded towards it. The traces of blood had been scuffed by many feet, but there seemed no reason to doubt that was where Cobblers had been attacked. I pushed the door open and walked in. No sign of the Dante professor today. The only person in the room was a young woman, sitting at the table, pen in hand, working on what looked like a grammar exercise. She was the brightest thing in the place, dark hair, caught up casually in a knot at the neck, big brown eyes, a complexion like a white peach, probably in her early twenties. Her feet were in felt slippers too large for her. She hadn't expected visitors and looked startled. When I said I'd come to inquire about Italian lessons she managed a quick smile, but the startled look was still there. Haltingly, she repeated what I'd said. Her accent sounded north Italian.

'I'm looking for a man named Bruno Franchetti,' I said.

A pause, then a shake of the head and an upward glance. '*Signor*, a lady.'

Almost at once, steps sounded on bare boards upstairs. Whoever was there had heard our

161

conversation, such as it was. A man came quickly down the stairs and wished me, in English, a polite good morning. He was in his mid-thirties, plainly but neatly dressed, with a clean-shaven olive complexion, high forehead and quick intelligent eyes. His hands were fine-boned, the fingers of the right one deeply stained with nicotine. He had a presence, a way of standing, that made this cluttered room seem no more than a camping place, as if he belonged somewhere more spacious. It wasn't arrogance, though. I liked him on sight and any suspicion of arrogance in men makes me bristle like a terrier seeing a rat. The young woman was staring at him with open worship in her eyes, but that probably wasn't his fault.

'You're inquiring for somebody, madam?'

'A man named Bruno Franchetti. I left a message for him here last week. I need to speak to him again.'

No change in his expression of polite interest. 'If you'd be kind enough to leave your name and address with us, I'll see if he can be reached.'

'Do you know where he is?'

A slight sideways and back movement of his head. 'But we'll do what we can.'

'There was a fight outside your premises last night,' I said. 'A friend of mine was attacked by several thugs. Do you know anything about that?'

'I regret, no. Nobody sleeps here at night. I'm sorry about your friend.' His voice was pleasant and his English good, with a strong Italian accent.

He picked up a piece of note paper from a shelf for me to write my name and address and

162

the young woman, anticipating what he needed, made a space among the papers and pushed a pen and ink stand towards us. The movement uncovered a book that she'd been using in her exercise. It was a well-used volume in a brown cloth cover with faded gold lettering and ink blots on the front. A dictionary, English into Italian, a volume small enough to slip easily into a traveller's luggage and printed by hundreds of thousands. The top right-hand corner of the cover was scuffed, the binding worn away with layers of stiff grey paper showing inside, rounded from much handling. Below the title was a large ink blot, extended by a bored convent schoolgirl into the shape of the island of Sicily. I found myself opening it, though I didn't need to because I knew exactly what I'd find on the first page. *Liberty Lane*, in the self-important hand of a thirteen-year-old, with a flourish underneath it, taking up half the page. Then, underneath it, the same person's writing, but more measured after the passing of twelve years: *To Robert, Soave s'il vento. May the winds be kind. Liberty 1840.* I'd tucked it into Robert's bag just before he'd got on to the coach that carried him away. The girl was looking at me like a scared chamois so perhaps I'd moved suddenly or made a sound. A man could dive into those dark eyes and forget everything else. Jealousy brings a terrible certainty and, without having to think about it, the picture came into my mind of a dark night by the landing stage at Dover and a man helping a young woman into a coach.

163

'Where did you get this?' I said.

The girl looked at the man, appealing for rescue. 'I really can't remember,' he said. 'We have so many dictionaries here.'

'It belonged to a friend of mine,' I said. 'A man named Robert Carmichael. Do you know him?'

He smiled. 'Quite a coincidence. No, I don't know the gentleman. Keep it if it has any value to you.'

I couldn't have given it up even if I'd wanted. He glanced at the door, waiting for me to go. I turned to the girl and tried to make my tone conversational, even kindly. 'So you're learning English. Have you been here long?'

'Not long, no.'

'It's a long journey from Italy, isn't it?' I said.

'A long journey, yes.' She glanced towards the man. He nodded, as if approving the conversational exercise. Short of throwing me out bodily, he couldn't do much else.

'And the seas can be rough.'

'The seas can be very rough, yes.' Some animation in her tone now. Her hand described rough waves.

'Enough to make one feel ill.'

'Feel ill, yes.' A nervous smile even. The admission of seasickness was a bond, or so she thought.

I picked up the pen, dipped it into the inkwell, wrote my name and address. The man took the sheet of paper I handed him. 'We'll see what we can do.' His tone said, *So now go.*

Tabby and Plush were waiting for me across the street. In the shock of finding the dictionary,

164

I'd even forgotten what we were there for, until Tabby said, 'Well?'

'No good,' I said. 'They didn't hear or see anything.' They were disappointed in me, as if they'd really expected me to produce the attackers for instant vengeance. 'We're doing no good here. We should go home, see how Cobblers is.' All the way back, the dictionary felt welded to my hand.

TWELVE

I took over the night watch from Mrs Martley at midnight. She was tired and I'd managed to sleep for some of the evening, a relief from thinking. I sat in the chair by the bed with a shaded candle on the table giving a steady half-light. Now and then Cobblers stirred and snuffled, but mostly he slept. Sometime after four he woke up and tried to get out of bed. I told him he was safe and to go back to sleep.

'Need a piss.' He hauled himself to a sitting position on the side of the bed, groaning at the pain from his ribs. There was a bed pan, but he wouldn't use it with me there so I had to go out on the landing. When I got back he was standing, looking round.

'Had a jacket.'

'It's downstairs. Mrs Martley's washed the blood off. Why do you want it? Are you cold?'

'Going. Can't stay here.' I wasn't sure if this was his normal way of speaking or because of his knocked-out teeth. I told him that he was staying until he got well and managed to get him back into bed, propped up on pillows. 'So, did they get them?' His certainty that the gang would be out for revenge was total. Since he didn't seem ready to go back to sleep I asked him if he could remember anything about the attack.

166

'Two of them, might of been three, one watching.'

'Did they say anything?'

'Not a word.'

'Did they come out of one of the houses?'

'Don't know. Just there.'

'Would you recognize them again?'

'No chance. Collars pulled up, scarves or mufflers over their faces.'

'Did they know you were following the man Slater?'

'Likely.'

'How far behind him were you?'

'Half the street. Harder following at night with nobody round.'

'Do you know what sort of time this was?'

'Clocks struck two before it.'

'And the man Slater came out of his lodgings?'

'Somebody went in first, then they came out together.'

'So there were two of them?' It sounded as if somebody might have brought a message to Slater urgent enough to take him out at that hour of the morning. 'You're sure one of them was Slater? It was dark.'

'Sure. Funny way of walking, like he's been wound up with a key.'

He was sounding tired. I rearranged the pillows and watched as he slid back into sleep. Had Slater realized he was being followed and deliberately led Cobblers into an ambush? Everything hinged on this man, and we knew so little about him.

Was it simply coincidence that connected him both with the death of Lesparre and whatever Robert had got himself involved with? His interest – even his obsession, from the way he patrolled the streets – was with foreigners in London, particularly those plotting revolutions in their home countries. If not part of the police force he must at least be closely connected with it, or why was he in Sergeant Bevan's company? And, of course, from there my mind went back to the nagging question of what Robert was doing. The answer, if I faced it squarely, was obvious: Robert was rescuing a dark-eyed Italian beauty. More than that, he was rescuing a dark-eyed Italian beauty who'd got herself involved in politics. Robert's political beliefs, like mine, were radical. We'd both supported, from a distance, the cause of Italian unity and he'd looked forward to finding out more on his travels through Italy. Only it hadn't stopped at acquiring information. Robert had a quality of knight errantry about him and a broad streak of romanticism. I'd teased him about it sometimes. Only it had turned into more than a case of rescue. Otherwise, why hadn't he brought her to me to look after? The answer was obvious. So think of something else. Think of Amos coming in the morning and a canter in the park on Rancie and . . . oh ye gods. The squawk of sheer misery I let out made Cobblers stir and groan, so after that I just cried silently until it got light.

By the time Mrs Martley reported for duty Cobblers was awake and I'd mopped myself up to look like a halfway efficient nurse. She'd found or bought a clean nightshirt for him, almost certainly the first time he'd seen such a garment. The plan was that she would apply comfrey salve to his ribs and slip the nightshirt on. This would involve taking off the filthy and bloodstained undershirt he was wearing, which – I was sure – she'd carry downstairs in the washing, tongs and stuff straight into the fire. Cobblers clutched the blanket to his chin and gave me a look that said: *Save me.* I knew she had no chance of getting his undershirt off with me present, so I left them to it, brewed coffee in the parlour, hacked some slices off the loaf and took them on a tray through the small door to my study. I was hungry, couldn't remember when I'd last eaten and stopped thinking beyond the next mouthful because thinking was doing me no good. A note from Gore House had arrived the day before, only I'd been too dispirited to read it. I unfolded it and found the usual few lines from Lady Blessington asking me to call. Later, perhaps. As I was sweeping crumbs into my hand to put out for the pigeons a commotion broke out in the yard – a hissing of wheels on the cobbles, a shout from Mr Grindley in the work-shop, a horse whinnying. I looked out on a vehicle far too smart for our disorderly yard, a gentle-man's racing curricle drawn by two bright bays, one of them trying to rear. The wheel spokes were lacquered shiny black, picked out with stripes of green and yellow, the upholstery yellow too, exactly matched by the waistcoat of the man in the driving seat, tall and broad shouldered in

169

a brown top hat with a gold cockade. When I pushed up the window and looked out, he raised the hat to me with a flourish.

'Morning, Miss Lane. Would you care for a drive?'

For a moment, it struck me as heartless that he should bowl up looking so chipper when he knew I must be sick with worry about Rancie, but Amos wasn't cruel. Since we couldn't have our usual morning canter round the park, this must be his idea of consoling me. It wouldn't work, but that was no reason to add ingratitude to my sins. I dabbed eau de cologne in various places to freshen myself and changed quickly into my riding habit, which seemed the only thing dashing enough for such an equipage. Amos got down from the driving seat to help me in then vaulted in on the other side and picked up the reins. One of the bays tried to rear again as we turned out of the yard into Adam's Mews but he controlled it, missing the granite block that stood in the gateway by a coat of lacquer.

'Half-brothers,' he explained. 'Matched sweet as a nut for looks, but that one's new to the game.' By the time the curricle went back to its owner he'd have them pulling together as if they'd done it from birth. We turned into Park Lane and went northwards at a fast trot. A few early riders and carriages were out and the curricle and bays brought admiring glances. Amos liked to advertise. I waited while he got the horses settled, knowing he always delivered news in his own good time.

'She's all right,' he said. 'A touch restless but she'll settle.'

'Amos, you've found her already. Where is she?'

'Where she should be. Back in her stable.' We turned into the Bayswater Road and had to slow to a walk because of the traffic.

'But where from? Where's she been?'

'Carlton Gardens.' One of the most fashionable addresses in London, overlooking Green Park and no more than a mile away from where I lived. 'In the stables there, along with the prince's horses, all eating their heads off with nobody to pay the bills now the owner's got himself in prison.'

'Prince Louis's stables?'

'No other.'

'The wretched woman must have taken her there. How did you find her?'

'Like I said to you, it wasn't hard following her. They'd turned right in the mews, so that meant Mayfair or Piccadilly. There's a man I know, down on his luck, who drives a cab round those parts so I got him to ask around and sure enough, he had a friend who'd seen them going east along Piccadilly. The friend had noticed because a boy threw something at the horse and the lad on his back turned round and gave him a mouthful that would have blistered the ears of a stoker. So I asked a crossing sweeper or two and found one of them with eyes and a brain who'd seen them going down St James. From there, it was just a matter of asking round stables and I'd had dealings with most of the big ones at some time or another.'

He said it casually, but I knew it must have

taken hours. 'And you just walked into Prince Louis's yard and found her?'

'Not straight away. Their head groom was there, doing his rounds for the night. I knew him a bit from seeing him out in the park. When I described her, he pretended he didn't know what I was talking about, but she must have heard my voice because she let out a whinny you could have heard in Middlesex. He'd put her in the foaling box, out of the way at the end of the yard.'

'Did he say how she'd got there?'

'According to him, one of the prince's friends brought her in and said she was to be looked after. So I asked him if the prince's friends made a habit of horse stealing and he said not usually, but with that one you never knew what she'd do.'

'He said *she'd*?'

'Yes, though he pretended he hadn't when I picked him up on it. He said he didn't know much about any of the friends, just the horses, and there was nobody in the house except servants wondering who's going to pay their wages. When I said I was going to take her with me, he just shrugged and let me get on with it. It was late by the time I got her back, so I left it to this morning to tell you.'

She was there in her box at the livery stables, her pet cat curled up on her back, pleased to see me but not over-excited. I cadged an apple for her and scolded her for her treason in letting the woman take her so easily. I wanted to reclaim

172

her by riding her and decided I might as well go over to Gore House as requested. Amos – now busy with his duties as head groom – gave instructions to have her tacked up and said he'd send a boy with me.

'No need,' I said. 'I don't suppose the woman's going to take her off me at pistol point in broad daylight.'

He was uneasy. 'It's not that I'm bothered about. It's just in my mind that somebody might be watching you.' He tried to make it sound casual, but didn't quite succeed. I looked at him. 'Probably nothing,' he said, 'but when we left your yard this morning, I had the idea somebody was looking out for us, the other side of one of the gate posts. I didn't get a proper look at him because of keeping my eye on the horse.'

It shook me, because Amos didn't fuss unnecessarily. It reminded me of my own feeling of being watched in the park the other day. When he insisted on sending the boy to Kensington with me, claiming that one of the ponies needed the exercise, I didn't argue.

Lady Blessington was in the library, looking a lot fresher than I felt. We drank coffee and talked, though not much to the purpose. I'd decided not to tell her about the attack on Cobblers or the dictionary. If she knew how things stood, or rather did not stand, between Robert and myself she'd have been sympathetic, but I didn't want sympathy.

'It's kind of you to come,' she said. 'But in

173

fact it's Alfred who wants a word with you. About what, I don't know. He's in the conservatory.'

A footman took me there, though I could have found my own way. As always with Count D'Orsay, the setting was nicely judged. In conservatories, as in gardens, a man and a woman may be alone together respectably. He was standing by a vine, looking critically at a cluster of small purple grapes.

'Just as well we're not depending on them for our wine. Thank you for finding time to see me, Miss Lane.' We both stared at the grapes. All his life he'd been a true dandy, which was more than a matter of correct dress, important though that was. The code of the dandy was never to show emotion. He should allow himself to be burned at the stake without showing more than a polite interest in the procedure and regret at what the smoke was doing to his linen. And yet Count D'Orsay was worried, unsure how to start. 'I'm sorry to say I have not been entirely open with you,' he said at last. I waited. 'We've given you the impression that the arrival of Mr Lesparre here was more or less by chance.'

'I gathered from Lady Blessington that he didn't know many people in London.'

'I promise you, Marguerite has been entirely honest with you. She's told you the truth – as she sees it.' Another wait. He'd taken a vine leaf between finger and thumb and was rubbing it. If he went on like that he'd suffer a stain on his fingers. 'I'm depending on your discretion because I wouldn't want Marguerite to know this. The fact is, I haven't been entirely open with her

174

either.' He released the vine leaf, took a deep breath and looked me in the face. 'The man who called himself Lesparre was blackmailing me.' My turn for ostentatious lack of emotion. 'May I ask what about?'

'French politics. More specifically, Prince Louis's attempt. I was more deeply involved than Marguerite knows. I knew what they were planning all along. I helped him to some extent by putting him in touch with people who know about finance. He had enough for the attempt itself, but if he'd been successful at Boulogne and set up a government, he'd have been dependent on the international financial market for survival, at least for the first few months until he was established. He needed guarantees, or at the very least promises not to be hostile. I did what I could.'

I thought I could guess why. There are circles of people who think they or their friends have a right to rule and D'Orsay was part of one. Friends in his case, because he had no great liking himself for the dirt and digging of politics. Prince Louis, with the glow of the Napoleonic legend about him, was a much more appropriate ruler of France in his view than the plodding, unpopular king, Louis Philippe. His circle had probably pictured themselves having a private little celebration banquet at the Tuileries palace. 'And Lesparre knew how you'd helped the prince?' I said. I could see how that would lay him open to blackmail. With the foreign secretary and half the cabinet on her guest list, even Lady Blessington would be embarrassed by an already scandalous son-in-law actively supporting revolution.

'Goodness knows what he knows or how he knew. I'd never met the man before he arrived at the back gate three weeks ago.'

This time I didn't try not to look surprised. 'He's not a friend of yours?'

'No. That's what I had to tell Marguerite. What other reason could I give for hiding him here?'

'So he just arrived out of the blue, claiming to be a friend of the prince?'

'Pretty well, yes. Marguerite was out. I was in my study and the gateman sent up a note for me that he said some foreigner had just left. I know now that it was the valet, Bruno. The note was in French, very curt, saying a gentleman in distress wished to see me at the back gate at once. There was another note folded inside it, one of my own. I'd written it to the prince, setting up a meeting for him with a banker acquaintance.'

'Would that have been so very damaging?'

'In itself, possibly not, but the question was what else he had. It was obviously a threat. I decided I had to go down and meet this gentleman in distress. There were Lesparre and his valet by the back gate. He claimed they'd managed to escape from the debacle at Boulogne with the prince's papers. He had them with him. He showed me more of my own letters to the prince. There were other papers there as well, hundreds of them, not all about me by any means.'

'The papers in the satchel?'

'Yes. He was very blunt about what he wanted. I was to give him refuge at Gore House while he used the papers to try to negotiate the prince's release from prison or a lighter sentence, at least that's what he claimed at the time. If I helped him, he'd give me back my own letters. I had to make a decision quickly. I agreed. By the time Marguerite got back, we'd concocted this story about Lesparre being a friend of mine and meeting him in the prince's company. I hated deceiving her, but what else could I do?'

Quite a lot of things, it seemed to me, including knocking Lesparre down and grabbing the papers from him. I'd heard D'Orsay had been quite an athlete in his youth. But with the valet there, it would have been two to one, so perhaps I was being unfair. 'But Lady Blessington thought she remembered him from one of her salons.'

He smiled sadly. 'It's one of Marguerite's little vanities. Hundreds of men pass through her salons and she likes to think she remembers them all. Once I'd introduced Lesparre as one of the prince's circle, that was enough.'

'And he convinced you he was from the prince's circle?'

'Not a doubt of it. He knew details about the prince and his friends that he could only have known from being close to him.'

'But then a spy would, wouldn't he?'

'You think he was?' D'Orsay sounded weary but not surprised. He and Lady Blessington had discussed it.

'Somebody told me Lesparre had been spying

on the prince. The person claimed he'd betrayed the whole Boulogne operation.'

'The prince knew about the French government spies. He said they were useless.'

'Are the English government spies any better, I wonder?'

'But why should . . .?' As the significance of that hit him, he let worry register on his face. 'You mean Lesparre might have been spying on me?'

'It's possible, isn't it? Palmerston doesn't like revolutionaries. Somebody at a high level stopped that inquest.'

'But I'm not . . . I mean, I was only trying to help a friend.' He sounded so honestly hurt, like a misunderstood child, that I almost laughed. Could D'Orsay be so naïve? Hadn't it occurred to him that his confession to me gave him a motive for murder? The blackmailer was dead and the threatening papers had disappeared. The killer must have known his way round Gore House. Who had more chance than the man who lived there? 'You won't say anything about this to Marguerite?' He was near pleading.

'She should know. Wouldn't it be better for you to tell her?' But he wouldn't. All I'd promise him was that I'd keep his secret for now and only tell Lady Blessington if it became essential in future. He wasn't happy with that, but had to accept it. I left him standing and staring at the unsatisfactory grapes and followed pathways between beds of dahlias and chrysanthemums to the stables.

*　*　*

178

Amos's lad followed me faithfully home on the pony and seemed competent, so I said goodbye to Rancie in Abel Yard and left him to lead her back across the park, far too crowded by that time of day for any attempts at horse theft. The news of Cobblers was good. He was sitting up and taking nourishment more solid than beef tea but had lost a skirmish with Mrs Martley when Plush tried to smuggle in his clay pipe and tobacco. Plush was back in the mews and Tabby was asleep in her cabin in the yard. Although it was still only mid-afternoon I decided to follow her example, stripped to stockings and chemise and stretched out on the day bed in my study. I woke some hours later to dusk, a tap on the door and Mrs Martley holding what looked like an invitation card.

'Some lad just delivered this.'

A stiff rectangle of pasteboard, printed. I took it over to the window, looking for a handwritten message, but found nothing. Simply a single ticket for a front stalls seat at Covent Garden, a new Italian opera that I'd never seen before, taking place that evening. A puzzle. I have many musical friends, but few of them with the means to buy expensive seats. Even if one of them had hit a lucky streak, why no message? There seemed one possible explanation: people can meet casually at the opera without attracting attention. Perhaps somebody wanted to talk. There was still time, so I put on my blue silk twill with the blue-and-green Indian shawl, pinned my favourite dragonfly in my hair and told Mrs Martley not to wait up for me. A couple of pennies sent one of the boys in the mews running to find a cab and I was soon lurching over the cobbles for an unexpected evening at the opera. As far as I could see from inside the cab – which isn't far – there was nobody watching me at the gate.

THIRTEEN

The seat was at the end of the third row of the stalls, and if my neighbour – a plump woman in overstretched sage satin with a nervous husband in tow – wanted to talk to me she was hiding it very well. By the time the overture started I'd seen two or three people I recognized and exchanged polite nods and smiles, and two or three others had pointedly ignored me for reasons I could guess. Still, nothing of significance. Not far into the first act it was obvious that the composer was a faithful disciple of Donizetti, but without the flair. It was pleasant enough to the ear, but the warmth of being so near the footlights reminded me that I hadn't had enough sleep. Once, in a long duet between heroine and about-to-be-exiled tenor, I tipped sideways against my neighbour's shoulder and got a glare that would have curdled milk. He would always, always be faithful and she would always, always wait. I really was not in the right mood for it. The tenor left at last and the villainous baritone appeared, declaring his love for the heroine, threatening vengeance when she refused him. At least his voice was good enough to keep me awake. The heroine warbled another aria about being faithful and was applauded at such length that her kidnappers, already on their way out from the wings, had to loiter looking embarrassed, but they finally carried her off to much *coloratura* screeching. By that time I was hoping that anybody who wanted to speak to me might manage it at the interval and let me go home, when the heroine's sister came on stage. A rustle in the audience of waking up or sitting up showed that this was what some people had been waiting for. She was slim and tall, dark hair flowing over her shoulders, face beautiful and fine-boned with a touch of arrogance, like a statue of Minerva. She had that quality of taking possession of the stage by right, so that everybody was looking at her and waiting. Madam Gordon, the posters had said. The name had meant nothing to me but her looks did. When the orchestra launched into the introduction to what was clearly going to be another major aria, I wondered what would happen if I stood up in the stalls and shouted *horse thief*. Of course, I did nothing of the kind but sat as if some force pinned me to the back of my seat as she lamented, in recitative, her sister's kidnapping and then took wing into an aria expressing determination to bring her back. I guessed that the composer must have known her, because for most singers the music would have been almost impossibly challenging. It ranged from mezzo soprano to low contralto, with passages that verged on the baritonal and called for almost superhuman breath control. She took all its challenges like a fine horse soaring over fences with air to spare. I've heard sweeter singers, but never one with such an amazing range. At the end of it the applause was thunderous but she stayed in character, staring out as if not seeing the audience, challenging the world to bring back her sister. For all my anger, I couldn't help joining in the applause. When it died down another tenor, who'd been standing there practically unnoticed, decided that was the right moment to declare his undying love for her. In another aria, shorter but just as demanding, she told him she couldn't even think about love until her sister was free. Fall of curtain. Interval.

I stood aside to let the rest of the row get out, then sat down again, staring at the lowered curtain. One of the house's footmen appeared at my side with a piece of torn paper on a salver. Four words were scrawled across it: *My dressing room afterwards.* No apology or explanation. She'd given no sign of noticing the audience at all, unlike some singers who come close to waving to their friends, and yet she'd known I was there. The audience came back. The curtain rose on kidnapped sister in the bandits' cave, lamenting her cruel lot, fending off another attempt on her virtue by the villainous baritone. A new bandit arrived, telling the kidnappers he's been sent to join them, and provoking even more excitement in the audience because the new bandit was, naturally, big sister in man's attire. The reaction of the audience to the first act was nothing compared to this. My neighbour's satin-covered arm quivered with pleasurable disapproval. Her husband, and most of the husbands as far as I could see, were on the edge of their seats. Gasps, indrawn breaths and a few nervous giggles combined in the soughing noise a retreating wave makes, competing with the orchestra. Her knee breeches were closely cut, over shapely white-stockinged calves and black leather pumps, above them a frilled white shirt, embroidered bolero and blue cummerbund, and her hair up under a hat with a sweeping feather, altogether more exotic than the lad's costume she'd worn at Gore House, but the same swagger. While the unobservant bandits sang a hunting chorus, she mimed the discovery of her sister in the cave and when the bandits marched out to hunt the two of them sang a tender duet, voices blending well. The thing was pretty ridiculous, even by operatic standards, but Eleonore, alias Madam Gordon, brought conviction to it. It ended, many arias and choruses later, in a scene where big sister challenges the villain to a duel with sabres. It was one of the most realistic stage fights I've ever seen. She knew what to do with a sabre and as she forced the baritone back towards the scenery the poor man looked genuinely alarmed. Finally, she jerked his sabre out of his hand and a couple of bandits had to hop aside smartly as it clattered on the stage. When cheers broke out from the audience she condescended to notice them for the first time, saluted with her sabre and bowed. After a final chorus about the triumph of virtue, with the audience cheering and some of the men on their feet, I was on my way to the dressing rooms.

I'd been backstage at Covent Garden before, but even if I hadn't known my way it would have been simply a matter of following bouquets. Several footmen were loaded with them and some gentlemen who hadn't waited for the final chorus were bringing in their own. The air was heavy with the smell of tuberoses, grease paint and gas. The soprano who'd sung the kidnapped sister had left her door welcomingly open to the men and bouquets. The door next to it was shut, with a small queue of gentlemen waiting outside. When the door opened they surged forward, to find the way blocked by a square middle-aged woman in a black dress.

'Madam is not receiving this evening.' She gathered up an armful of bouquets then noticed me at the end of the line. 'Madam says you are to come in.'

To some groans from the gentlemen and a few remarks I didn't much care for, I followed her inside. Eleonore was sideways in an easy chair, legs hooked over the arm, still in her bandit costume though she'd wiped off most of her make-up. A bottle of champagne and two glasses stood on a table beside her. She gestured to them and raised an eyebrow.

'I'm not sure that I care to drink with somebody who stole my horse,' I said.

She smiled and twisted round to fill both glasses to the brim. 'You'd have got her back – eventually.'

'We don't wait.' I was shamelessly sharing the credit that was due to Amos.

'I know that now. You did well, you and your groom.' She raised her champagne glass in salute. 'I've been finding out more about you. If I'd known as much before, I'd have hidden her properly. Failure in reconnaissance.'

'Why did you take her?'

'To open negotiations.'

'You could have done that in any case.'

'Yes, but it's better to start with the other side at a disadvantage. I could see you're attached to that horse.' The way she said it made it clear that she saw attachment to something as a weakness. Then in a different tone she said, 'I'm not surprised. She is a very good horse. You wouldn't consider selling her?'

'No.'

'Nor would I, if I had her. Besides, I couldn't afford her. I'm a pauper, a soldier of a defeated army.' She gestured with her champagne glass around the room, with the maid arranging bouquets in a variety of vases, another half-dozen bottles of champagne on a table, a brocade cloak thrown casually over the back of the chair. Our eyes met, hers catching the smile I couldn't help. 'Oh, for heaven's sake sit down and let's take your accusation aria as sung.'

I sat and drank. 'You took something else of mine. A picture.'

She unhitched her legs from the chair arm, twisted round and sat upright, facing me. 'You said you were looking for that man. Why?'

'And why don't you want me to find him?'

'Why did you have it?'

'Because I'm looking for that man. Do you know where he is?'

She gave me a long look. 'I'll answer your question when you answer mine.'

I took my time, considering how much to tell her. 'A man has been killed. His valet should be told about it.'

She'd been about to take another sip of champagne and froze with the glass halfway to her mouth. Then she caught herself and drank, slowly. 'Who?'

'The man you wanted dead.'

Just one heartbeat of doubt, then she was acting again as if a proscenium arch with looped-back velvet curtains had been lowered into the space between us. She drained her glass, put it down carefully on the table and swung to her feet, turning away from me. One of the bouquets seemed to catch her eye. She walked across the room in her bandit pumps of soft leather, picked up a card from among the flowers, read it and shrugged. Her maid had slipped out while we were talking. She said, still turned away, 'Who do you mean?'

'Are there so many men you want dead? Lesparre.'

Another bouquet, another card. 'When?'

'The same night somebody tried to set fire to Gore House. The same night the police arrived. I think you know more about that than you admitted. Were you at Gore House that night as well?'

She turned round, with an odd, strained look on her face. Surely not guilt – she'd be too clever to let that show. 'No, but I should have been.' She sprawled back across the armchair, facing me, with her knees crooked over the arm and poured herself more champagne. 'The valet's a better man than the master.'

'Meaning he's not a traitor? So did he hang Lesparre?'

'Hanged, was he? Where?'

'From the loft where he was hiding. You really didn't know that?'

'Not until you told me.'

'And yet you bothered to steal the picture. I'd like it back, please.'

'I haven't got it. I must have dropped it as I was riding away.' She was lying, but no matter, I could always get D'Orsay to draw me another one. 'So you thought Bruno killed Lesparre?' She sounded no more than politely curious.

'He knew his way round Gore House. He knew about the hiding place in the loft.'

Her face went totally serious. She put her hand inside the frills of her shirt and brought out what looked like a battered silver ring on a chain round her neck. 'You see this? It was given to my father by the emperor himself, from the emperor's own finger, for saving his life at the battle of Austerlitz. If I swear on it falsely, may I be forever defeated in this world and damned in the next. I swear that the valet did not kill Lesparre.' She tucked the ring away.

'You're sure of that, but you say you don't even know where he is. Have you spoken to him in the past week?'

'No. I don't know where he is. I'm trying to find him.'

'So we're both of us looking for him. Maybe we should join forces.'

'So that you can accuse him of murder and hand him over to the police?'

188

'I don't think I'd do that.' I was surprised to hear myself saying it. In the first shock of Lesparre's death I'd wanted justice on the man who'd killed him, but justice and trust in the police weren't so simple any more. 'I want to know and to help my friends.'

'Should I trust you?' She asked it in a considering way, as if she really wanted my opinion.

'About as much as I trust you,' I said.

Her laugh, clear as a carillon, made petals tumble from bouquets. 'You know, I like you. No trust, then, but a temporary alliance. Let's drink to it.' She refilled our glasses. We drank. 'So have you discovered anything?'

Typical of her to make me go first but I could see nothing to be lost by it. 'He has Italian friends, hasn't he? I think he's had some connection with the Italian mutual aid office near Hatton Garden. But if they know where he is, they're not saying.'

She was unimpressed. 'They wouldn't.'

'Somebody's been spying on the place.'

She laughed. 'Of course they have. Your London has as many spies as it has rats: the Czar's Russians, Louis Philippe's French, Metternich's Austrians, most of the Italian states' and probably the Vatican's as well, plus your own police spies. It would be a positive insult not to be spied on by two or three of them at least. I'm sure they're watching Mazzini and his people.'

'You obviously know a lot about it.'

'It was my main duty for the prince. The entire collection of them were interested in what he was going to do next, so I kept an eye on them for him. Singers travel everywhere and know

189

everybody. How did you know about the Italian place?'

'I think a friend of mine may be connected with it in some way.' Her eyebrows went up. Probably her quick ears had caught something in the way I'd said *friend*. 'There's one man in particular taking an interest in the place. He's either a police officer in plain clothes or connected with the government in some way. He's keeping watch on foreign exiles in London, almost obsessed by them. Could you see if any of your connections know anything about him?' I described Slater as best I could and gave her his name. 'But I don't even know if it's his real name.'

'Slater.' She thought about it, then was suddenly on her feet, shoulders hunched, head forward. 'Very long fingers, hair like pondweed. Walks bent forward a little, small cold eyes.'

'Yes. You've met him?'

Instead of answering immediately she got up, opened the door and called, 'Emilia.' Her maid appeared. 'Last week's cards, where are they?' The maid produced a silver bowl from a cupboard and Eleonore came back to her chair and started rummaging through it, setting cards flying, some of them landing on the floor in front of me. They were the gentlemen's cards that would have accompanied the hopeful bouquets. One of them even had a gold cravat pin piercing it. She found the one she was looking for and held it out to me, just the name printed in embossed copper-plate, *S. Slater*, and two lines underneath it in tiny handwriting: *I should be obliged if you could find a minute or two to speak to me about this account.* 'It came last week. The bouquet was white roses, very commonplace except for one thing – it had a bill addressed to Prince Louis tucked inside it.'

'A bill for what?'

'The steamer. The one we took to Boulogne. As far as I know, it's still in the harbour there under guard. Five thousand pounds, quite a ridiculous sum in any case, but of course he knew it would never be paid.'

'Did you see him?'

'Of course. He claimed to be a representative of the shipping line that owned the steamer. He had their notepaper and quite a lot of the details, but they'd be easy enough to get. His manners were polite enough on the surface but there was a feeling of threat about him – as if he wanted me to know he was more than he was pretending to be.'

'I know what you mean, yes.'

'He said he was approaching me because I was the only well-known associate of the prince still in London. He said *associate* in a way that implied quite a lot of things, but I didn't give him the satisfaction of being offended. I laughed and said he should apply to the French government to get the steamer back.'

'Was that the end of it?'

'Not quite. He asked me if there were any other of the prince's friends in London, still pretending it was all about the wretched steamer. He mentioned a few by name, including Lesparre. Naturally, I told him nothing.'

'And you've seen no more of him?'

'No. Have you?'

'No, but one of my assistants was following him and was attacked and injured quite seriously, near the Italian office. I think the man Slater had something to do with it.'

She nodded, as if that were only to be expected. I asked her how I'd get messages to her if I found out anything. Not at Covent Garden, she said, because there were only two more performances of the opera.

'Carlton Gardens?' She wouldn't admit to living at the prince's house but agreed that messages might be left with the head groom there. As we parted, I said I assumed Madam Gordon was a stage name.

'My married name,' she said. 'My husband was an English army officer, but he died.' She didn't sound as if she greatly regretted it. Her maid showed me out, through a foyer now empty of anyone but men sweeping the floor, their shadows wavering in the light from the few candles still burning in the great chandeliers. It was past midnight by the time I got back to Abel Yard but Tabby was waiting. She pounced as soon as I was out of the cab.

'Where've you been? Plush has sent to say he wants us.'

'Where?'

'Near the foreign place where it happened. Come on.'

'In these shoes?' Opera-going blue satin, with little heels. Tabby let out a piercing urchin's whistle and the cab that had been driving away stopped so suddenly that the horse came back on its haunches.

'You got money?' I nodded and we rattled away eastwards, not very fast because the horse was tired. So was I, but with Tabby in hunting mode there was no help for it.

FOURTEEN

It was hard to hear what Tabby was telling me above the noise of the cab, even when we'd turned out of the cobbled mews.

'Somebody's got Slater.'

'Got? Killed?'

'Not from what Plush said. Not then anyhow.' It was hard to make sense of it because I was hearing it at third hand. Plush had sent a message, verbally of course since none of the three could write, by means of some urchin from a Hatton Garden gang. It had been deliberately obscure in the first place because Plush wouldn't want another gang to know his business but Tabby thought she understood it. 'Our man had been taken off by some other men to the place near where it happened. Plush was waiting outside and I was to come.'

'What did he mean *taken off*?'

'Didn't go of his own accord, Plush means.'

I wished there had been time to send for Amos. 'When did the message get here?'

'Not long. Sometime after eleven.'

'What does Plush expect us to do? Rescue Slater?'

'I don't know what he expects. Won't this cab go no faster? I don't like thinking of Plush there on his own after what happened to Cobblers.'

She was on the edge of her seat the whole

journey – not, I guessed, from any anxiety for Slater. If she and Plush had any thoughts on that subject it would be regret that somebody else had forestalled their revenge. We paid off the cab at the corner of Hatton Garden and Cross Street and walked. There weren't many people about and very little lighting apart from candles through thinly curtained windows, so we didn't attract attention. One lad came out of a doorway and grabbed at my cloak – I don't know if he was begging or trying to steal it – but a quick chop from Tabby sent him flying. A few lamps were still burning in the church but the doors were closed. We stopped at the steps outside it and Tabby gave a quieter version of her whistle. Plush appeared from an alley two doors up, near the Italian office. It was a relief at least to see him undamaged. Tabby asked me to wait and went to talk to him on her own, then beckoned me over.

'He's in there.' She nodded towards the office. It was in darkness with no sound coming from inside. 'Two men took him in. Plush reckons they might have had guns or knives and that there was somebody in there waiting. He says there was a bit of fighting by the sound of it but it was three against one at least so he couldn't have done much. Then the two that had brought him came out with another man, not long ago, and went off up the street. Plush didn't follow them because I thought I'd better watch in case anything else happened in there, but it hasn't.' It was typical of Plush to let her do the talking for him.

* * *

We all three of us looked at the dark window, plastered with its innocent announcements of concerts and classes. Not a sound or a glimmer from inside. From further off, in one of the lodging houses, somebody was playing a mournful-sounding song on a concertina, then somebody else shouted and it stopped.

'There's probably a door round the back,' Tabby said. 'I'll go and have a look.'

'All right, but don't go in. Come back.'

While she was gone I tried to get more out of Plush. 'You were still following him, then. Where did you see him with the two men?'

'Near where he lives.'

'And he went with them without a struggle?'

'If they had knives he wouldn't have had much choice.'

'But you heard some fighting from inside?'

A nod. I supposed that Slater would be desperate by then, fighting for his life, probably. He must have made many enemies on his investigations and sooner or later some would strike back. But why did it have to be here of all places?

Tabby was back within a couple of minutes. 'No door, just another house.'

Still no sound from inside the building. The question was, had there been only one man waiting inside? If so, then the only person left there was Slater, injured or dead. I wondered whether to send Tabby or Plush for a policeman, but with their nervousness of blue coats it would be like sending two mice to fetch a cat. In any case, there would be too much explaining to do. Those were the excuses I made to myself but

196

there was another reason: this place and Slater himself were connected with Robert in some way. Until I knew why and how, I couldn't risk bringing in the police. I told them to wait and went to the door. It began to open as soon as I turned the handle. I went in with Tabby and Plush on my heels.

Nothing but darkness deeper than the street outside, a disorderly darkness full of meaningless shapes. I tripped on something and almost fell until a solid object jabbed into my stomach, pushing me upright. Things cracked and tinkled underfoot. I think Plush must have fallen completely because he was swearing from floor level behind me and Tabby was telling him to be quiet, a waste of breath in view of the noise we were making. Surely anybody alive and conscious in the place would be shouting out to ask what was happening. More stumbling and heavy breathing came from behind me, presumably Plush getting to his feet. Smells were eddying round in the dark – piss, whale oil from a lamp, the iron tang of blood. Something came over the side of my shoe and slimed against my instep. The three of us stood where we were, listening. Nothing.

'Anybody got a light?' Tabby said. I felt like asking her if she thought I took my burglar's lantern every time I went out for the evening. I wished I had it. A scraping sound came out of the darkness, then the spark of a flint lighter that seemed as bright as a bonfire by contrast. A small flame spread a widening circle of light round it, showing first a stub of candle, then Plush's hand still shaking from his fall, then the rest of the room, very dim at first then shapes rising like wreckage on a beach when the tide goes out. Wreckage was what it was – the big table where I'd seen the girl doing her grammar exercises tipped over on its side with its legs sticking out, chairs thrown over, a book case pulled away from the wall, scattering papers over whatever it was sliming the floor. The light spread. Tabby had spotted another candle in a tin holder attached to the wall and used Plush's stub to light it. The mess on the floor was blood and the vomit I'd stepped in, along with the shattered glass of a lamp.

'He made a fight of it,' Tabby said, half admiring.

'But where is he?' I said. Certainly nowhere in the room. I took the candle stub off Tabby and went through the curtained opening to what I'd guessed was a storeroom. No more than a cubicle with more books piled on a small table, a spirit lamp and a jug half full of cold coffee. There was no other door out of it and no further signs of struggle. The place was only a thin segment, probably backing on to another house, with the door we'd come in by the only way into the street. I went back to the other room, shaking my head to let them know I'd found nothing. They were looking up at the flight of wooden stairs in the corner of the room. Tabby started up it before I could stop her and I followed with the candle stub, now hot in my hand and splashing wax on to my good dress. The steps ended in a broad platform that had been used as a sleeping place, with a thin pallet on bare boards, a bolster and a tumbled heap of blankets, no other furniture and not even a door to close it off from the room below. It looked like a refuge in an emergency and I noticed a smear of blood and sick on the corner of one of the blankets as if somebody had trodden there, more fresh blood on the bolster. Tabby and I moved the blankets to make sure, but nothing and nobody underneath. Plush was at the bottom of the stairs.

'So what have they done with him?'

Above us was a rough trapdoor, secured only with a piece of metal that rotated on a screw to fit into a notch in the wooden surround.

'He's up there then,' Tabby said. Her voice sounded unsteady for once and Plush must have picked up her nervousness because he pushed past us, put a rough hand on my shoulder and jumped up to reach the catch. My yell of 'No' shook the flimsy walls and sounded loud enough to wake the street but Tabby moved faster than I did, pushing Plush aside as he jumped so that he lost balance, clutched at me, and we both fell back down the stairs together. He swore at Tabby as we landed.

'What did you want to do that for?'

'Like the other one,' I said. Most of the breath was out of me, my voice hardly working, but Tabby had understood.

The silence that followed the noise we made was broken by a sound so low and deep it was more of a vibration felt through the skin, a groan that might have come from an old tree creaking

199

in a gale, but muffled as if on the far side of the forest.

'He's up there, and he's still alive,' Tabby said.

'Yes, if we open that hatch we hang him.' I'd got back on my feet by then. Landing on top of Plush had broken my fall but winded him, so he was still trying to straighten up, wheezing.

'So he's trussed up there, standing on the hatch, just like the other one,' Tabby said. I thanked the gods for her quickness of mind. Unlike me, she hadn't stood under that other trapdoor and seen a body come hurtling down but her mind must have been dwelling on the account I'd given her. Ironic that she should have saved Slater's life, for the moment at least. 'So what do we do now?'

I went up and stood beside her, positioning myself as closely under the hatch as I could. 'Mr Slater, can you move at all? Can you move sideways off the hatch?' No answer, not even a groan. I sent Tabby downstairs for the other candle, but all that did was throw a better light on the impossibility of the position. He was there, certainly injured, possibly dying, and the only way we could get to him was by killing him.

'Through the roof,' Tabby said at last. There was some sense in it. A building like this would have no more than a covering of slates on a probably flimsy roof. By daylight and with ladders, or from the top windows of neighbouring houses, men could remove enough slates to get into the loft, but it would be a risky business. On our own and in darkness, we were helpless. Tabby threw herself down on the blankets. I thought she was simply resting after the shock, but her eyes were fixed on the ceiling of whitewashed boards, slanting up from the outer edge of the room, then flattening as it came to the trapdoor. 'Or the ceiling. Doesn't look that strong.'

The flimsiness made it too risky. If we broke through too close to the trapdoor it might collapse and we risked hanging him anyway. 'We'll have to go for help,' I said. I was on the point of telling them to wait in the room downstairs and keep the door bolted while I went to find a policeman when a knock on the door to the street froze all of us. Quite a soft knock, but confident and repeated.

'Who's there?' Plush wheezed, picking up a broken table leg for a weapon. Another knock.

'You two wait up on the landing,' I said. 'I'll see who it is.' I hoped against hope that it would be an unusually conscientious policeman on the beat, noting something wrong in the building. I left the candle with them and went carefully down the stairs, knowing the person outside would see me through the gaps in the advertisements in the window. I could just make out his shape, well enough to see that it wasn't topped by a policeman's uniform tall hat. No matter. Whoever it was, it changed the situation. If it were some innocent neighbour, he could be sent for help. If not, the three of us would simply have to make enough noise to rouse the street. I picked my way through the debris in the office, went to the door and drew back the bolt. My eyes were accustomed to the darkness inside, so I recognized him a heartbeat before he recognized me.

'Sergeant Bevan.'

A gasp he'd probably have suppressed if he could, then: 'Miss Lane, I suppose I should have guessed.' But his attempt to sound world-weary wasn't successful. The man was keyed up, expecting trouble.

'I suppose you're looking for Slater,' I said, letting him in. 'He's upstairs in the attic, standing on a trapdoor like the one at Gore House.'

He was carrying a dark lantern. When he slid the shutter round the wash of yellow light revealed the wreckage of the room and threw jagged shadows on the walls.

'What happened?' He said it evenly, as if asking a fellow officer for a report. I tried to reply in kind.

'He was brought here by two men, against his will. There was another man waiting inside. They've gone, some time ago.' The light from his lamp picked up the stairs, then the two figures standing at the top of them, glaring down at him. He was in plain clothes, but the smell of police was rank as a badger in their nostrils.

'Hello Tabby,' he said as he went up the stairs. She didn't answer and Plush turned his face away. Sergeant Bevan squeezed past him and stood directly under the hatch, as I had.

'Mr Slater?' Again, that tree-like groan, even fainter. Bevan frowned and glanced round him, taking in rapidly the problem we were facing. 'Will you be all right here? I'm going for help. Don't touch the trapdoor.' When he'd gone the three of us moved down to the ground floor.

'Does he think we done it?' Plush said.

'Goodness knows what he thinks.' I knew

there'd be a lot of questions to answer, but that would come later. From a distance, I heard the clack-clack of a police rattle sounding like a rocketing pheasant, some constable calling for reinforcements. Not long afterwards Bevan came back with a police constable in uniform and my two companions melted away like snow in the sun.

By now, all the activity was waking up the street. Windows were brightening into squares of candle-light and lamplight, sashes creaking up and people looking out, a few men on the street asking each other, in a variety of languages, where the fire was. Anybody not awake by then would have been roused a few minutes later when the constable started hammering with his night stick on the door of the house next door. The man who opened it looked scared and was shouldered aside as the constable rushed inside.

'Miss Lane!' A shout from Constable Bevan on the landing. I went up the stairs. He was standing under the hatch and gave me an order as if I were part of his team. 'I want you to stand here and keep talking. I don't think he's conscious, but in case. Keep telling him we're coming to save him and above all not to move. And not to worry about the noise from next door.'

'Noise?'

'We're going to break through from next door. I'll leave the door to the street open. If anything happens in here, shout as loudly as you can.'

By now, the noise from next door, with people protesting and a woman screaming, was so loud that I doubted if anything would be heard over it. Still, I obeyed instructions, saying soothing things up to the loft hatch and getting no reply. It struck me as another irony that for days I'd wished for a chance to talk to Mr Slater and now I had it and it was useless. By going down a couple of steps I could watch what was happening in the street, lit by a few hand lamps. By now, every constable on night duty in the Holborn area must have arrived, some of them keeping back the crowd that was gathering. A builders' cart with two men pulling it came dashing down the street, making people jump aside and yell out warnings. It stopped outside the open door of the neighbouring house and crow bars and heavy hammers clanged on to the pavement. Soon, a regular thudding came from next door, making the whole house vibrate. 'Don't worry, they're just making a gap,' I said. 'They won't be long.' It felt strange, this one-sided conversation with a man who might be dead by now of shock or suffocation. I wished they'd hurry, for my sake more than his. The thudding was nearer now, with a different rhythm of smaller concussions, probably bricks falling from the partition between the two attics, most likely a single thickness of bricks since these houses had not looked solidly built. Then a voice, seeming very close.

'Through, sir.'

Then Sergeant Bevan's voice, answering. I couldn't make out the words but it was probably an order to let him go first because when I heard the voice again, it was just above my head. 'It's all right, sir. I've cut the rope. We've got you.'

Then, more loudly, 'Tell them to bring the stretcher up.'

Boots thumped and shuffled on the hatch above my head, presumably men loading Slater on to a stretcher, whether alive or dead I didn't know. They'd obviously decided to take him out through the house next door so I heard nothing after that until the crowd was shoved aside to let an ambulance cart draw up outside. As the stretcher was carried out to it I could see nothing but a dark blanket and a white face above it. So not dead, not yet at any rate. When Sergeant Bevan came into the office I'd found a chair that wasn't broken and was sitting much where the dark-haired beauty had been.

'Thank you, Miss Lane. I'm sorry to have to leave you.'

'Will he live?'

'I hope so. He's profoundly unconscious. Of course, the sheer strain of waiting and wondering when the trap would open would do that to a man.'

'Yes, I've been thinking about that,' I said.

'Gore House?'

'It's no use pretending the two aren't connected.'

'I wasn't going to.' He sighed. It was still noisy in the street, the builders clanging tools back into their cart, the owner of the house next door wanting to know who was going to pay for the damage, but here in the wrecked office Sergeant Bevan and I were in our own world, as if in a cave by a stormy beach. On another case, we'd trusted each other – up to a point. I sensed that he was trying to get back to that.

'The question is was it revenge or repetition?'
I said.

'Explain.'

'If Slater were responsible for hanging the man at Gore House, then it might be revenge.'

'Or if somebody thought he was responsible, even if he wasn't.'

'True.'

'And if repetition?'

'Then whoever killed the man at Gore House has gone to a lot of trouble to try to kill Slater in the same way.'

'Yes,' he said, 'a lot of trouble.'

'And why here? Slater was keeping watch on this place, as I'm sure you know. What's his interest?' And, unspoken in my mind, *What's Robert's interest?* I hoped Sergeant Bevan didn't guess that. He knew about Robert and me from the earlier case.

He didn't answer for some time, then said, 'You know about the *Carbonari*?'

'Of course, the society fighting for a united Italy.'

'A secret society.'

'Given what's happening in most parts of Italy, they've no choice but to be secret.'

'Not just in Italy, but in London too. Probably run from London. You've met the leader, Mazzini.'

'I think I might have. I've read his articles, of course. He writes well.'

'Yes, you met him here in this room, two days ago.'

'How do you know that?' He didn't answer. 'Slater,' I said. 'Slater has been watching me.'

'Not you, specifically. This place.'

'Not just this place, dozens of places. The man goes all over London, every night.'

'I might ask you how you know that,' Bevan said. 'You've obviously been having him watched. Why?'

'It was you who brought him to me. He practically threatened me in my own house. Did you expect me to let it go?'

'I warned him it wasn't a good idea.'

'But he overruled you. So what is this man? A superior officer?'

'No.'

'Any sort of policeman?'

'Not exactly.'

'Surely you either are or you aren't?'

Things were beginning to go quieter outside, people going back to their beds although in an hour or two they'd be up again to start the day. It was that peculiar time in the early hours that doesn't belong either with the day that's ended or the one that hasn't begun. Perhaps it was that feeling of being out of time that made him honest.

'The police force is changing. We live in a world that's more complicated than pickpockets and fights in public houses. A man can be starting a revolution in France on Monday morning and snug here in London by Wednesday night. Or vice versa, of course. People in government are well aware of that.'

'So Slater is working for the government? Lord Palmerston?'

'I don't know that myself. I was simply given

207

orders by my chief constable to work under Slater's instructions and report to him on matters concerned with foreign nationals involved in politics. I'm still a police officer, but detached from normal duties.'

'Quite a long way detached. Has it occurred to you that Slater is obsessed?'

Another silence, then: 'I think it's fair to say that he is entirely devoted to his work.'

'And what work, exactly? Is he simply keeping a watch on these political foreigners or setting himself up as judge and jury?'

That stung him. 'I can assure you, my instructions are to keep within the law.'

'What about him? Can you be sure he keeps within the law? There was that business of the adjourned inquest for a start.'

He turned away, looking out at the dark street. 'There was genuine doubt about the identification.'

So I couldn't trust him in spite of his apparent openness. 'Slater was keeping a watch on this place and Mazzini. He was also going to considerable trouble to keep a watch on Gore House and Prince Louis's circle. Is there a connection?'

'In politics, there are always connections.'

'Is that you or Slater speaking?'

He turned back towards me, annoyed. 'I do have a mind of my own. I don't suppose you're naïve enough to believe that revolutionaries in exile are always right and governments always wrong.'

'No, and I'm not naïve enough to believe that

governments are always right either. And you were worried about what Slater was doing.' He didn't try to deny it. 'So what happens now?' I said.

'That depends on whether Slater recovers and what he can tell us. We'll have men here in the morning to talk to Mr Mazzini and his friends.'

Inevitable, but it worried me, so I went on the attack. 'Did you have an arrangement to meet Slater here this evening? Is that how you came to be here?'

'No. He failed to keep an appointment with me, not very far from here, so I decided to check places that I knew were of interest to him. This one first, fortunately.'

There were more questions to be asked, but I was suddenly hit with a tiredness that felt like a heavy blanket coming down over my head. 'I'm going home. Will you let me know what Mr Slater says, if anything?'

He didn't answer, just went outside, said something to one of the constables and came back. 'I've sent for a cab.'

We waited among the wrecked furniture, looking out at the street where the householder was still complaining to a couple of constables. 'A hard night for your men,' I said.

'They won't mind. Beat duty gets so monotonous, it's a relief when something happens.' He said it with a touch of nostalgia.

'But you sometimes wish you were back on the beat,' I said. He didn't deny it. Soon afterwards the cab came.

FIFTEEN

When I got down from the cab outside the yard
gates it was still dark but one of Tabby's gang
was awake, leaning against a wall. I asked him
if she and Plush were back.

'Long time ago.'

I gave him a shilling and asked him to go
across the park as soon as it got light and tell
Mr Legge at the livery stables that I shouldn't
be riding this morning but would see him on
Monday. I went upstairs, intending to collapse
on my bed, but remembered just in time that
Cobblers was in it so made for my study and
slept dreamlessly on the day bed until long after
Mrs Martley was up and about. I went down for
a jug of warm water and used the washstand in
her bedroom to get as clean as I could from the
night before, promising myself a bath by the fire
later. My best evening shoes and good silk
stocking were fit only for the rubbish heap and
our laundress would probably charge extra for
the petticoat. I drank coffee and ate bread and
butter at the parlour table, answered absent-
mindedly to Mrs Martley's chatter and thought
about the question I'd put last night to Sergeant
Bevan: repetition or revenge? If he knew the
answer – which I doubted – he hadn't told me.
If repetition, somebody unknown but connected
with Gore House had hanged Lesparre and tried

again with Slater. The elaboration suggested the murderer was trying to make a point beyond the killing itself, sending a message. Lesparre was a spy and Eleonore, alias Madam Gordon, was spying on the spy. Slater was spying on all of them and probably me as well, but seemed most interested in Mazzini's Italians, who in some way included Robert. On last night's evidence, somebody beside myself had been spying on Slater. If the attempt on his life had been repetition, then Slater had probably been close enough to finding Lesparre's killer to be a threat to him. Or her, come to that. I thought of what Prince Louis's groom had said to Amos: *With that one you never knew what she'd do.* The method of it would probably have appealed to her sense of drama and although the attack must have happened while she was at Covent Garden, either onstage or talking to me in her dressing room, there were probably plenty of exiled Napoleonic fanatics she could call on.

I poured another cup of coffee and tried it the other way – revenge. Slater himself had killed Lesparre. Shocking but possible. The man was devoted to his work to the point of being fanatical. Lesparre had been carrying papers that might be a threat to people high in the British government. Slater had strong links with the police and probably other resources he could call on. Somebody at a high level had stopped the inquest in its tracks. So assume that Slater had arranged for Lesparre to be hanged. Lesparre's friends and associates knew that and wanted him to pay for it in precisely the same way. But what friends and associates? If you believed the story he'd told D'Orsay, he had none in London, apart from the faithful valet, Bruno. Bruno knew the Italian office well enough to use it as his address. If he wanted to avenge his master he had the premises to hand and probably help from political exiles with no reason to like government spies. The *Carbonari* were every bit as zealous as the Napoleonic crowd and more or less on the same side. The late emperor had supported the cause of Italian unity and his nephew did too. Mazzini's supporters would probably have known that Slater was spying on them and might have been all too ready to help Bruno get rid of him in a way dramatic enough to be a warning to other spies. (Would the high-minded Mazzini have been involved himself? Probably not. Political leaders are good at not seeing things when necessary.) But did Bruno even know that Lesparre was dead and how he died? The other problem was that Eleonore had strongly implied that the valet was not a traitor like his master, which might explain the separation between the two of them after the first few days at Gore House. In that case, why should he go to the trouble to avenge him? The problem was that everything said by Eleonore Gordon had a *perhaps* attached to it.

Nothing happened on Sunday except Cobblers was allowed to get out of bed and walk round his room and started talking about going back home, by which he meant his heap of straw in the mews. Surprisingly Mrs Martley was the one who opposed this plan. She was proud of her successful nursing, his comparative cleanliness and healthy appetite. Two bowls of her stew and a large slice of apple pie convinced him to stay in possession of my bedroom for another day at least. Tabby and Plush didn't appear and I decided not to inquire, hoping that the near-hanging of Slater might satisfy their need for revenge. I rode out as usual with Amos on Monday morning and reported the latest events to him. His reaction was predictable.

'You should have sent for me.'

'Believe me, I wish you'd been with us, but there simply wasn't time.'

Back at Abel Yard a message arrived for me about midday, brought by a liveried messenger from a club in St James that I knew D'Orsay frequented. Since the club was only a few minutes' walk away he might have delivered it himself except I couldn't imagine D'Orsay in Abel Yard.

Dear Miss Lane,
I had occasion to visit my shoemaker this morning, who told me something which may be of interest to you. On Friday a man arrived at his premises with a pair of shoes with split seams and what purported to be a message from me asking that he should re-stitch them and make a similar pair two sizes larger and charge them to my account. He immediately

213

recognized the shoes as mine. The man fits the description of the valet. Since the shoes were required urgently he immediately set to work on the repair but was puzzled and mentioned it to me when I visited him this morning. The man was naturally concerned that some accident or illness might have increased the size of my feet. I was happily able to disabuse him of this idea. (I imagined him writing with a shudder of horror at the spectre of gout or bunions. D'Orsay's small shapely feet were part of his legend of Apollonian perfection.) *I thought I should let you know this as soon as possible. I hope the information may be of use. Please let me know if I can assist in any other way.*

I'd kept the messenger waiting in the yard so sent off an immediate reply: *When are the shoes to be collected and where? Has your shoemaker an address for the valet?* D'Orsay's response came back within the hour: *This Wednesday afternoon, no particular time stated. Burlington Arcade, third left from Piccadilly. No address given or asked for as the shoemaker assumed it was mine. Should he finish repairing the shoes?* I replied that he could do what he liked about the shoes but should tell the shoemaker to keep the valet waiting in his workshop as long as possible and not talk about it to anyone else.

I walked directly across the park to the stables and found Amos in the tack room preparing a poultice to draw out pus from a hoof. He had a saucepan simmering on a spirit stove and smells of warm linseed and bran filled the air. He listened, stirring all the time, then gave his verdict.

'That's not a ferret. It's a weasel.'

'Just what I thought. It's too neat, isn't it? On Wednesday I ask D'Orsay for a way to track the valet, and he tells me about the shoes. Two days later, the man arrives at the shoemaker's with them.'

'So who's D'Orsay been talking to?'

'He'd tell Lady Blessington, of course. I think he'd have the sense not to tell anybody else, except perhaps Disraeli then . . .' I let the thought trail away. Disraeli was capable of keeping secrets as tight to his chest as winning cards or flinging them around like birdseed, according to whatever his current schemes were.

'So the world and his wife, then. Only some-body had to have the shoes. I suppose they were the same ones the valet took.'

'No doubt of it. A shoemaker would recognize shoes the way you recognize horses. Besides, the man fitted the description of the valet.'

'That's it then, he's trying to turn our ferret back on us and flush us out. The question is, why?'

'Perhaps he wants to talk to us. If he's found out somehow his employer is dead, he might want to know more.'

'Complicated way of trying to talk to somebody.'

'So what, then?'

'What does a farmer do to a rabbit when he's got it ferreted out?' With the side of his free hand, he made a chopping motion.

'You think so? Why?'

'Because he thinks you're getting too close to him.'

'That's assuming the valet killed Lesparre.'

'He's the one my money's been on from the start.'

I didn't argue, but the picture of Eleonore and the emperor's ring came back into my mind. I'd hesitate to believe anything from her, but it must have made an impression. 'Anyway, I'll need to be there. You can be waiting somewhere near, if you like.'

Amos tapped the spoon against the saucepan. 'I don't like. You stay away from this. I'll wait and keep an eye on the shoemaker, pick up the valet and take him somewhere we can ask him questions.'

'No. In Burlington Arcade you'd stand out like an oak tree in a flower border. I can wait there for hours and not be noticed.'

The stubborn look that could have been carved on stone with a chisel came over his face. He dipped a little finger into the mix to test the heat of it, turned off the stove and walked out of the tack room with the saucepan and a handful of cotton strips. Uninvited, I followed him across the yard to a loose box where a groom was waiting, holding a dark bay seventeen-hand hunter type by the head collar rope. It was always good to see Amos at work, even when he was annoyed with me. The chisel-carved look left his face as soon as he came near the big horse and the soothing noises he made to it were like doves in a tree. He lifted up a hoof the size of a soup bowl, packed the poultice mixture round the frog and bound it in place with strips of cotton. Then he produced from his pocket a cloth sugar bag and tied it over the whole foot. The horse put it gingerly to the ground and a surprised look came into its eyes, as if wondering where the pain had gone. When Amos signed to the groom to undo the head collar rope, it limped over to the hay rack and started munching.

'He'll do,' Amos said. Back in the tack room, his bad temper had gone as if the poultice had drawn that out too and we started planning. If we accepted the idea that the shoe business was a trap, the question was how to turn it to our advantage. Some time on Wednesday afternoon the valet would come to the shoemaker's, knowing I'd be watching. I'd have to let him see me otherwise he wouldn't bother making the attempt. We should assume that he'd have friends on the watch too. (Possibly friends from the Italian office. Don't think about that.) Amos insisted he wouldn't let me out of his sight and he'd find a way of being in Burlington Arcade inconspicuously, though how he'd manage that without losing a foot in height and another in shoulder width I didn't know. At least two of Tabby's gang would be on the watch at both ends of the arcade.

'If they'll do it,' I said. 'They've had some bad shocks with this business.'

'If Tabby thinks you're in danger she'll make

217

sure they do it. And I'll bring a couple of my lads along as well.'

Back home, I started tidying my office, found Lady Blessington's bracelet and pendant on the table and remembered I should have returned them days ago. I walked along the Serpentine in a fine autumn afternoon and arrived at Gore House in the unsocial period between the end of tea and dinner. I found Lady Blessington alone in a sea of papers at her library table, the giant poodle stretched out at her slippered feet. She was as courteous as ever, but I sensed some reservation. Possibly it was no more than irritation at being interrupted while chasing yet another deadline. In any case, I had my reservations with the occupants of Gore House now, not knowing how much to tell them or even how much they were telling each other. On the walk over I'd decided not to mention D'Orsay and the shoes, but Slater was another matter. I said there had been a development in the case: a man had almost died – might still die – in exactly the same way as Lesparre.

'He was a man named Slater, a government spy keeping watch on foreigners.' I described him as well as I could. 'Have you met or seen anybody like that?'

She shook her head. 'He hardly seems the sort of person we'd meet, does he?'

I produced the lapis lazuli pendant and garnet bracelet from my pocket and put them on the table in front of her. She almost jumped out of her seat.

'Where did you get those?'

'From the person who stole them, Eleonore Gordon. I should have brought them back days ago, but with so much happening it slipped my mind.'

She stared. 'Madam Gordon? But we know her. She sang at one of my receptions. She's very close to poor Prince Louis. Why should she go around stealing jewels?'

'Because she wanted an excuse to get back into the house and look for Lesparre. She's been in here at least twice in disguise. The plan was to put Lesparre on trial for betraying the prince and kill him.'

As I told her the story her head sank into her hands and the poodle came and sat with its muzzle in her lap, looking up at her with its amber eyes as if sympathizing with her confusion.

'So did she kill him?' she asked through her fingers.

'I'm honestly not sure. I think she might be capable of it.'

'She scares me a little. I think she even scares the prince.'

There weren't many people who scared Lady Blessington. I left knowing that I'd brought her no comfort and by no means sure that she'd deserved it.

On Wednesday morning Amos and I rode together as usual and settled the details for the afternoon, though he still wouldn't tell me how he'd manage to keep me in sight and not be noticed. 'I'll be there when I'm wanted, don't you worry.'

I wasn't worried, I said. Not about that at any rate. It struck me that I was already breaking my temporary alliance with Eleonore Gordon by not telling her about the developments in the search for the valet, but that didn't worry me either. I was sure she'd do the same for me.

SIXTEEN

If you need to trap a person, Burlington Arcade is about the best place that can be devised: an avenue of luxurious shops – milliners, glovers, jewellers, hatters, watchmakers, lacemakers – running from Piccadilly to Burlington Gardens. The people who work there may know back entrances and side doors, but as far as the public is concerned the shops on either side run as continuously as a glass tube. Once a person is inside, he has to come out either by the north or south entrance. It's always well populated by strollers and patrolled by top-hatted beadles so that a cry of *Stop that man*, uttered in a suitably commanding voice, would have half a dozen people on his back in seconds. The problem was we might be the ones in the trap. It was the only reason I could imagine for Bruno to dangle such a convenient piece of bait in front of us. He surely wouldn't have gone to that trouble simply for the pleasure of having us waste our time. In spite of all the work I'd put in to convince Amos that I wouldn't be in danger, my heart was beating faster than I liked as we took up our positions at a quarter to midday. According to the plan Amos and I had worked out, Tabby and Plush were stationed close to the north entrance in Burlington Gardens looking like ordinary street urchins lurking to run errands for pennies. Close to them,

221

ready to move on Tabby's say so, would be one of Amos's grooms from the stables, a man nearly as large and muscular as Amos himself. *He'll do what's wanted and not make a cackle about it*, Amos had said. Another of his friends would be waiting at the south entrance, on to Piccadilly. Since the shoemaker's shop was close to that end, the chances were that the valet would arrive that way – if he showed himself at all. Assuming that he was waiting for us to walk into his trap, that end would be where he'd expect to find us. If he needed a quick getaway, his best chance would be to mingle with the crowds in Piccadilly. Another problem was that we didn't know whether Bruno would be acting on his own or with accomplices. My post was outside the window of the milliner's shop opposite the shoemaker's. The milliner's black velvet backing for her creations made it a good mirror of the premises on the other side. I'd have to rely on my memory of Bruno in the sketch but I expected no difficulties. Shoemakers who charged D'Orsay's sort of prices would not get a vulgar rush of customers. If he did go inside, we'd have to hope that the shoemaker followed D'Orsay's instructions to keep him talking. That would give me time to signal to Amos, then walk up the arcade and raise a hand to Tabby, waiting at the other end. As soon as he came out, I'd walk over to talk to him and our forces would close in from both ends. If he broke away from me in either direction, they'd be in his path. Almost foolproof. As Amos and I saw it, the main problem would be to hustle him out without attracting the attention of the police. We wanted him for ourselves.

Twenty minutes or so after I'd taken up my position there was still no sign of Amos. I wasn't worried exactly, but the creeping feeling up and down my spine wouldn't have been there if I knew he was watching my back. I tried to concentrate on the people: the plump lady in a beaver fur cloak too hot for the weather that made her face as red as a baked plum, followed by a small maid loaded with parcels; the thin girl in an old cloth coat looking into a jeweller's window as if feeding on the sight of emeralds and sapphires; the beadle pacing slowly along, eyes turning from side to side. Burlington Arcade is famous for, among other things, its beadles, dignified top-hatted men patrolling to deter pickpockets, beggars or other riff raff. They're usually former soldiers, tall and imposing men. This one, though, was even bigger than the average, getting on for seven foot tall if you included the top hat and so broad in the chest that the brass buttons of his black coat were under strain. The shivery feeling slipped away from my spine like a lizard going under a rock. The beadle came to a stop beside me and raised his hat, like a good employee passing the time of day with a customer.

'No sign of him so far.'

'Amos, how did you manage it?'

'One of my grooms has a brother who works here. He was happy enough to let me join the strength for the afternoon when I passed him ten shillings.'

I made a mental note to refund it from petty cash. 'Is everyone in position?'

'Ready and waiting. Just hope he doesn't keep us hanging about too long.'

He kept us waiting for two hours and fourteen minutes. In that time, I got to know the contents of the milliner's window very well: the plum-coloured bonnet with the pink silk lining and the silver trim (gaudy), the straw with the green velvet ribbons and appliqué leaf shapes (too light for autumn) and the blue silk on cane hoops with a lighter blue net frill to frame the face (useful in my work since I could pull the hoops forward and the frill round my face to hide it, but not so useful that I could justify the probably outrageous price). I knew all this down to the last detail of stitching after the first hour, also the contents of the glove maker's window to the left and, in rather less detail, the gentlemen's shaving accoutrements – cut-throat razors, silver bowls and badger-hair brushes – in the narrow window to the right. There was also a problem that should have occurred to me when making our plans: some of the rooms over the shops are convenient places for gentlemen to meet what a friend of mine calls *les papillons d'après-midi*, the afternoon butterflies. Noticing me lingering and showing an unaccountable interest in male toilet items, a couple of men leapt to the inevitable conclusion and I had to put Arctic ice floes into my voice to convince them of their mistake. To avoid attracting attention, I had to extend my beat and walk up and down the arcade, further than I liked away from the shoemaker's door. The truth is, I'm bad at waiting and that's a weakness in my strange profession, where waiting is sometimes the only thing to be done. Tabby has a kind of genius for it. She can stay unnoticed in the same place for hours and not miss a detail of what's going on, from a hole in a stocking to a pimple on a man's cheek. Amos is good too. He hasn't quite Tabby's skill at observation, but he can slow himself to the rhythm of a patient animal, waiting for the need for action. Sometimes, when I came close to him in his regular pacing up and down, he'd give me a questioning look and I'd shake my head. That was careless of me and I've nobody but myself to blame for what happened, although I don't think it was caused by being too conspicuous in the arcade. It went back further than that. A carriage clock in a window two up from the milliner's was showing sixteen minutes to three when I turned round and saw Bruno no more than fifty yards away from me. As we expected, he'd come in from the Piccadilly end and was almost at the door of the shoemaker's. He was our man, no doubt about it. D'Orsay's sketch had been quite a good likeness – a neat man with dark glossy hair showing under his hat, a pale oval-shaped face with dark eyes and a quick, neat way of moving, the cut on his cheek healing to a slim pink scar. It was easy to imagine him as a valet, deft and unobtrusive. His black cutaway coat and trousers were good quality but a shade too small for him, tight across the chest and an inch above the ankle, probably the gift from D'Orsay's wardrobe. With

225

no more than a passing glance in my direction he opened the door and went inside the shop.

Amos must have recognized him from my description because he was already looking in my direction and nodded when I raised my hand. At the other end of the arcade, Tabby ducked outside as soon as I signalled to alert Plush and Amos's friend waiting in the street. I took up my position at the milliner's window, but this time looking directly at the shoemaker's door. I couldn't see the counter inside the shop from there but hoped the shoemaker was drawing out the business as instructed. Bruno came out more quickly than I'd expected, less than a minute after arriving and no parcel of shoes in his hand. In the one glance I had of his face he looked worried, glancing up and down the arcade, up on the balls of his feet ready to turn either way. Amos was only two or three strides away. I walked towards him, opening my mouth to say we'd like to talk to him. I was planning to say it in English then French but didn't have a chance at either because before he could decide which way to turn, a crack and a shattering of glass, then screams, sounded from the far end of the arcade. The falling glass and the screaming and shouting seemed to go on for some time – longer than the sound that had come just before them: the crack of a pistol shot. Bruno spun away from it, towards our end of the arcade. His hand went to his jacket and came out holding a long-bladed knife. Amos was a step away now, reaching out a hand to grab Bruno's shoulder.

'No.' I heard my own voice screeching and launched myself at Amos. It was like colliding with a hay stack and in normal times my weight wouldn't have moved Amos an inch, but reaching out had put him off balance and he rocked sideways, just enough for Bruno to dart under his arm and out into Piccadilly. I yelled 'Stop him' but it was no use because everybody's attention was on what was happening at the far end of the arcade. Beadles and police were rushing in that direction, top hats flying off and rolling round the feet of alarmed shoppers, a lap dog yapping, people coming out of shops asking each other what was happening. Amos gave me a reproachful glance and ran into Piccadilly after Bruno, colliding with a pair of police constables rushing in. One of them tried to grab Amos by the arm and a fight might have broken out between them if I hadn't got there in time.

'He's nothing to do with it. The shot was up at that end.' I wanted to tell them to follow Bruno instead but other voices were urging them to the far end of the arcade. Besides, Bruno had done nothing wrong as far as the police were concerned.

'What did you want to do that for?' Amos said when they'd hurried away to join the confusion. 'We almost had him.'

'He had a knife. Didn't you see?' I could tell from his expression that he hadn't – Bruno had drawn it so quickly, like a man practised in it.

'I'd have managed.'

'A real knife, not a penknife.' Long and sharp enough to stab Amos to the heart. I wanted to get my hands on Bruno, but not at that cost.

'We'd better go and see what's happening.' I was worried now for Tabby and Plush. Everybody had congregated a few shops down from the Burlington Gardens end. The floor was covered in glass fragments and jagged edges were all that was left of the window of an elegant pastry cook's shop, with more glass twinkling among the pink and green marzipan fancies in the display. Police and beadles were trying to keep back the crowd, who'd progressed from fear to excitement at being witnesses to the most alarming event Burlington Arcade had suffered for a long time. Or rather, near witnesses, people who might have been witnesses if they hadn't been inside shops, or looking the other way or in the wrong place altogether. It was becoming obvious, from the various voices and the already weary look on the faces of the beadles and police, that nobody really knew what had happened. Certainly a shot had been fired and it had gone through the window. A scent of powder still lingered among the sweat, lavender water and sugar smells and a pistol ball had been found embedded in a glazed grape tartlet. The assistants in the pastry cook's thought it had come from the far side of the arcade and one of them had seen a tall man in a cloak and top hat. Somebody else claimed to have seen a second man with a pistol and one school of thought was that two gentlemen had been fighting a duel, though nobody could explain why they'd do it in Burlington Arcade in the middle of the afternoon. There was no sign of Tabby or Plush, not surprising given the presence of the police.

* * *

Amos and I pushed our way through the crowds and out to Burlington Gardens. Both of them were waiting on the far side of the road, along with Amos's friend.

'You didn't get him then?' Tabby said, seeing our faces.

'No. Did you see what happened there?'

'Nah. We were waiting outside, like you told us, for him to come out. We heard the shot and Plush was all for going in and seeing if you'd been hurt, but I said we should do what you told us and you'd be all right with Mr Legge. Which was just as well we didn't because then we wouldn't have seen him coming out.'

'Him?'

'The one that fired the shot, I reckon. I saw him walking in a bit before – tall, in a black cloak and hat. Then there was the shot and straight afterwards he came out again, walking fast but not running, and away up the street.'

'Did he have a pistol?'

'Couldn't see under the cloak, but I reckon he might have, otherwise he'd have got his hand to his hat quicker before it nearly came off, then we wouldn't have seen what we saw.' The glint in her eye showed she had a treasure for me.

'So what did you see?'

'He wasn't a man at all. Tall enough for a man, but when the hat nearly came off her hair started falling down and there was a lot of it, not a man's hair. She saw I had my eye on her and looked me straight in the face, as if she was daring me to say anything.'

'Dark hair, dark eyes?'

229

Tabby nodded. Amos whistled and looked at me. 'Same one as took Rancie?'

'Of course the same one. There can't be two like her. But what in the world did she think she was doing?'

Amos thanked his friend and sent him away, then he, Tabby and I held a council of war by the horse trough in Burlington Gardens with Plush as a silent onlooker. There was one obvious conclusion: Bruno knew his trap had worked and we were there, or why had he come out of the shop so soon after going in? Eleonore Gordon knew Bruno would be there because something more than coincidence must have brought her to Burlington Arcade at the same time with a pistol in her pocket.

'Or knew we'd be there,' Amos said.

I thought about it. 'That would mean she's had somebody watching us. But why?'

'Because she wants him and she thinks we're more likely to find him than she is,' Tabby said.

'And we nearly had him,' Amos mourned. The business of the knife still rankled. His view was the simple one that he'd held all along: Bruno had set up a trap intending to kill me. I disagreed. I couldn't see why I'd be such a threat to the man, and in any case he'd only produced the knife after the pistol shot, not when I walked up to him.

'So how did she know?'

'She might have had somebody follow us from this morning,' Tabby said. 'I'd usually know, but that one's clever.'

I ignored the grudging admiration in her voice. 'It's just possible. We'd allowed a lot of waiting time in the arcade, enough time for her to do something. But that would mean she'd had somebody watching us all the time, on the off-chance.' I thought of the times, too many to count now, of when I'd had that quivering feeling down my spine and tried to dismiss it. 'Or it was her trap all along.'

'Just what I was thinking,' Tabby said. Amos looked at me, questioning.

'She's looking for Bruno, but with all the people she knows you'd think there'd be easier ways of finding him,' I said. 'Besides, she approves of him.'

'We don't know who she was trying to shoot,' Amos said. 'She and the valet could have been in it together.'

'To kill me? But why? Besides, I have a feeling that when that woman fires at a target, she doesn't miss.'

'Long shot with a pistol,' Amos said.

'In any case, it can't have been her trap. It all started with D'Orsay's letter to me and she wouldn't have known about that.'

Silence. I wondered if they were thinking what I was, only not saying it because the man was my friend. D'Orsay had handed us the present. But what reason could he have for being in partnership with an absconding valet? We'd come to no conclusion by the time Amos had to go and supervise evening feed at the stables. As we parted, Tabby let me know she'd be sleeping in her cabin in the yard that night. The tone was casual but the implication clear: I needed guarding. When I got back it was only chance that made me go up the smaller of our two staircases direct to my office. Mrs Martley said later that she'd left a note on the parlour table to tell me, naturally expecting that I'd go there first. So when I opened the office door, bonnet in my hand, letting my cloak slip from my shoulders, I wasn't expecting company. There, sitting in my best chair with his hat, coat and walking cane laid neatly across my chaise longue, reading one of my books (the *Odes* of Horace as I discovered later) was Mr Slater.

SEVENTEEN

For a man who'd been nearly dead four and half days ago he was looking better than might have been expected, but then he hadn't looked healthy in the first place. The left-out-in-the-rain look was more pronounced, eyes deeper in their sockets, face with the weary look of a predator after an unsuccessful day's hunting. He wore his stock high up against the chin, so perhaps his neck was hurting. At least he stood up when I came in. I took my time before giving him the nod that allowed him to sit down again, carefully moving his things to one side of the chaise longue so that I could lay my cloak and bonnet down, then taking my chair on the opposite side of the table.

'Your housekeeper kindly permitted me to wait for you,' he said.

'So you didn't bring the sergeant with you this time.'

'Officially, this visit is not happening.'

'So no tea again.'

'I'd prefer an explanation.'

'Really? I was thinking that you might have come here to thank me for saving your life. Tell me, do you know who attacked you?'

He shook his head. 'They took care that I shouldn't. Scarves over their faces.'

'English or foreign voices?'

'They didn't speak.'

I stared at him, not trying to hide my disbelief. Tabby had said that two men, probably with knives or guns, had walked him to the Italian office, then there'd been a fight inside. He expected me to believe that they'd never let a scarf slip or uttered a word? He flicked the question aside like a man driving off a mosquito, as if getting almost hanged made an annoying distraction.

'That's not what I want to discuss. What were you and your people doing in Burlington Arcade this afternoon?'

'So your people were there as well. No wonder it was crowded.'

'I see you came to no decision on shaving brushes. I wondered if you were shopping for your friend.'

'So you had a man . . .' I stopped, realizing that he wouldn't have left it to anybody else. He'd been among the gentlemen's toiletries inside, watching me with those unblinking eyes. I felt cold.

'Were you and Madam Gordon working in partnership?'

'No.'

'I thought not. Between the two of you, I'm caught between Scylla and Charybdis.'

As far as I remembered my Homer, Scylla was a multi-headed monster who ate men six at a time and Charybdis was a horrible black whirlpool. Odysseus had decided that Scylla was the lesser risk.

'So since you've come here, that makes me the man-eating monster.'

Not a flicker of a smile from him. 'I tried to warn you when we first met. I still don't think you realize in what you're interfering.'

'I think I do: one murder, one attempted murder, blackmail and an assault on my assistant. And I think you know something about all of them. Did you kill Lesparre or arrange to have him killed?'

'No. Why should I do that?'

'Because those papers he was carrying were inconvenient to the government and its friends. Your employers.'

'And you believe you're living in a country whose government employs assassins?'

'What I believe doesn't matter. Somebody tried to kill you in exactly the same way as Lesparre was killed. There's a reason for that and you must know it.'

The raptor's eyes met mine as if trying to see through into my brain. 'I think you know it too, Miss Lane. You're interested in the Italians after all. Everything turns on them. Napoleon was going to give them their united Italy once he'd overrun all Europe. The next generation thought they had a second chance in so-called Prince Louis and he encouraged them. He's been a sworn *Carbonari* all his adult life. Mazzini and Madam Gordon and her friends are like that.' He held up two pale bony fingers, pressed together. The knuckles were calcified with arthritis.

'And the Italians tried to kill you because they thought you'd had their ally Lesparre killed?' I was trying to clear my mind, wondering whether to tell him anything at all, but it felt like that black whirlpool. I made my choice, for better or worse. 'That certainly wasn't the case with Eleonore Gordon. If she thought you'd killed Lesparre she'd probably have sent you a case of champagne. As far as she's concerned, he was a spy and a traitor.'

Did that surprise him? If so, he gave no sign of it. 'You believe that? That woman wouldn't tell the truth about anything as a matter of principle. Why was she so determined to protect the valet from you this afternoon?'

'You think that was what she was doing?' I guessed we'd come to the reason for his visit. He was as puzzled as I was, so it was a contest between us to see how much information we could get for how little we gave away. I'm too impatient to be good at chess and I guessed he was very good indeed.

'Of course. That shot was simply to distract attention so that he could get away from you.'

'The question we should be asking is why he was there in the first place,' I said.

'Collecting his shoes.'

Was that Slater's first mistake? Collecting shoes, obviously – why else should a man go to a shoemaker – but *his* shoes, gentleman's shoes repaired for the valet. Only D'Orsay, Amos, Tabby and I should have known about that. 'You read Count D'Orsay's note,' I said. 'The messenger from his club.' I remembered no more than a man in club livery, standing in the yard waiting for me to write my reply. Nobody notices messengers. The faintest flicker in Slater's eyes told me I was right. 'Is every club messenger on the

236

government's payroll?' I said. 'Do you pay boot boys and chambermaids to spy on people as well?'

'When necessary.' No hint of shame in his voice or eyes. 'You find that distasteful? You prefer to live in an open and honourable world, of course, just as you prefer to have your waste and rubbish carted away and the rats in your basement disposed of when you're out having afternoon tea with friends.'

I pretended to applaud, palms not quite meeting. 'Do you make that speech to yourself when you're walking the streets at night? Spare me the rhetoric. Suppose we both of us admit that we were tricked this afternoon. Bruno wanted me to be there, and you got drawn in too.'

'Go on.'

'That note was altogether too pat, what we wanted to hear. Bruno knew very well that we'd be waiting. I don't suppose he guessed that you'd read the note as well, but it would have made no difference.'

'If you're right, why should he do that?'

'That's what I don't know. Perhaps to flush me out and confirm I wanted to find him. But it was a dangerous game to play for something he could have guessed anyway. We could have had him.'

'And the reason you didn't was Madam Gordon's performance.'

'Yes, it would be her style – risky, theatrical.' We looked at each other, in agreement now except I think he'd have used harder words about her.

'So Madam Gordon set a trap and you fell into it,' he said. 'That means she and Bruno are allies.'

237

If so, it meant too that she'd found him before I did and – in spite of our peace treaty – said nothing about it. After all, I'd intended to do the same thing to her.

'If you'd taken him, what did you plan to do with him?' Slater said.

'Ask him if he'd killed Lesparre.'

'I thought I was the candidate for that honour.' He was still one of them, though I didn't say so. 'So what was his motive? Wasn't he the devoted valet?'

'He might have been once, but I don't think he stayed that way. I thought at first that he was loyal to the prince and had found out that Lesparre was a traitor.'

'And now?'

'Since you're still interested, he must be a threat to authority in some way. Did he kill Lesparre and take those papers you're so interested in? Is he still threatening people with them? If so, I think the threat reaches a long way up. Either Bruno stole them, which probably means he killed Lesparre, or . . .' I tried to bite back the *or*, hoping he wouldn't notice. What I'd been going on to say was something that had just occurred to me: *Lesparre never had them at all. He was making too much display of that satchel. Bruno had them all along.* No reason to give Slater more than I need.

'Or what?' So he had noticed.

'Or was in league with whoever did.' He guessed I was hiding something so I changed the subject. 'Cobblers will live, by the way, but he was badly hurt. That's the lad you had kicked

238

and beaten nearly to death. Was that all part of removing household waste?'

He blinked for the first time that I'd noticed. 'So it was you set him on following me?' Then he hadn't noticed Tabby and Plush. It had been too much to expect Cobblers to live up to their standard. 'Why? Or can I guess? You're anxious for your friend Mr Carmichael. I wish him no harm, in fact I'd like to talk to him. Do you think you could get him to meet me?'

I had to fight the urge to stand up and kick him hard in a kneecap. 'So that you can ask him to act as one of your informers?' I wasn't going to admit that I had no way of sending messages to Robert, even if I wanted to.

'So that I can suggest he advises his friends to leave the country. I can understand that it would be inconvenient for them to return to Piedmont, but France is near enough. There are so many conspirators there that they'd hardly be noticed.' A softening like a fleeting touch of sun on dark water came over his face, probably what he thought of as a reassuring smile. 'He's really not in as much trouble as he thinks he is. Believe me, it's happened before. A naïve, generous-hearted young man on his travels sees all the world's problems as something he's been put on earth to solve.' (Particularly if the problems have dark hair, wide eyes and a tendency to sea-sickness, I thought, not daring to give myself away by looking at Slater as he went on talking in that voice that was trying so hard to sound casual.) 'Quite often no lasting harm comes of it, provided he listens to advice. Apart, that is, from his first experience of ingratitude.'

I might have protested that Robert was not naïve nor, come to that, particularly young, being in his thirties. As it was, I changed the subject again. 'You're assuming that Madam Gordon and Bruno got together and planned what happened this afternoon. Are you certain of that?'

'How else would she know he'd be there?'

'From following you and your men?'

'No. More likely from you.'

'Equally, no.'

'It had occurred to me that the two of you had made some kind of pact.'

I shook my head, thinking it wasn't really a lie. A pact implies equality of favours and Eleonore was certainly not dealing fairly.

He began to stand up, a careful and probably painful business. All that night walking must have taken a toll on his knees and hours of standing on a trap with a noose round his neck would not have improved things. I handed him his hat, coat and cane and saw him downstairs and out of the yard gateway. He didn't thank me for my time and I didn't invite him to repeat the visit. I went back upstairs to my study and began worrying again at the problems. How had Bruno known what bait to use in his trap? How had Eleonore Gordon known what he was doing? Visits were in order to both Gore House and Number One, Carlton Gardens. I spun a penny and it came down for Gore House, so that's where I went on Thursday morning.

EIGHTEEN

Lady Blessington was out in the garden, supervising the remaking of her spring bulb border dressed in serviceable green twilled silk and a straw bonnet with matching scarf tied under the chin. She didn't even try to look pleased to see me. There must have been something in my face.

'What is it now?' She drew us aside from the gardeners.

'You said your staff has been with you for a long time.'

'Well, they have.'

'With one recent addition. You might ask your housekeeper if she told Ronson to replace those candles along the corridor. Isn't that usually a housemaid's job?'

She looked like a child caught out at something. 'Ronson?'

'Yes, Ronson. How long has he been working here?'

She took a deep breath. 'Shall we go and look at my dahlias?'

We walked and came to a halt in front of a bed blazing with oranges and crimsons. I noticed that some plants had been newly staked.

'Badgers,' she explained, seeing where I was looking. 'They got in one night and made a terrible mess.' I decided not to tell her that the badgers had been Eleonore Gordon and me crashing through them. 'Miss Lane, I think you may have guessed that I have not been entirely honest with you.' I waited. 'What I'm going to tell you I should not want anybody else to know under any circumstances, especially Alfred. He's a sensitive man and would be deeply hurt if he thought I mistrusted him in any way.' I was still waiting. 'The fact is Alfred's been a little incautious.'

'Over Prince Louis?' I hadn't intended to help her, but it was a new experience to find Lady Blessington having difficulty saying something.

'You guessed? Yes, I'm afraid he was much more deeply into the attempt than most people think. He helped the prince plan it, put him in touch with people. He might even have gone on that steamer with them, except he does get so terribly seasick.'

That again. 'Yes, I did hear rumours,' I said.

'So you can imagine how very inconvenient it was when those two turned up at our gates. Poor Alfred, I felt so sorry for him. There he was, telling this story about how he'd met Lesparre in the prince's company and he couldn't in all conscience turn him away. Alfred really is not very good at lying.'

'Lying?' Jolted, I looked up and met those confiding grey eyes.

'Yes, he tried to convince me that Lesparre had even attended some of my salons. He has this idea that I entertain so many people that I can't possibly remember all their names and faces. I assure you, I do. Everybody I've ever met is stored here as surely as if they were pasted and labelled in an album.' She tapped her forehead. 'And I'd never met Lesparre before, or the valet come to that. Until Lesparre arrived here I didn't know him from Adam and neither did Alfred.'

I decided not to tell her that D'Orsay had already confided in me. 'So why did he let them in?'

'Isn't it obvious? They were blackmailing him. I don't know whether they were on the prince's side or the other side, but they knew how deeply he was in. I suppose he'd put something in writing, which was really very silly of him.'

'Not telling you was even sillier.'

'My dear, you know how men do hate to lose face. He was probably simply buying time while he decided what to do or hoping Lesparre would give up once he realized he has no money to speak of.'

'Why didn't you tell me this when you called me in?'

'Because it was Alfred's secret, not mine. When I involved you, I was trying to call Lesparre's bluff. He was claiming that he couldn't leave this house, so I'd show him a way it could be done and try to flush him.'

'And up to then you'd just sat there with a man you knew was a blackmailer under your roof. I must say I admire your nerve more than your judgement.'

She looked sideways at me. 'You're really angry with me, aren't you? No, I didn't just sit there, but you're going to be even more angry when I tell you what I did.' More waiting. The poodle wandered up and she caressed its neck and ears, murmuring to it. When it walked away she took another deep breath and spoke. 'I consulted Mr Disraeli.' Then, seeing my look: 'Well, why not? You weren't back then so I couldn't ask you. Besides, he's Alfred's friend and he does know all kinds of people and he's really brilliant at finding out what's happening behind the scenes of things. I sometimes tease him that he's like one of those wicked old Italian cardinals, secretly pulling strings all over the place, though I suppose he could hardly be a cardinal being Jewish and . . . I'm talking nonsense, aren't I?'

'Suppose you just tell me what happened.'

'I told him exactly what I've just told you. He said the thing to do was to get our hands on whatever papers Lesparre was using to blackmail Alfred. I said that would be difficult because Lesparre made a great business of never letting that satchel out of his sight. Disraeli said every man let his guard down at some point. He suggested introducing somebody among the servants to watch Lesparre and get it from him. So that's what we did.'

I felt like groaning. 'So you brought in Ronson.'

'Yes. That's why I wasn't very eager for you to talk to the servants, but at least the wretched man kept his nerve when you were interviewing them all, though you probably had some suspicions.'

'He was listening at the door when we talked about how to find the valet.'

'I dare say he was. I suppose that's what they're trained to do, like gun dogs.'

'Is he still here?'

'Yes. I'm waiting for Disraeli to come and take him away.' From the way she said it, I had a mad vision of Disraeli arriving with a large basket and carrying him off like an unwanted pet.

'Where did you find him?'

'I left that to Disraeli.'

'And where did he find him?'

'I think he's by way of being a paid inquirer. You know sometimes when there are embarrassments in a household . . .' Her voice trailed away.

'I know. I'm one of them, remember.'

'Oh, my dear.' She put her hand on my arm, contrite. 'I didn't mean you. I don't think of you in that way. I wish you'd been here from the start. You'd have been far more use than Ronson.'

'So he failed to get the papers?'

'Yes. I had hopes of him at first. I tried to steer him into duties where he'd have chances to be in contact with Lesparre without making the other servants suspicious. Several times he reported that he was close, then something would happen and he'd have to start again. I don't really blame him. You saw how close Lesparre kept those papers.'

'I need to speak to Ronson again.'

'Don't you think you should talk to Disraeli first?'

'Heavens above, is there some kind of etiquette with spies?'

I must have sounded as angry as I felt because she looked hurt. 'I wish I knew. Believe me, I'm as bewildered with it all as you are – more, probably. But would it do any harm to speak to

245

Disraeli? I expect he'll be here this afternoon. Why don't you wait and speak to him then?'

Lunch for the three of us was as strained an occasion as might be imagined, given that Lady Blessington and D'Orsay were keeping things from each other, both probably keeping things from me and I from them. Soon afterwards the first of her 'at home' regulars arrived and by four o'clock a dozen or so visitors, all but two male, were drinking Lady Blessington's tea, most of them clustered round the sofa, where she was sitting in rose silk with fringed turban, managing to look as if she hadn't a care in the world beyond making sure that the maids were refilling cups as necessary and that the men who preferred whisky were being offered it. Disraeli was holding forth as usual with the other men giving him fidgety attention, unwilling to encourage him but unable to tear themselves away from the story. I waited for the end of it – something to do with a man accidentally shooting his host in the hinder parts on a grouse moor – and caught his eye while the others were laughing. He put down his cup, asked leave from Lady Blessington and came over to me. We withdrew to a corner alongside an ancient Greek urn with satyrs.

'Am I in your bad books again, Miss Lane?'

'Why didn't you tell me D'Orsay was being blackmailed?'

'I was in a delicate position. Lady Blessington had told me about his problem in confidence.'

'And neither of you thought to tell me. I was supposed to solve it but only knew half the story.'

'It was wrong, I admit it, but we were simply trying to encourage Lesparre to go away. If we'd had any idea how things were going to develop, we'd have done things differently.'

'So the best you could think of was getting the man Ronson introduced into the household.'

'It was an outside chance, we knew, but it seemed worth trying.'

'And he was obviously unsuccessful.'

'Yes, not entirely his fault. We'd evolved a plan that might even have worked if somebody else hadn't preceded us.'

'From the little I've seen of Ronson, he'd wreck any plan. Where did you find him?'

'He's occasionally employed by some banker friends of mine on a confidential basis.'

'Do your banker friends often suffer from blackmailers?'

'Other things – credit worthiness for instance.'

'So another spy.'

'That's not a word they like to use. He sighed and looked serious. 'There is something I should tell you, in confidence of course.' He paused, waiting for my promise.

'You'd better tell me anyway. I'm as deeply in as the rest of you by now.'

He stared at a pair of satyrs doing something that shouldn't have occurred in a polite drawing room. 'D'Orsay was far from the only one who was threatened by those papers. Half the bankers in London are in the same position.'

'They supported Prince Louis?'

'Any sensible banker hedges his bets and until Boulogne the prince was definitely in the field.

It wasn't as if they were taking big financial risks. Their letters guaranteeing credit would only apply if Prince Louis come to power in Paris.'

'But we'd be talking a lot of money?'

'Millions.'

'So big names?'

'Some of the biggest.'

'And those were the letters Lesparre had?'

'Very probably, yes. If they got into the wrong hands, especially if they were published in the press, they could do serious damage.'

'And did the government know the bankers were behind him?'

'Only behind him if he succeeded, remember. Nobody would lend him ten sous for a glass of bad wine now.'

'But the Foreign Office knew about the bankers?'

'They wouldn't be doing their job if they didn't. Nobody in government would be stupid enough to put anything in writing, but financial guarantees might be traced back by people with the right contacts.'

'And now they've disappeared again? I suppose you know from Ronson that they weren't in that satchel Lesparre was guarding so carefully.'

He looked me in the eye, seeming genuinely worried. 'The problem is that they probably haven't disappeared. A banker of my acquaintance received half a letter yesterday.'

'Half?'

'A page of his letter of guarantee to Prince Louis, cut down the middle, an obvious threat.

He's waiting to know what will happen next, expecting blackmail.'

'So somebody's got hold of the letters and is using them as Lesparre was?'

'Yes.'

'And that presumably is the same person who killed him.'

'Also yes, which makes things worse than they were. At least we knew who Lesparre was and where he was.'

'Coming back to Ronson . . .'

'What I've just told you is all part of that. When D'Orsay confided in me about his problem, I'd already had an approach from a banker friend of my acquaintance on similar terms. He and others were also being blackmailed by Lesparre. They decided to consult me as the person most likely to know what to do about it.' His eyes were still staring into mine, anxious and urgent. As always with him I had to decide how much to believe. He was a true politician, seldom lied if he could help it but to tell the whole truth about anything would be as indecent as stripping naked in public. The banker story rang true because he had many friends in high finance. What he wasn't saying was that his debts were so monumental that he couldn't refuse favours to them. His recent marriage to a rich widow had helped to some extent, but when she fondly agreed to settle all his debts, he hadn't dared tell her the half of it. That was common knowledge in London, at least among the few hundred people who mattered. I decided to believe him, for the while at least.

'And Ronson?'

249

'When D'Orsay consulted me, I decided that I could help him and my banking acquaintances in the same way, by getting in a man to recover the papers. Naturally I couldn't tell him about the others, but it was a god-sent opportunity to get a man into Gore House. The question then arose, what man? We couldn't recruit a thief or some disreputable agent. It had to be somebody known to us. Ronson had shown intelligence and initiative in the past so we decided he was our man.'

'He was being well paid, I suppose.'

'A hundred pounds were promised as a bonus if he secured the papers.'

A year's salary for a clerk; chicken feed for the banker. 'Cheap at the price,' I said. 'You get what you pay for, or don't get in this case.'

'You underrate Ronson,' Disraeli said. 'He was reporting to me discreetly when I came to visit Lady Blessington and was making some progress. He was almost ready to move.'

'He struck me as nervous.'

'Of course. He was in a difficult position when you questioned him. He must have played the household servant pretty well if you didn't guess.'

'There was this ridiculous business of reporting a robber climbing out of a window. He didn't really see it, did he?'

'No.'

'So why did he say he did?'

'He had his reasons. I apologize if it complicated your investigations. Are you making progress?'

'Fair trade,' I said. 'You want to know

everything that I know, but you're keeping something back. I want to speak to Ronson.'

He hesitated a moment. 'I'm sure that can be arranged. He'll be leaving Gore House anyway now he's no longer needed here. I'll let you know when . . .'

'I mean I want to speak to him now before he leaves. I'm sure Lady Blessington will have no objection.' I took a step as if going straight to ask her.

'Wait.' He was definitely alarmed. 'There's something you should know first.' I looked at him over my shoulder. 'And you're going to tell me?'

He sighed. 'If you'll permit, we'd better sit down.'

I led the way to a sofa in the far corner. I could tell Lady Blessington was aware of us, though all her attention seemed to be on the people talking to her. D'Orsay was nowhere to be seen. As Disraeli told his story his pose was relaxed, one knee bent, body turned towards me, mildly amused expression on his face. If anybody had glanced at us it would have looked as if we were exchanging social gossip.

'As I said, Ronson was making progress. He'd learned a lot about the household routine and Lesparre's habits. Twice he came quite close to getting that satchel but the second time it looked as if our man was getting suspicious. When he reported that, it was clear we had to do something quickly. The first thing we tried was putting opium in his after-dinner coffee to make him sleep heavily, but Ronson thinks he might have detected something wrong with the flavour. He took no more than a sip.'

'How disobliging of him.'

'As it happens, Ronson is quite an amateur of chemistry, attends public lectures and so forth. He came up with a very ingenious suggestion. You've heard of nitrous oxide?'

'Laughing gas? You were planning to put him in such a state of hilarity that he'd simply hand it over?' It was as much as I could do not to laugh out loud myself. Disraeli frowned.

'It also induces drowsiness. Ronson's suggestion was that we should wait until Lesparre had to go up to the loft for some reason then bore a small hole through the hatch and introduce the gas through a tube from a portable container. Its effect in a confined space should have been enough to make him less wary than usual, even if it didn't send him to sleep. When the fire broke out, Ronson thought that was his opportunity and was ready to act, only they didn't send Lesparre up to the loft. So he took advantage of the confusion and sent a lad running for the police pretending he'd seen a burglar. When they arrived, up Lesparre went and soon afterwards there was Ronson with his gas apparatus and a brace and bit.'

'But Ronson got the gas instead of Lesparre.'

He stared. 'How do you know that?'

'When I saw him, he'd been sick. He said it was from the fire, but none of the others was affected in the same way. So what went wrong?'

'Lesparre must have heard him drilling. From

252

what I can gather, he had to do it from a kind of ladder on the wall, not very well balanced, with the oiled silk bag containing the gas down on the landing. Suddenly the hatch came crashing down and he was kicked hard in the face from above. He fell face down on the bag and it split so his lungs and throat were full of nitrous oxide. By the time he'd got back some self-possession, the hatch was closed again. All he could do was pick himself and his apparatus up and invent the story about inhaling smoke in the fire.'

'Exactly what time did this happen?'

'Sometime after the police arrived. Probably quite soon after.'

'I still need to speak to him.'

He walked over and said something to Lady Blessington. She glanced at me, nodded and called one of the maids over. Disraeli followed me along the corridor, through the door to the servants' hall and into the housekeeper's room, looking as exotic as a humming bird in a hen coop. Ronson appeared almost at once. He was still wearing his servant clothes and green baize apron but his hair was sleeked down, his complexion clear, his bearing more confident. He glanced at Disraeli then at me, his look questioning.

'You've met Miss Lane,' Disraeli said. 'This time you can tell her whatever she wants.'

Ronson's bob of the head was respectful, but not servile.

'We should go upstairs to where it happened,' I said.

Disraeli made no objection, apart from the lift of one eyebrow. I stood back to let Ronson lead the way. A dozen fresh candles in holders were ranged on a shelf, ready to go up into the bedrooms. I picked up one of them and a lighter and we started the familiar climb up the back stairs to the top landing by the servants' bedrooms. Disraeli stood at the bottom of the wooden steps and looked up at the hatch, blinking in the deep shadow.

'Please show us exactly where you were standing when you were trying to drill through the hatch,' I said to Ronson.

He went to the ladder fastened to the wall and climbed almost to the top, just as I'd seen Stedge do.

'You knew the ladder would be there?'

'Yes, I'd reconnoitered.' The tone and vocabulary were quite different, senior clerk rather than under-servant. Perhaps Disraeli's choice hadn't been so ridiculous after all.

'Wouldn't Lesparre have heard you coming upstairs?'

'I wore felt slippers, the kind we wear when we're polishing the marble floor in the hall.'

'It must have been difficult to drill from there.'

'It was. I had to wedge my shoulder under the ceiling so that I could use both hands.' He demonstrated: difficult but not impossible. I lit the candle.

'Can you show me where you drilled?' He came down a step and pointed. It was difficult to angle the candle to get enough light on it, but sure enough there was a hole the thickness of a little finger. I asked Ronson to come down and gave the candle to Disraeli so that I could climb up a couple of rungs and look for myself. The hole looked to be no more than about an inch deep. 'You didn't get far,' I said.

'The hatch was thicker and the wood harder than I'd appreciated. But I'm convinced I'd have achieved it, if it hadn't been for the interruption.'

I climbed down. 'You mean, being kicked. Tell me exactly what happened.'

'The hatch was suddenly drawn aside from above. The shock of it made me drop the brace and bit and I nearly fell but managed to hang on. Then something struck me hard in the face, a boot sole I think, and I fell. Either the force of my landing split the gas bag, or possibly the brace and bit punctured it. The next thing I knew my face was stinging and burning and I was choking. I must have rolled down the next flight of stairs, just trying to get away. I freely admit that for some time I was hardly in control of my faculties.'

'Hardly surprising,' I said, because he sounded ashamed of himself. 'Was anybody coming after you from the loft?'

'No. After some time, a minute or two perhaps, I recovered enough to drag myself up to the top landing and collect the gas bag and tube and the brace and bit. The loft hatch was closed again and there was no sound.'

'You didn't report it to anyone?'

'No. Her Ladyship had given me firm instructions that Count D'Orsay should not under any circumstances know what I was doing. As far as I knew, he was still downstairs with the police, Her Ladyship with them. I decided all I could do was wait and report to Mr Disraeli on his next visit.'

'And you still said nothing, even when you knew Lesparre was dead?'

'I thought hard about it and decided it wasn't relevant. Again, I thought the decision should be left to Mr Disraeli.'

And he'd decided to say nothing to me. He must have realized what I was thinking.

'I agree with Ronson, Miss Lane. It simply wasn't relevant. All it adds to what we know is that Lesparre's last action in this world was to kick Ronson off a ladder.'

'If it was Lesparre.' They both stared at me. 'All that Ronson knows is that something, probably a foot, struck him in the face. 'I take it that you couldn't identify the foot?'

'I'm not even sure it was a foot. It felt like being kicked, that's all.'

'At some point there must have been another man up in the loft, possibly more than one. Isn't it possible that Lesparre had already been knocked senseless or tied up and it was one of his attackers who kicked you off the ladder?'

Silence, then Ronson said, 'Yes, it's possible.'

'Pretty cool of him, or them,' Disraeli said. 'Here they are, almost discovered, but they go ahead with the plan of trussing up Lesparre.'

'Cool, yes, but they were deeply committed by then. They might as well finish what they'd come to do,' I said. I looked down at planks of the

256

half-landing where we were standing. Sure enough, under the half-finished borehole in the hatch were little spirals of bright new pine from Ronson's brace and bit. Perhaps he'd been unlucky in his timing and his crazy plan might have worked. There seemed nothing more to be learned there so we went back down to the housekeeper's room. I suggested that we all sit down at the table. Ronson waited for a nod of approval from Disraeli before settling himself. He looked a shade less self-possessed than when we'd started. Perhaps it was more alarming to think of being kicked by a murderer than his victim.

'So all this happened while the police were still in the house,' I said.

'Yes. I know they were on the ground floor when I went up to the loft. I had to make the attempt quickly in case they went and Lesparre was allowed to come down.'

'You didn't consider using the other way into the loft, by the chimney.'

'I knew there was a way, because one of the servants had mentioned it, but I didn't know in any detail. It would have taken too long to look for it.'

'And all the time you were here, it was your duty to keep a watch on Lesparre so that you could try to get those papers?'

'Yes, and I failed.' He turned to Disraeli. 'I very much regret that, sir.'

The sadness in his tone sounded real. A hundred pounds in hand and an increased reputation for dealing with bankers' embarrassments would have been prizes worth winning.

'You did your best,' Disraeli said. 'I'm sure you won't lose by it.' I was touched by his humanity and remembered there was real warmth under the posing, one of the reasons why I'd liked him in the first place.

'So what will happen to Ronson?' I asked as we walked back to the drawing room together.

'He'll leave here this evening. He'll get half his hundred pounds at least.'

'I might want to speak to him again. Will you make sure to find out where he can be found?'

He promised. I didn't tell him that there was no *might* about it and I'd definitely want to speak to Ronson again. With Disraeli there, I'd decided not to ask Ronson whether he'd overheard and passed on the conversation with D'Orsay about the valet's shoes. Unless D'Orsay himself had done it – which I couldn't entirely dismiss – Ronson must have had dealings with the valet. That opened up complications I wasn't ready to share with Disraeli or his banker friends.

We went back to join Lady Blessington's group round the sofa. Disraeli settled as if he intended to stay there for the rest of the afternoon but I took my leave.

'We'll see you again soon?' she said. The words were conventional but the look in her eyes hoped it wouldn't be too soon. A footman was waiting in the corridor to show me out but I thanked him and said I had something to ask the housekeeper and I knew the way. Mrs Neal was in her room, working on what looked like complicated accounts. So much had happened in the

258

household that she was only slightly surprised at the question I asked her.

'Yes, of course. We scrubbed it several times over with soap and carbolic as soon as we were allowed up there and sluiced it so thoroughly that we had water running down the back stairs. I oversaw it myself because the girls were squeamish.'

So Ronson had been lying. Perhaps I should have gone back to have it out with Disraeli there and then, but I couldn't face a re-entry to the salon. We all make mistakes.

NINETEEN

On Friday morning I walked to Carlton Gardens, making a detour along Burlington Arcade out of curiosity. Its wounds were healing already. A smell of glazier's putty mingled with sugar at the pastry cook's, the beadles were patrolling with the regularity of clockwork toys and the crowd of shoppers and window gazers was even thicker than usual, with the lucky ones who'd happened to be there embroidering events for those who hadn't. Attempted robbery now seemed the most popular option, though nobody was explaining why an armed thief would be so desperate for marzipan fancies. Number One, Carlton Gardens was on the north side of St James's Park and overlooking the gardens of Marlborough House. In spite of that and the morning's autumn brightness, there was a gloomy look about the place. Most of the blinds were down, a few yellowed elm leaves shifted in the breeze around the steps and the front door knocker wasn't as bright as you'd expect on such a mansion. A whinny from the stable yard at the back reminded me that Rancie had been kept captive there and made my feelings about the place even less cordial. It seemed a long time before anybody answered the door and then it was not the butler but a maid in a long brown apron with her cap awry as if she'd been doing heavy work. When I gave her my card and said I'd like to talk to Madam Gordon she stared at me a moment then shut the door without speaking. It was five minutes or more before she opened it again, still wordlessly. I followed her along a corridor with gold-framed watercolours of European cities that anybody might have owned and up a staircase carpeted in blue and gold. Two spiky palm trees, rather dusty, stood at the foot of it and two more on the landing, framing a deep doorway topped with plaster acanthus leaves. The maid knocked again then scurried away and left me standing. The door was opened from the inside and Eleonore Gordon stood framed in real and plaster leaves like a portrait. She wore dark blue silk, with her hair caught up by tortoiseshell combs in a style that looked careless but probably wasn't. She stepped back to let me into the room.

'So you're making war on pastry cooks now,' I said.

'I had to do something since you were trailing half the spies on the government's payroll after you. Did you know that?' She closed the door. The room was dim with the blinds half down.

'I didn't know, not then. You saw them?'

'We recognized several people we knew, but then we expected it. You were setting a trap for Bruno. I thought we had an agreement.'

'I'd have honoured it if we'd caught him and it was mainly due to you that we didn't.'

'Either he'd have got away or he'd have been in Slater's hands. We didn't want that.' She moved over to the window, pulled a cord and let the blind rattle up. The light came in through high windows that could have done with cleaning, showing a place that was half drawing room, half museum, or perhaps shrine. A marble bust of Emperor Napoleon on a porphyry column dominated it. Portraits of the Empress Josephine, Letizia Bonaparte and Queen Hortense stared out from the walls as if avoiding having to look at each other. Eleonore folded back a silk covering from a glass-topped cabinet. Inside, a locket with a curl of dark hair, a tricolour sash, several rings, all clustered round a golden reliquary set with sapphires, diamonds, emeralds like minor planets round the sun. 'The talisman of Charlemagne,' she said, pointing to the reliquary. 'The emperor always carried it with him.' I guessed she was trying to send me a message: our minor affairs of murder, blackmail and mistrust were no more than satellites to something much greater. Or perhaps the message was to herself because she looked more tired and strained even than by candlelight in the stables at Gore House.

'How did you know Bruno would be going to the shoemaker's?' We both said it at once. Our eyes met across the cabinet, sabres crossed. We might have stayed like that all morning, so I decided to answer first.

'I was told he'd brought shoes and was due to collect them. Somebody sent me a note about it, but the messenger was in Slater's pay. I didn't know about that until afterwards. It was a trap, of course, but I wanted to know who set it and why.'

'Shoes.' She said the word like kicking something.

'Was it your trap?'

'No.'

'But you were following me. Were you trying to protect the valet when you fired that shot? You didn't want him in our hands or Slater's.'

'I wasn't following you. We knew he'd be there.'

'Because he'd told you?'

She said nothing.

'If you're trying to protect him, you're protecting a murderer and a blackmailer,' I said. 'You told me the valet was a better man than his master but he's every bit as bad. Lesparre was a blackmailer and he knew it. He was even holding most of the blackmail letters for him. I suppose Lesparre was worried that somebody in Gore House would be trying to get them back. But Bruno was greedy and decided he wanted all the profit for himself. He got into the attic and trussed up Lesparre so that he was certain to die, then carried on blackmailing people.'

'You have evidence that he killed Lesparre?'

'There's a man named Ronson who helped him. He was supposed to be on the other side, but Bruno must have offered him more money.'

She moved over to the window and looked out, taking her time. When she spoke she kept her face turned away. 'The valet wanted me in the arcade so that he could kill me. Perhaps he wanted to kill you too, but me more.'

'I'll gladly resign the honour to you. So you've changed your mind about him? You swore on the emperor's ring that he didn't kill Lesparre.'

She shrugged. 'One may be mistaken.'

263

This was a new mood for her – quiet, almost humble. It must have cost her a lot to admit to a mistake.

'So we're back where we started,' I said. 'Both of us looking for the valet.'

'So we have a truce again.'

'A truce, yes.' But not a peace treaty.

'This man Ronson, you know where he is? Can I speak to him?'

'No. I'll speak to him and tell you what I find out.' Some of it, probably.

'A blackmailer exposes himself. At some point, he must collect the money.'

Our minds were working along the same lines, but I didn't tell her so. She came over from the window and stretched out her hand for me to take, arm moving from the shoulder in a fine operatic gesture. 'So next time you tell me what you're planning and I tell you.' Her fingers felt strong and cool. She walked down the stairs to the front door with me, not bothering to call a servant to show me out. Perhaps there weren't many of them because the prince's house had an almost empty feel. At the top of the steps, just before she closed the door on me, she said something in a voice so casual it might have been a remark about the weather.

'Your friend has left London. Stoke Newington. But they'll be on their travels again soon.'

The door closed before I could ask anything. As I walked away I imagined her upstairs again in that shadowy room, carefully drawing down the blinds and replacing the cover over her holy relics. And plotting, as always. She'd known that those last few words would tie me to her more surely than any promise. As long as she knew more about Robert than I did, there was no question of parting company.

I got back to find a note had been delivered from Disraeli, a hasty scrawl. *Miss Lane, we need urgently to speak. Please call without fail any time after three this afternoon.* A few minutes after three I walked round the corner to his house in Park Lane. A couple of carriages outside suggested he and his wife were entertaining company. Mary Anne was suspicious of me – goodness knows why – and I had no invitation but I'd been her guest in the past so could not be turned away. The gathering in her gilded, damasked and bulgingly upholstered drawing room was all female but as the footman had shown me in I'd asked him to let Mr Disraeli know I was calling. Sure enough, he came down ten minutes after I arrived, curls fetchingly disordered, apologizing to the company for being so lost in one of his own books that he hadn't noticed the time. As usual, all the women in the room fluttered to him like pigeons to corn. He scattered compliments and polite teasings, then came over to where I was standing by a window with my teacup.

'Miss Lane, shall we go and talk in my study?' Mary Anne's disapproving eyes followed us to the door.

I'd never been in Disraeli's study before and at any other time might have been amused at its stateliness. Its high windows with swagged velvet

265

curtains overlooked Park Lane and it was crammed with marble busts of classical writers, ranks of tooled and gilded books, a desk so ornate it looked as if it should open up into an organ keyboard and play Handel, and oil paintings of Italy. Her taste, perhaps. A plainer desk in a corner piled with books and papers was probably where he did his work. The minute we were through the door his social cheeriness dropped like a cloak and he was as grave as I'd ever seen him. He hardly waited for me to sit down before collapsing into a chair opposite.

'Ronson's dead.'

'When?'

'Sometime last night or very early this morning. He lodges in Cannon Street. I took him away from Gore House in my carriage yesterday evening and dropped him off at the first cab rank we came to. I had to give him money for the fare. Money was what we talked about on the journey. He was concerned that he should be paid quickly and kept saying that the failure to get Lesparre's papers wasn't his fault. I made a note of his address and promised I'd have some money sent to him this morning. It seemed the best thing to do in the circumstances.'

Of course. Ronson knew too much to be left discontented, even if he had been the loyal servant that Disraeli supposed.

'So I spoke to one of my banker friends this morning while he was at breakfast and he said he'd send fifty pounds over to Ronson's address by messenger. Naturally, the messenger was told to bring back a receipt. He got no answer when

266

he knocked on the door, but it wasn't locked so he pushed it open and walked in, shouting good morning in case Ronson was still in bed. He fell over him on the floor. His throat was cut.' Disraeli ran his hands through his hair, looking shaken. 'Of course, the messenger ran out yelling for the police. They came quickly. From the way the blood had coagulated and the body cooled they estimate that Ronson had been killed quite some time before the messenger found him, probably in the early hours of the morning. He rented two rooms, a living room and a bedroom. Both rooms were disordered, as if the murderer had been looking for something. The police assume it was money. As far as they're concerned, this was a killing committed in the course of a robbery and Ronson was just a chance victim.'

'And you hope they go on thinking that, even if we know it wasn't?' He didn't answer. 'Did you know Ronson was lying to you?'

He stared. 'About what?'

'That attempt with the laughing gas, for one thing. Of course, he never had any intention of carrying out such a ludicrous plan. It was just to make you believe he was working hard at trying to get the papers. But once I started asking questions among the staff, he knew he had to make it look as if he'd really tried it. Only he was being too clever by half. He forgot that Mrs Neal is a good housekeeper. Typical male arrogance. Just think about it. After they'd taken Lesparre's body away, that landing under the hatch was covered with filth. As soon as she could, she had every maid in the place up there under her personal supervision, scrubbing and sluicing away. Any trace of wood borings would have been swept away along with the rest, and yet when I checked after I heard Ronson's story, there they were. So he did the drilling after Lesparre's death, not before it, and that story of being kicked in the face and swallowing gas was a lie.' I could see it was a blow to his vanity. With his pose of knowing everything, being outmanoeuvred by a hired hand would sting.

'But you said yourself he'd been sick and had blotches on his face.'

'Yes, but I was wrong about the reason. He probably would be sick and blotched, after helping the valet overpower Lesparre and prepare him for hanging.'

'You think that's what happened?'

'What else makes sense? The valet decided he could be a better blackmailer than his master. You know yourself that the blackmailing's still going on even though Lesparre's dead. Bruno must have guessed that Ronson was spying – not difficult given Ronson's methods – and tempted him with a lot more money than your banker friends were offering.'

'Then Bruno killed him?'

'Yes. Ronson wasn't any use to Bruno once he was out of Gore House, so there was no point in Bruno sharing the blackmail money with him. I know Bruno carries a knife because he was going to use it in Burlington Arcade.'

'So that business was you.' He sat back, thinking. 'So where do we go from here?'

'A good question. We have a double murderer

and blackmailer at large, with a cache of papers that could rock the bankers and the foreign office and we don't know how to find him.'

'A blackmailer's vulnerable at some point.' Almost exactly what Madam Gordon had said.

'Yes, he has to collect the money and Bruno may not have many allies, especially now he's killed one of them. The thing would be to get one of his victims to agree to hand over money and have people there waiting for him.' Disraeli nodded slowly but I sensed he was thinking fast. 'You'll tell me what's happening?' I said. 'I think I've deserved that.'

He came downstairs with me, sparking into his usual teasing style for the ladies in the drawing room, and I paid my compliments to Mary Anne and left. One thing struck me as I was walking back to Abel Yard. All along I'd thought Disraeli might have been more deeply in the prince's confidence than he pretended and perhaps involved in the negotiations with bankers that might have changed the government of France. Naturally he'd disowned the prince when he failed, but one discreet letter from him in Bruno's haul would be enough to sabotage his career. He wouldn't have to look far for a blackmail victim: no further than himself.

TWENTY

Through the weekend, I tried not to think about any of it but mostly failed. One of the things was the remark that Eleonore Gordon had thrown out so casually. *Your friend has left London. Stoke Newington. But they'll be on their travels again soon.* No reason why they shouldn't have gone to Stoke Newington as well as anywhere else. It's only a short omnibus ride out of London and only a determinedly metropolitan person like Eleonore would have regarded it as outside the city at all. On the Saturday I almost worked myself up to the stupidity of taking that omnibus ride. The more I thought about the conversation with Eleonore, the more it puzzled me. I couldn't understand why, after swearing to the valet's innocence, she now calmly accepted his guilt. I was keyed up, twitching with restlessness, aching to be anywhere but Abel Yard or the familiar walks in the park with fallen leaves shifting in a breeze from the east under skies that had turned grey. I knew that it would take Disraeli several days to set the trap for Lesparre, presumably in consultation with people above my level, and nothing could happen until then. Even when it was set, I doubted if he'd let me know. He'd made no promises. Also, I was having nightmares. I'd expected it after Lesparre's death, but they'd held off while things were happening fast and pounced now, when I had too much time to think about them. Perhaps it was the effect of being back in my own bed because Cobblers had reclaimed his heap of hay in the mews or perhaps Ronson's death had triggered them. Even though I knew he must be an accomplice in murder, I couldn't help remembering him as the sick and nervous under-servant I'd first met. In these nightmares, some of the bad things I'd seen over the last few years would merge in with each other in a black whirlpool of blood and staring eyes. In the recent addition, Stedge, D'Orsay and I were back on the half-landing at the top of Gore House, trying to wrap his body up in the sheet, only the sheet shrank smaller and smaller and bits of him kept flopping out, especially the left arm. That was especially cruel of the nightmare because his arm really had flopped out. I remembered noticing that the signet ring had gone from his little finger and the flesh over the knuckle was torn and bloody. The ring had been too small, even for his little finger, and his killers must have torn it off violently before tying his hands beside his back. This extra act of greed and cruelty bothered me more than it should.

On Saturday afternoon a diversion came, but one I could have done without. Sergeant Bevan moved up beside me as I was walking in the park alone, raising his hat politely.

'Your housekeeper thought I might find you here. May we have a word?'

'If you must.'

He didn't react to my ungraciousness. 'I thought you might like to know that Mr Lesparre has been properly identified and the inquest concluded. The unfortunate man took his own life while the balance of his mind was disturbed, probably from what happened in France.'

'All very tidy. Who identified him?'

'A gentleman came forward who'd known him in France. Much as we thought, small estate near Bordeaux, staunch Napoleonist. Of course they'd had to bury Lesparre by then but in cases where identity is in question we bring in an artist to do a study of the face. The gentleman was quite sure it had been his friend.'

'That's odd, since he claimed to have no friends in London. Was the gentlemen French?'

'So I understand, with a London hotel address. Sebastian Morel, resident at the Olivia Hotel, Great Russell Street.' He wished me good day and walked away.

Having nothing better to do on Sunday, I walked to Great Russell Street. To my surprise, there actually was an Olivia Hotel, a modest place mainly for the scholarly who wanted to be near the museum and book dealers. Not to my surprise at all, the helpful clerk had no knowledge of a Sebastian Morel or indeed any French gentleman for the past month or so. I wondered why Sergeant Bevan had wanted me to know that. He surely wouldn't have pointed me in that direction if the identification had been done by one of Slater's men. I sensed the hand of Eleonore Gordon somewhere in it, though why she might have decided to close the case on Lesparre so tidily I couldn't imagine. Another thing not to think about. The ringless hand flopped out in my nightmare again but this time when I woke in the morning the memory of it connected with something else and my restlessness couldn't be denied a release.

'Eastbourne,' Amos said. 'Are you needing some sea air?'

It was our ride out, early on Monday morning, Amos on a big dark bay, nice temperament but not enough class about him for a career in the cavalry. He said he'd be just the thing for a hunting farmer of his acquaintance out Bromley way and he'd maybe pick up a couple of carriage horses while he was down there. When I'd told him about Lesparre being formally identified his view was that it tied up matters as well as they were likely to get tied and we could get on with other things.

'Identified by a man who doesn't exist. I don't like being taken for a fool. I'm certain Eleonore Gordon has something to do with it.'

'All the more reason for letting it rest, then. I've been hearing a few things about that one.'

'I will let it rest, once I've settled this thing that's bothering me. I shan't be away for more than two days, I hope. What I need to do is take this nearer where it started.'

'Boulogne?'

'Not quite that far. We know Lesparre really was with Prince Louis at Boulogne, because he couldn't have got his hands on the papers otherwise. The question is how he and Bruno got from Boulogne to London.'

Amos sighed, humouring me. 'Probably not the

direct way. They'd have the French police out, rounding up the rebels.'

'Yes, so not any of the regular cross-Channel services. Lesparre told Lady Blessington they came over on a fishing boat. That may be true.'

'Could be fishermen or smugglers, probably comes to much the same thing.'

'So they wouldn't put them off somewhere busy like Dover or Folkestone. My guess would be somewhere around Eastbourne or Hastings, then they'd have to get themselves to London. They wouldn't know about coach routes, so that would probably mean a night in an inn or hotel while they found out.'

'Hastings is busier. Three regular coaches from there to London and the overnight mail.' Amos knew all the timetables by heart.

'Yes, so probably the one that would be most watched, either by French agents or our own. So my guess is Eastbourne. That's where I'll start, at any rate.'

'Eastbourne Safety Coach, leaves the George and Blue Boar in Holborn eight in the morning, Tuesdays, Thursdays and Saturdays. Billy Wells will probably be driving it. Give him my regards and say he's to look after you. You'll take Tabby?'

'Yes, if she'll come.' She'd been distant with me since we'd rescued Slater. That was no surprise, but it didn't make my mood any better. I found her in the yard when we got back and she agreed to come, but without enthusiasm. I sent her to Holborn to reserve two inside places on the Safety Coach for the morning and took an afternoon walk to Gore House. Lady Blessington

274

received me in her dressing room where her maid was doing her hair, ready to meet her guests. My request surprised her.

'Another picture of him?'

'The first one got lost. Could he do one of Lesparre too, for me to take away this afternoon?'

She put a scarf over her hair and went along the corridor to D'Orsay's room. 'He's working on it. Will they do on the same page? He says it won't be more than rough sketches, having to work in such a hurry. I suppose I can't ask why you want them.'

I said I'd tell her if they produced any result and wandered in the garden while I waited. Later she called me in for tea and handed over the drawings. They were rougher than D'Orsay's usual work, but he seemed to have caught a better likeness of Bruno than before. I asked her to give my compliments to D'Orsay and went home to pack my travelling bag.

Tabby and I were in good time at the George and Blue Boar for the Eastbourne coach, she in her sober grey with hair pinned up, and if her expression that said all this had nothing to do with her was not quite appropriate for a lady's maid, nobody was surprised by that at eight o'clock on a drizzly morning. We were full up inside as far as Caterham, but from then on Tabby and I shared the coach with only a lawyerly looking man who slept most of the way. We made a half-hour stop at East Grinstead to change horses for tackling Ashdown Forest and came down on the other side with the brakes grinding and the green fields of Sussex stretched out in front of us, cloud shadows chasing across them in a stiff breeze from the sea. After so long inland, I always feel a lift of spirits when travelling towards the coast and for a while I played with the idea that I was going on across the Channel to France and the warm south, following the swallows, who would be well on their way by now. What was to stop me, after all, except a thoroughbred mare and Amos and Tabby, glaring at the countryside as if it had insulted her. Those, and an unanswered question. As we came nearer the end of our journey, and the reality of why I was travelling, I'd convinced myself that I was only doing this to get away from thinking about Robert and there was no sense in it at all. We arrived at the Lamb Inn at Eastbourne just after five in the afternoon and found it unexpectedly busy, considering it was well out of season. The military had been on manoeuvres and the place was full of junior officers braying to each other, lounging on chairs in the public rooms and corridors with their legs stretched out, sending the servants running in all directions. We got some insolent looks as the manager did his best to find a room for us. One of them must have laid a hand on Tabby because I felt a flurry behind me, heard a male squawk and turned to find a spindly lieutenant massaging his shin, face screwed up in pain. She explained later that it hadn't been nearly as effective a kick as she intended because her petticoat got in the way. It was a relief when they found a room for us looking out over the yard, narrow bed for me, palliasse on the floor for my maid. We had supper brought to the room, good mutton chops from the salt marshes. The military were a nuisance in more ways than one because I'd hoped to settle my business by questioning the staff in the evening and catching the morning coach back to London, but everybody from manager to scullery maid was too busy to be interrupted. In the morning most of the officers went on their way, only to be replaced by another invasion complaining loudly about the hardships of life in camp at Beachy Head, demanding steaks and brandy for breakfast. We wandered round town looking at the grand new buildings then walked out to the fort. I explained to Tabby about tides but she didn't seem convinced. We watched small boats moving in and out of the harbour on a choppy sea with white-capped waves and I wondered if a similar boat had brought two refugees from Boulogne about a month ago. If we got nowhere in Eastbourne I'd move up the coast to Hastings and try there. I hoped we wouldn't need to go on to Dover. It had bad associations for me.

When we got back to the Lamb the soldiers had moved on and the place had an exhausted air. I ordered tea and bread and butter in the parlour and sent Tabby upstairs to fetch the sketches. The maid who brought the tea in was tongue-tied with shyness and couldn't remember seeing either of the men. I found the manager but it turned out that he'd only been there for two weeks, deputizing for a man who'd hurt his leg. When he saw I was determined on getting an answer from somebody he sent in one of the senior maids, an intelligent-looking woman in her early thirties with wiry dark hair trying to break free from her muslin cap and lively brown eyes. As soon as I showed her the pictures, she nodded and smiled. Yes, she remembered them, foreign gentlemen, nice mannered. They'd been there just over a month ago. She couldn't remember where they'd come from – not from the regular coach, she thought. They'd stayed for two nights, then taken the morning Safety Coach for London.

'Did you have a chance to speak to the valet?'

'Of course. The gentlemen's valets usually take their meals at the servants' table, with us. I sat next to him both nights, a pleasant and well-mannered person but he didn't talk much. He was a foreigner, of course, but when he spoke his English was good. He seemed to me a little sad.'

'Sad?'

'His eyes were. Well, perhaps more like serious, thinking about things. Of course, he wasn't a young man. You expect valets to be younger than their masters, don't you? But I don't see why really.'

'And you had no doubt at all that he was a valet?'

She stared. 'No. Why shouldn't he be? He behaved like one and he knew things valets know. The first night, there happened to be another gentleman's valet at the table and the two of them were talking about how stiff a cravat should be starched. You can tell, can't you, whether a person

278

really knows about things? I only need to look at a girl sweeping crumbs off a tablecloth to tell if she knows what she's doing or not.'

I asked her if anybody else remembered the gentleman and his valet and in due course boots appeared – an elderly man, not a boy. He was equally certain.

'Yes, I remember him. Came down early and cleaned his master's boots himself, said he was very particular about them. Decent enough, but not talkative. Sad? I wouldn't know about that. Half past five of a morning, you don't get many whistling.'

So that was it, all we needed. We could go back to London in the morning and I found the manager to book two seats on the coach for London. But I'd forgotten that the service from Eastbourne only ran on Mondays, Wednesdays and Fridays, so we had a day and a half to wait. I could have taken a local service along the coast and caught a morning coach from Hastings or Dover but it didn't seem worth the fag. What had happened had already happened and the thing now was to decide what to do about it. I booked seats for Friday, and on Thursday after-noon Tabby and I went on another walk, this time for a look at the lighthouse. As it happened, we got back to the Lamb just after the coach from London had arrived. Judging from the luggage waiting to be carried upstairs, it had brought several passengers, but now that the military had moved on the Lamb had plenty of rooms free and they'd already been taken upstairs. As I lingered in the hall, wanting to see the manager about early breakfast next morning, a young man came hurrying down. He was an unexpectedly exotic sight in a seaside resort out of season, dark haired and pale faced with fine features and eyes sunk deep into their sockets, but very bright. Even in the simple act of descending the stairs he seemed to be crackling with nervous energy. He gave me a quick glance, pounced on the pile of luggage, seized from it what looked like a lady's dressing case, then bounded back upstairs two at a time like a man who'd snatched something from a tidal wave. I found the manager and went on my way upstairs. On the first landing I heard from one of the rooms a man and a woman's voices, speaking Italian, though I didn't grasp more than a few words about a headache.

When I came downstairs about an hour later, for a breath of air before supper, another man was standing just outside the porch, looking towards the sea. From the back view of him, he looked calmer and less exotic than the other man. I guessed they'd been fellow travellers in the same coach. I wished him good evening as I passed and what happened then was like walking into a stone wall. He gasped, a gulp of breath so sharp that it sounded painful. His expression as he turned round to me couldn't have been more astounded if a mermaid had come swimming out of the inn and accosted him.

'Liberty.'

'So it's a headache she's got this time, is it?' I said. 'She does seem rather prone to ailments.' I knew there were a hundred other things I could have said, all of them less malicious and more dignified. Better still, I should simply have walked past in silence after that first good evening and recognition. Jealousy turns you into something else and the moment I'd realized who was standing there I'd guessed the identity of the woman with the dressing case and seen her thick dark hair and wide eyes as clearly as if she too were there.

'Liberty.' Robert said it again, as if trying to cope with the reality of me. 'How did you know we'd be here?' He sounded alarmed as well as puzzled.

'Don't flatter yourself. I'm here on other business. I'd not the slightest notion that you and your Italian friends were coming here. He's her brother, I suppose.'

'And nobody's followed you?'

'Why in the world should anybody follow me?' I could think of two or three reasons, but I wasn't going to tell him that. 'Now, if you'll excuse me . . .' I started to walk away, not caring where I was going.

He grabbed me by the arm, quite painfully. 'Libby, listen . . .'

I pulled away. 'I have things to do, so I'll wish you a pleasant voyage. May the winds be kind.' I started walking again. I'd gone no more than three paces before he jumped in front of me, blocking the way.

'I'm not going anywhere.'

'Well, I am.' I turned and started walking in the other direction. He jumped in front of me again. If any idler happened to be watching it must have looked as if we were playing a children's game.

'I mean, I'm not sailing with them. Libby, will you please listen?'

If I'd opened my mouth I'd have said something else mean and sarcastic. If I'd turned away he'd just have bounced in front of me again. I started walking along the road that was deeply rutted with coach tracks, heading parallel to the sea. Still white crests on the waves and a breeze that made me hold on to my bonnet. He was walking beside me.

'I don't know how much you guessed.'

I was tempted to say, *Pretty well everything*, but kept my tongue firmly clamped. He went on talking, keeping the appropriate distance of a lady and gentleman out for an evening stroll.

'You can blame me for plunging in too deeply, if you like, but in the circumstances I don't see what else in all decency I could have done. I even asked myself what you'd want me to do, and had the same answer.'

I was nearly biting my tongue through by now but kept looking at a small boat with an off-white sail, tacking for the shore. The sail had a brighter patch of white in it.

'I know you and I share much the same views on Italian politics.' His voice was level, reasonable. 'I think I mentioned in one of my letters that I'd met some interesting Italians in Paris, in exile from Piedmont. They gave me letters of introduction to some of their friends in Turin, so when I parted company with O'Leary I decided to go on there. Perhaps I should have turned for

282

home instead. It would have certainly saved me some trouble.'

That was one way of putting it, I thought. There was another smaller boat, with a faded red sail. Robert took a long breath.

'Turin was in a state of some agitation, not unusual I gather with the regime so unpopular. A group thought to have connections with Mazzini had tried to assassinate a minister and come pretty near succeeding. One of the group had been shot dead at the scene and others were in hiding. One of those others was a young man my friends in Paris had said I should call on. I won't go into details, but it turned out that his only hope was to smuggle himself out of the country. That was the young man you might have seen when we arrived this afternoon.'

Words were pounding in my brain louder and more insistent than the waves breaking on the shore: *Don't ask about the woman. Don't ask about the woman.*

'Then there was Beatrice,' Robert said. We walked on a few more paces. 'There can't be many young women as courageous and loyal as she is. She's given up everything in the world for the man she loves – family, reputation, country, everything. It staggers me to think about it.'

A seagull flying overhead, wry neck turned down to look at us, let out a derisive screech, the comment that I was suppressing. Robert went on talking, not noticing.

'He's well aware of it, of course. That's why he's been so insistent on secrecy, to protect her. He tried to persuade her not to come with us, to

283

wait in Turin until he sent for her, but she said if they did that she might not see him again.'

My mind was so tightly clenched that it wouldn't function. 'Who are we talking about?'

'Guido, of course. Guido and Beatrice, his fiancée.'

'She's his fiancée?'

'Yes. As soon as we got to London, in spite of the risk of being spied on, he insisted on going in front of a priest and making a formal declaration. They'll get married in Geneva.'

I still couldn't get my mind away from that little room with the girl and the dictionary. 'So you and she . . .?'

'I'll admit to you, they've been a terrible responsibility. I thought my part in it would be over as soon as I'd got them safely delivered to Mazzini's people in London, but I was drawn into it. He's a remarkable man, Mazzini. I'll introduce you to him.'

'I've met him.'

'And London's not as safe as I expected. I promise you, you take a different view of your country when you're helping to guard a wanted man – spies on every street corner.'

'I know.'

'I wanted so much to let you know what was going on, but Mazzini had made me swear not to tell anybody Guido was here. Sometimes when I was watching you in the park, it was all I could do not to walk up to you. But it wouldn't have been fair to involve you. I knew you'd have plunged in and it might have brought you into trouble too.'

'So it was you, watching me?' My mind was moving again, but slowly.

'You felt it? I'm glad of that. Tomorrow it will all be over. The boat will come into a cove just down the coast to take them over to France and other friends will meet them and see them to Switzerland. They'll feel safer there. I'll wave them off and be a free man again. Oh, it is so good to be able to talk to you.' He stopped, turned and took my hand, bringing me to a stop too. 'So, did you guess? Is that why you came here?' He smiled, but it was an uncertain smile, breaking against something that must have been there in my expression.

'No, I didn't guess. I'm here for another reason, but it does involve your friends from the Italian mutual aid office. You know a man nearly died there?'

His face turned serious. 'Of course I know. Mazzini was horrified. He's sure it was an attempt by Austrian agents to discredit him. He knew the man Slater had been spying on him, but he wasn't worried about it. He says you might as well complain about the rain in London as the spies.'

'There's a Frenchman, a blackmailer and a murderer, who uses the place for his correspondence.'

'Liberty, who have you been listening to? You sound like one of those people who think all foreigners are threats.'

'The government spy was standing there for hours waiting to be hanged. Another man actually was hanged.'

'And you think my friends were involved in

285

that? So it's not a coincidence that you're here. I shouldn't have said what I said. Forget I told you. Do that for them at least.' He let go of my hand, spun round and started walking back towards the Lamb. I fell in beside him.

'Do you think I'd tell anybody? What do you think I'm doing?'

'I don't know and I don't care.' He walked faster. I could have kept up with him but it would have been undignified and, worse, useless. I stood watching the sea and the boat with the patched sail that seemed no nearer harbour. The seagull, or another one that sounded the same, was still screeching. When Tabby and I went down to breakfast on Friday morning the three of them were already gone.

TWENTY-ONE

The Eastbourne Safety Coach was nearly an hour late into Holborn on Friday evening because of a wheel needing repairs at Caterham. I put Tabby and her bags into a cab and asked her to tell Mrs Martley not to wait up for me. I walked fast to Covent Garden but arrived only ten minutes before the curtain was due to rise. People were still queuing for the cheaper seats, sweepers nudging them aside trying to tidy up, sellers of nosegays and sugared almonds in paper cones harassing latecomers getting out of carriages. It was to be the last performance this season of Madam Gordon's extravaganza *The Faithful Sister* and *House Full* strips were pasted across the playbills, gentlemen fallen on hard times sidling up to likely prospects to offer their seats in boxes, strictly against regulations. The piece had been a success and her reputation had a lot to do with it. No chance of speaking to her so close to the performance so I went round to the artists' entrance, where my friend the doorman let me in to stand at the back of the stalls. Her performance was even more enthusiastically received than before. As soon as the curtains came together at the interval I made for the dressing room corridor just in time to see her whisking into her room, slamming the door behind her. When I knocked her maid opened it.

287

'Madam is changing. She's not seeing anybody.'

After the cheers at the final curtain I was back again, queuing up behind the gentlemen with bouquets. The maid came out and gathered the flowers as efficiently as a reaper stacking sheaves and sent everybody away.

'Madam is tired. She is still not seeing anybody.' I got a special glare. 'You too.'

So there was nothing for it but to wait outside. I mostly stood near the artists' entrance but every few minutes went to the front of the building in case she came out that way. Members of the orchestra came out carrying their instruments, chatting to each other and lingering in the street. A few gentlemen, top-hatted but of the humbler sort, lingered for the dancing girls who emerged giggling, arm in arm with friends, feigning surprise at finding the gentlemen there. Soon afterwards the back-stage staff began to leave too and half a dozen cleaners went in. The gas lights at the front of the house went out, with only a few windows still alight inside the building and the glow of the doorman's lamp at the artists' entrance. It was past eleven o'clock, the temperature falling fast. I pulled my cloak round me and walked up and down to keep warm. At around half past eleven the doorman came out and whistled for a cab. When it arrived Eleonore's maid appeared, weighed down with several bags. I moved closer to the door, expecting Eleonore to follow, but the doorman helped the maid load the bags into the cab and she drove off alone. By now I was more than half convinced

288

that I'd somehow missed her and was about to ask the doorman if she'd gone when I noticed that somebody else was waiting.

I don't know how long he'd been there because he practically merged with the darkness, standing on the opposite side of the street from me and about a hundred yards away. He wore a long coat and a low-crowned black hat and stood stock still, his eyes on the artists' door. It might have been me he was watching and yet I didn't have the ants' feet shiver you feel when you're under observation. He knew I was there but wasn't particularly interested. He wasn't tall but he stood upright and didn't have the air of an elderly man, so definitely not Slater. He might have been some besotted admirer waiting for a glimpse of his idol. If so, it must be Eleonore herself because everybody else had left, but he was too plainly dressed for an opera-goer and carried no bouquet. I walked up the street towards the front of the house, passing him. He glanced at me, but no more than that. After a couple of minutes I walked back and he was still there. A flash of light startled me then a smell of tobacco floated across the street and I realized he was lighting a cigar, or rather trying to light it. It must have gone out after that first draw because the flint flashed again. As he bent his head to it the small flare against the darkness illuminated the side of his face as brightly as a wax candle, for no more than an instant but enough to see the slash of a fresh scar across his cheek.

I kept walking, willing myself not to go faster. At the side door, the doorman had his head down on his folded arms, dozing at his counter. He jerked awake as I came in.

'You still here?'

'Is Madam Gordon still in her dressing room?'

'Yes, but she's not . . .'

'Urgent message for her. And don't let the man in the black coat in.'

He tried to ask a question but I ignored him and went as fast as I could along the dark corridor. The only light was a glow round the door frame of one of the dressing rooms – hers. I opened it without knocking and went in. She'd changed out of her stage costume and was conventionally dressed in a black skirt and jacket, sitting back in an armchair with a lamp on the table burning low. If I'd startled her, there was no sign of it in her posture or expression, apart from an upward tilt of the chin that asked what I thought I was doing.

'Lesparre's outside,' I said.

A blink. At last I'd managed to surprise her. 'How did you know?'

'When they landed in England the older man was the valet, the real valet. Lesparre must have ordered Bruno to impersonate him when they got to Gore House and pretend to have the papers. I suppose he knew he'd be safer blackmailing people in hiding as the valet. Did you know that all along?'

'No. Not until I saw that picture you had and you told me it was the valet. I'd seen them both. I knew it was Lesparre.'

'Until then, you really thought it was Lesparre at Gore House?'

'Yes. Bruno had tried to get a message to us to let us know what was happening, but it got here too late, after he was dead. He thought somebody was spying on him.'

'Somebody was, a man named Ronson. He's dead too – or did you know that?' She shook her head, as if it didn't matter either way. I thought of Lady Blessington's belief that she'd seen somebody at night in her garden. I hadn't taken much notice of it at the time, but it was probably the real Lesparre, spying out the house's weak points. The weak point had turned out to be Ronson. 'So the valet died instead of the master. You said he was the better man.'

'Yes, Bruno was loyal. He'd have been horrified at what Lesparre was doing. That's why Lesparre had to kill him.'

'Was it you who sent a man to identify Bruno's body as Lesparre's?'

Another nod. 'Yes. It would make things tidier when we dealt with the real Lesparre. Officially, he's dead already.'

'So the loyal valet's buried in a pauper's grave under a traitor's name.'

'He'll be recognized where it matters.'

'A statue in the Place Vendome when the prince comes into his own?'

She glared at me. 'He doesn't deserve your sarcasm.'

'He doesn't, true. Why was Lesparre able to use the Italian office?'

'They knew nothing about Bruno but the name, and Lesparre knew enough about him to deceive them.'

'Why didn't you tell me Bruno was Lesparre? I thought we had a pact.' But then, I hadn't told her everything and she knew it.

'I didn't trust you.' A simple statement, said without offence.

'And now Lesparre's waiting outside to kill you.'

'Yes. I expected him to try it in Burlington Arcade, only you got in the way.'

I hadn't anticipated thanks for trying to save her life and clearly wasn't going to get any. 'The question is what are we going to do now?' I said. 'I suppose the safest thing will be to wait here till morning.'

She looked at the travelling clock on top of the hamper, considering. She didn't often hesitate about anything so perhaps the prospect of an assassin with a knife waiting outside was fluttering even her nerves.

'Perhaps you're right.' She said it reluctantly. 'But I should go and tell the doorman. I don't want to keep the poor man up all night.'

Surprised by her consideration, I said I'd go, but she was on her feet.

'No, you wait here. I shan't be long.'

She shut the door behind her and her footsteps faded along the corridor. Ten minutes or more passed. She seemed to be taking a long time to deliver a simple message so I decided to see if anything was wrong. I thought at first that the door handle was sticking and tried it several times, with increasing force. I couldn't believe what should have been obvious from the first try: she'd gone and locked me in.

I banged and shouted for a long time but nothing happened. The noise I was making in the great maze of backstage rooms sounded no more than a wasp in a box. In between bangs and shouts I wondered why Eleonore had done it. Had she gone out defiantly and stupidly to meet her assassin, thinking she could defeat him? She hadn't even taken her sabre but perhaps she had some other weapon. Had she decided, fatalistically and operatically, to go to her death? Or did she think I'd been trying to trick her? The last seemed much more likely. In which case she'd find out her mistake when she came face to face with Lesparre. I banged and shouted some more and at last there were footsteps in the corridor and the doorman looked in.

'What happened? Did you get locked in?' He looked no more than faintly amused.

'Where is she?'

'Madam Gordon? Driven off with her friends.'

'What friends?'

'Came up with a carriage to collect her, as they often do. Two foreign gentlemen – French, I think.'

'And she went with them willingly?'

'Why wouldn't she? I've seen them quite often, here waiting for her. They seemed in a cheerful mood tonight, probably going to celebrate her last night here.'

'Cheerful!'

'Cheerful enough to give a ride to the man waiting on the corner. I suppose he was looking for a cab but had no luck at this time of night.

So they stopped the carriage and her two friends got down and persuaded him to get in with them. He seemed to be saying no at first, not wanting to put them out I suppose, but they insisted and in he got.'

'And you're sure Madam Gordon was in no trouble?'

'Why should she be? I heard her laughing.'

I couldn't believe it. Far from being Lesparre's victim, Eleonore and her friends had kidnapped him. She'd set a trap, guessing he'd be waiting for her on this last night, and he'd walked into it. I must have looked dazed because the doorman kept asking me if I was all right. He had his keys in his hand, waiting to lock up and go home. Probably to get rid of me he offered to whistle up a cab and I accepted.

Back home, with the fire gone out, the house in darkness and Mrs Martley snoring up above, I collapsed into an armchair and knew that the thing had gone beyond anything I could do about it, even if I'd wanted to. Eleonore Gordon and her associates had their traitor and were probably even now putting him on trial, probably in that room full of Napoleonic relics and the emperor staring out from his porphyry column. There was only one possible verdict and I was sure he'd be dead by morning. He'd killed at least two men, probably tried to kill another, and yet the thought brought a chill that had nothing to do with the cold of the room. Then I had other thoughts of a dark-haired woman and a man with a pale face and bright eyes, probably near the French coast by now, and of Robert by the sea, offended beyond repair by my suspicions. I never thought I'd agree with Slater about anything, but for those dark hours I pretty well shared his feelings on foreign revolutionaries.

TWENTY-TWO

Amos came round in the morning and we took our ride together, with the breeze still from the east and clouds gathering. I told him everything that had happened, apart from the bit about Robert.

'So what are we going to do?' he said.

'Should we do anything? Am I supposed to tell Sergeant Bevan I think Eleonore Gordon and her friends probably killed a man last night – a man who's officially dead already?'

'Depends how much trouble you want to make for her.'

I'd been thinking about that most of the night, remembering the fear the valet must have felt, pinioned in the dark waiting for the trap to open. The world owed Lesparre no favours. What I couldn't admit to Amos, hardly even to myself, was a kind of admiration for the woman because she knew what she wanted and took her risks. 'I don't think I do.'

'But you do want to know for sure what's happened.' He was grinning, thinking he knew me well.

'Do I?' I meant it as a real question but he didn't take it that way.

'Course you do. Suppose I go round to Carlton Gardens when we've done and have a chat with my friend the head groom.'

'It's a Saturday. You haven't time.'

296

He nodded towards the cloud bank. 'Half my regulars won't come out in this. I could take Tabby with me, drop her off on the corner and leave her to keep an eye on the place.'

'You're not to let her take any risks.'

'That one's got the sense she was born with.'

When we got back Tabby was at the far end of the yard, helping Mr Colley settle his cows after their milk round, wearing her urchin gear. She raised a hand to Amos but wouldn't look at me. I didn't know what I'd done to offend her this time, but Amos could do no wrong in her eyes. He slipped out of the saddle and went for a word with her while I fed Rancie an apple. They came back together and Amos lifted her on to the back of his cob, riding astride, then swung himself up in front of her. I got back on Rancie. He'd offered to deliver her back to the stables, but I thought an extension of my ride might clear my head and make me feel better. It didn't, and by the time I walked back across the park the drizzle had started. I thought of Amos smoking his pipe in the stable yard of Number One, Carlton Gardens and Tabby lurking somewhere outside and wished I'd told him not to go.

For most of the day nothing happened. Then late afternoon a note from Disraeli arrived, delivered by a footman in the odd brown livery of his household.

Dear Miss Lane,
The trap was baited from yesterday afternoon onwards but the rat has failed to appear. Have you any further suggestions?

That made it two signs of desperation: one that Disraeli was asking my advice, the other that he'd stayed in town for the weekend, practically social death when all the people who mattered disappeared to their friends' country estates. I scribbled a reply saying I was sorry the plan had failed but could offer no suggestions, took it down to the footman and watched from my office window as he picked his way delicately over the cobbles and out of the yard. I half wished I'd gone round and told Disraeli that his rat had been caught by somebody else and was probably dead by now, for the interest of seeing his reaction. At some point I'd need to let him know that Lesparre, alias the valet, was no longer a blackmail threat. Presumably the papers were in the possession of Eleonore and her allies by now.

Amos arrived around seven in the evening in good tweed jacket, best breeches and boots, hair still damp from the pump and a trace of carbolic soap mingling with his hay and tobacco scent. He'd obviously tidied up after evening stables, knowing that Mrs Martley would insist on treating this as a parlour visit. Like Tabby, she approved of him more than of me. The fire blazed, tea was made and a range of newly baked biscuits, cakes and tarts that I didn't even know we possessed appeared on a snow-white table cloth. Amos absorbed them as neatly as a bullfrog taking flies while keeping up a teasing conversation with her, threatening to arrive with a nice white pony and take her for a ride in the park with us. She gasped and protested at the idea, but a certain gleam in her eye said she half wished he would. He waited until she'd gone down to the pump to refill the kettle before reporting.

'The groom says there've been a lot of comings and goings, more than at any time since the prince left. The travelling chariot was out till the early hours last night. Two French gentlemen who visit the house quite often and have the run of the stables took it out last night around ten o'clock and told him he needn't wait up to put the horses away, they'd do it themselves. He was surprised they wanted the travelling chariot because it's more than twenty years old, came with the rental of the house and hadn't moved for years. There was a nice phaeton in the stables he thought would have suited the gentlemen a lot better but they would have the chariot. You can see why, of course.'

'A closed carriage with room for four, even if one of them was struggling.'

'Right. He heard them coming back sometime between one and two, Madam Gordon with them. He doesn't know if there was anyone else because he didn't look out, but there might have been. The maid told him the two men stayed in the house overnight. Two more gentlemen arrived this morning separately, one on foot, the other on a bay thoroughbred. The one with the bay was foreign, probably French, but he doesn't know about the other. They've all been shut up in the house all day, no sign of any of them outside.'

Mrs Martley came in so he switched to praising

her fruit cake, but a lift of his eyebrow told me there was more to come. As he drank a third cup of tea I thought I might have been wrong about Lesparre being tried and executed the night before. The arrival of two more men this morning suggested a court convening. For all I knew, they'd do it in a parody of the normal style with prosecution, defence and judge. If I'd sent word to Sergeant Bevan in the morning, Lesparre might still have been alive. Perhaps that made me part of the hanging jury. When Amos went, I walked with him to the yard gates and we talked by the mounting block.

'I brought Tabby back with me,' he said. 'She got talking with the lad who does the knives, takes out the kitchen slops and so on. He told her they're all moving out tomorrow.'

'Madam Gordon too?'

'Yes. Her maid's been packing up all day and one of the other servants who can read says her trunks are labelled for Paris. Another thing, the two gentlemen who drove the travelling chariot have ordered it to be ready for nine o'clock tomorrow morning. He's not to drive it, one of them will, like last time.'

'To take them to the Channel boat?'

'No, that's later in the afternoon. The morning one would be a short journey, they said, back by midday. What do you reckon to that?'

'A closed carriage, with no coachman as a witness. Is she going with them?'

'I don't know, but there's one way to find out. There'll be plenty of carriages around St James tomorrow morning, people going to church and

300

so on. They won't notice another one. I'll pick you and Tabby up at half past eight in the landau, if that suits.'

'Yes, that will suit.' He was taking it for granted that I wanted to know the end of it, and I did.

The landau with Amos on the box in sober black coat and top hat arrived in the yard a few minutes before time on Sunday morning. Tabby, in her maid's dress and still not very conversational, got in beside me and Amos drew the hood of the landau well up. Even at this early hour he was right about the traffic in the area around Carlton Gardens, but he managed to draw up with a clear view of the back entrance of Number One. At twenty past nine the gates from the stable yard were opened and the travelling chariot drove out and past us, only yards from where I was sitting behind the landau hood. The man driving it was very much the gentleman in a well-cut black coat and tall hat, in his mid- to late forties, profile as sharp and severe as the head on a coin, complexion brown from the weather, as if he'd done a lot of travelling. He handled the reins as if he knew what he was doing. The horses were dark bays badly matched for height, the blinds firmly down over the windows. That, and the age and dull black paint of the carriage, gave the whole thing the look of a funeral. I thought that was pretty well what it was. When you're quitting a rented house – as Eleonore and her associates seemed to be – you try not to leave any unpleasant souvenirs for the next people to find. They were spending Sunday morning tidying up. Where they planned to dump or bury Lesparre's body was anybody's guess, but if they intended to be back by midday it couldn't be far. Hampstead Heath was my prediction. Amos, in a short conversation before we started, put forward the theory that Lesparre was still alive and they were taking him somewhere to hang or shoot him without interference. If so, we'd have to intervene. I'd seen the heavy stick he'd slipped beside him in the driver's seat. I was convinced that Lesparre was dead already, that they'd have killed him in that shadowy room under the marble gaze of the emperor. Amos waited for another carriage to come between us then turned the landau neatly and followed the travelling chariot at one remove out to Pall Mall and eastwards into Cockspur Street. After that my Hampstead Heath theory came apart because instead of turning northwards the chariot kept on eastwards into the Strand, and then Fleet Street. We were in the City by then, church bells pealing from steeples all around but fewer carriages on the streets and the chariot broke into a fast trot. Amos took his time about following their example because by now we'd lost the vehicle that had been a buffer between us. We were some two hundred yards behind as we drove up Ludgate Hill and into a mass of carriages outside St Paul's. The chariot slowed to a walk but picked a way through them, down towards the river and London Bridge. It didn't cross the bridge but kept on heading eastward, parallel to the Thames with only wharves between us and the river.

'Going to dump him in it then,' Tabby said, the first words she'd uttered all the journey.

'Perhaps.' But both vehicles were still moving at a good trot and an odd idea was coming into my mind. We were close to the Tower of London now, and Traitor's Gate. Had Eleonore Gordon chosen that as an appropriate launching place for their traitor? The chariot came to the western edge of the Tower Moat then swung up alongside it at a walk now, heading up towards Tower Hill. For pity's sake, was she going to have the man beheaded? But instead of stopping there it went straight on and turned the corner down the eastward side of the tower. Amos drew up the landau, jumped off the box and looked in on us.

'Nothing down there but the river. If we follow them down they can't miss us.'

'Irongate and Irongate Stairs,' I said. 'There's a wharf for boats.'

'Looks like whatever they're going to do, they'll do down there then.' It seemed a dangerous choice to me, visible to shipping on the river, but perhaps they thought there was not much risk of that on a Sunday. 'You two wait here and I'll come back and tell you what's going on. They won't notice just a man on his own.'

It made sense, but I didn't like watching him going alone round the corner and Tabby looked like a dog straining after its huntsman. He was back in a surprisingly short time.

'There's a scrubby sort of public just round the corner, the sort sailors use. They've drawn up outside there.'

303

I could hardly believe it, that they should come all this way across London to a low public house. 'Have they gone inside?'

'I don't know. There's a lad come out to hold the horses but . . .' He stopped, because against all expectation in this remote part of London another carriage had appeared from the direction of Tower Hill, a smart-looking cabriolet with the hood up. As it went past us at a trot I glimpsed a youngish man driving and what looked like an older man beside him. The driver gave us a glance but we were partly screened by the landau. They too turned the corner into Irongate. 'Busy round here,' Amos said.

'More friends arriving.' My heart was hammering. These new arrivals surely weren't coincidence. For some reason, the prince's friends had chosen this unlikely time and place to finish off Lesparre. When it came to it, I couldn't stand here, within shouting distance, and let them do it. 'Amos, is there a back entrance to the public? If there is, you and Tabby wait there. When you hear me shouting out from the front, you shout as well, loud as you can. Don't go in. They probably have pistols as well as knives.' With the new arrivals there would be at least four men guarding Lesparre plus Eleonore as well. We couldn't take them on, so all we could do was provide a distraction and hope it would be enough to stop the execution. What we'd do after that, I'd no idea.

Amos shook his head. 'Me at the front, you two at the back. Don't know if there's a back door, but there usually is. I'll yell like a drunken sailor wanting a drink.' He shifted the horses a couple of paces forward and looped the reins round a pump by a horse trough, a thing he'd never have done except in a grave emergency. I didn't argue, wondering fleetingly what a drunken sailor would sound like in Amos's inland accent. 'All right, but give us a start and wait till we're in position. Tabby will whistle.'

Tabby and I rounded the corner together. The boy outside the public – a place too down-at-heel even to have a name board – was now holding the reins of both the chariot and the cabriolet, not dealing well with three horses so that the carriages were blocking the street. He didn't notice as we slipped along the side wall of the public, squeezing past sour-smelling barrels. There was a back door, giving on to a narrow courtyard with slimy flags, hemmed in by a brick wall patched with green mould. Beside the door was a window about eighteen inches square with only cobwebs for a curtain. I looked through it into a narrow scullery with a big stone sink and not much else. The door between the scullery and the main room was half open. I could see two men's backs through it. It looked as if they were sitting down at a table. They didn't move for a minute or so, then one of them shifted aside and a hat feather waved on the far side of the table. So she was there, and from the movement of the feather she was doing the talking. Tabby was pulling my arm, pursing her lips ready to whistle. I shook my head and went on watching. One of the backs was straight and broad, the other thinner and bent forward, intent on whatever Eleonore was saying. Then the man with the stooped back turned suddenly and looked out towards the scullery. Tabby and I had made no noise, but something must have bothered him. I gasped and stepped sideways from the window.

What's up? Tabby mouthed at me.

'Slater.' Even through cobwebs, there was no doubt about that damp buzzard's face. I was sure too, even though he hadn't turned, that the younger man was Sergeant Bevan and it had been the two of them in the cabriolet. Tabby's face was a question mark. I took her arm and moved her away from the window. 'Go out to Mr Legge. Tell him the plan's changed. He's to keep quiet and watch. Stay there with him.'

Another glance at my face and she went, quiet as a cat. I risked a look through the window. Slater had his back turned to me, concentrating again on whatever Eleonore Gordon was saying. If it hadn't been for the squalor of the surroundings and the stale beer smell, I might have been watching a not particularly heated board meeting. Ten minutes or so later they all stood up. I had a quick glimpse of Eleonore in profile and beside her, briefly turned in my direction though not seeing me, the man I still thought of as the valet, Lesparre. His round face was impassive, his hair sleeked back. If he was a man facing execution he was carrying it off well. Only that couldn't be the case. Whatever game Slater was playing, he and Bevan couldn't stand by and see Lesparre killed. The only answer was that they'd come to an agreement with Eleonore. She'd decided to hand over Lesparre to the authorities to put on trial for murder. Why, I didn't know, but it would probably take Machiavelli himself to unravel Madam Gordon's plotting. I waited for the room to empty then went back up the side of the house. Amos and Tabby were tucked in by the beer kegs. In the street, five men and Eleonore were clustered in a group near the carriages. At the end of the street the tide looked full, coming almost to the top of Irongate Stairs. A lift of the eyebrows from Amos asked me what was going on.

'Slater and Bevan are arresting Lesparre.'

'Don't know how they're going to find room for another person in the cabriolet,' Amos said. 'Only takes two.' It seemed to me an irrelevant remark, but Amos had understood before I did. 'See that ship down there? I'm no sailor, but wouldn't you say that's the Blue Peter she's flying?'

Again, it seemed to me irrelevant. Some of the smaller continental ships sailed from Irongate Stairs, so conveniently close to the city. It wasn't surprising that one was preparing to leave on the tide, even on a Sunday. Then three people from the group started walking down towards the river, Madam Gordon, Lesparre and Slater. They walked down the steps and a minute later a rowing boat slid away into the river, the boatman pulling towards the ship flying the Blue Peter and one passenger sitting opposite him, back turned to the shore. By then, Madam Gordon and Slater were walking back up Irongate towards us and I'd stepped out from hiding and was standing almost shoulder to shoulder with Sergeant Bevan, knowing it didn't matter any more. He was watching the rowing boat as if trying to will it back.

'So you've done a deal with her,' I said.

'He has.' He slid the words sideways out of his mouth, not turning.

'She hands over Lesparre on the promise that he'll be allowed to escape. That suited Slater, of course. If you'd had to put him on trial for murder and blackmail he'd have come out with things that would have embarrassed a lot of people.'

No reply. The rowing boat was alongside the ship by now, Madam Gordon and Slater halfway up the street. He was saying something to her and she was nodding thoughtfully.

'What about those letters and papers? Did she get those from him?'

The slightest of nods.

'And hand them over to the police too?'

'Some of them, I believe.'

'A compromise?'

'Aren't most things?'

Slater and Madam Gordon were almost back with us, so he moved aside from me. I knew that what she'd have demanded in return would be a good word put in for Prince Louis, from somewhere that would matter in the cat's cradle of international politics. She knew when to fight and when to make allies. Perhaps she'd learned that from her hero. When they came up to us she and Slater also moved aside from each other, no goodbyes. Slater ignored me, though he must have seen me, caught Sergeant Bevan's eye and nodded him towards the driver's seat of the cabriolet. Bevan took his place stiffly, a man controlling his anger. One of Madam Gordon's gentlemen was already on the box of the chariot, the other letting down the step for her to get inside. She put her foot on the step and paused, looking straight at me.

'I thought you wanted vengeance on the traitor,' I said.

She gave me a radiant smile. 'Oh, we'll have that, don't worry. We'll know where he goes. It's only delayed.'

Then she saluted me with an imaginary sabre, the other gentleman folded the step, got in beside her and closed the door and off they went. By then, the ship was moving slowly out with the tide.

TWENTY-THREE

On Monday I did nothing. On Tuesday I rode out to Gore House on my own. Nobody was watching me. My spine remained free of shivers. Lady Blessington met me in the garden. She'd been expecting me, although I hadn't told her I was calling.

'He called yesterday. It's over then?'

Disraeli, freed now of blackmail. D'Orsay also, and freed of suspicion. An inconvenient guest dead or sailed away, which came to much the same thing. I wasn't sure how much she knew, or how much she wanted to know. She lived at a level when things rearranged themselves quickly.

'And I gather that Madam Gordon has an engagement with the Paris opera. A remarkable woman.'

'Remarkable, yes.'

'We really are so grateful to you. Would you accept this as a small memento?'

The lapis lazuli pendant, set in heavy gold and worth two hundred or so, too valuable for a gift and too small for a fee.

'Thank you.'

'We'll see you again soon, won't we? You'll call with the gossip?'

'Yes.' I should, but probably not for a while.

I delivered Rancie to the stables and walked

310

back across the park. Tabby was in the yard, in ragamuffin gear, staring at the chickens. She looked sulky and I couldn't blame her. She had no interest in the survival or disintegration of governments, ministerial reputations, military coups. Nothing that happened in the greater world would affect, for better or worse, the lives of her and her friends who lived day to day on their wits and the toughness of their bodies. And yet she sensed a wrongness. A man we'd been hunting had sailed away. Slater, whom she hated, had been part of that and I'd done nothing. Above all, the hurt done to Cobblers was not avenged. I was convinced now that Lesparre had strung Slater up and left him to die, but Tabby, his reluctant rescuer, didn't care about that. I'd failed her. She came across the yard to me, scowling. It was goodbye, I thought. Tabby was leaving me too. We walked to the mounting block by the gates.

'Something to say to you.' She sounded as sulky as she looked. 'You know that man Slater nearly got hanged. It was us. Plush and the others. I didn't know about it till afterwards. That is, I did sort of know what they were going to do but I didn't know, if you see what I mean, like when you won't let yourself.' She kicked a piece of dried horse dung and sent it duck-and-draking over the cobbles.

'They were going to kill a man, and you knew it?'

'Luck of the draw, Plush said. They weren't going to tie him up that tightly, not like the other one at your friend's house. He might have got loose or he might not have. Either way, it would pay him out for Cobblers.'

'I can't believe this: you were going to let a man hang.'

'Well, I could tell you didn't like him. Anyway, I wasn't in the end. That's why I came and told you that something was happening. When I thought about it, Plush and the others hadn't given him very fair odds, so I thought I ought to even them up a bit.'

I couldn't find words at first. I'd known Tabby lived two separate lives, but had begun to flatter myself that the more principled one with me was gaining the upper hand. But then, it had been my involvement with Gore House that had led her into this. 'You know you might have been an accomplice to murder,' I said at last.

She shrugged. Official words meant nothing to her. 'I took you there and I stopped you opening that trap, didn't I? And I couldn't give Plush and the others away.'

Still shocked, I realized there was some justice in that. She could even claim to be the one who'd saved Slater's life. It struck me too that if I'd known this last week the conversation with Robert might have gone very differently. He and his Italian friends were innocent. I might have wondered if she'd somehow known about our talk and decided to confess, but Robert and I had been alone and even Tabby couldn't transform herself into a seagull.

'What made you decide to tell me?'

'I told Mr Legge and he said I should.'

* * *

'Hard to blame her,' Amos said.

It was the last day of September and we were riding in the park together on a cold morning with the frosts that would kill Lady Blessington's dahlias not far away. We cantered along the Row and back. I was still downcast, not inclined to talk, but Amos was as jaunty as I'd ever known him, a glint in his eye and a light hand on the reins.

'That bay with the bad foot, he's healed nicely, walking sound.'

'I'm glad to hear it.'

'I've found a buyer for him, gentleman home from abroad looking to spend some time with his friends. I've told him nothing but walking for a week, then a bit of trotting, but he's patient, he can wait. That's him coming now.'

They were a couple of hundred yards off, the bay walking out and his rider relaxed and easy in the saddle. Amos kept his eyes on them as they came closer and I supposed he was looking for any signs of lameness. Judging by his expression, he was finding none. I didn't want to disconcert the buyer of the horse by adding my stare to Amos's, so I kept my eyes on Rancie's mane until the rider was close enough for Amos to wish him a cheerful good morning. The voice that replied brought my head up and my astonishment must have communicated itself to Rancie because her head came up too and she whinnied to the bay so that I only just heard the rider's voice wishing me good morning by name, first 'Miss Lane' then, on a questioning note, 'Libby?'

He turned the bay in beside me, hat in hand, eyes still questioning. I said, 'Good morning,' then, after a pause that even in my ears seemed to go on for a long time, 'Robert.' Amos had reined back, riding a few lengths behind us. 'Am I forgiven?' He was smiling, but still anxious. My heart was hammering so fast that for a wild moment I wanted to touch my heel to Rancie's side and gallop off, letting the cool morning air blow away the confusion in my head. But if I'd galloped the bay might have followed and that would have undone all Amos's patient work on his hoof.

'If I am.' We rode on together, Rancie walking out to match the bay's stride, not saying anything. There would be time for talking later. Plenty of time.